Spread Your Wings

CAROL ANN GRANT

ISBN 978-1-964462-70-7 (Paperback)
ISBN 978-1-964462-71-4 (Hardback)
ISBN 978-1-964462-72-1 (Ebook)

Inquiries and Book Orders should be addressed to:

Leavitt Peak Press
17901 Pioneer Blvd Ste L #298, Artesia, California 90701
Phone #: 2092191548

Chapter One

'Yes Mr. Reynolds, right away.' How she didn't slam the phone down on the cradle she would never know. Muttering to herself she pushed back from her desk, and ignoring the others in the small office, wound her way around them into a closet sized kitchen. Slamming cup and saucer down on the counter made her feel better as she busied herself with making coffee. Taking long deep breaths didn't seem to help at all.

'You going to use a days worth of coffee for one cup?' Toni Birkwood ambled into the tight space and deftly snatched the beans from her friend's hand and carefully poured some back into the airtight canister before setting the machine to grind.

'Arrrrrgh' Aurora snarled. 'Yes Mr. Reynolds. No Mr. Reynolds. Three bags full Mr. Reynolds. He makes me sick to my stomach.' She looked up at the clock. 'What time does that say Toni?' She folded her arms across her chest to stop herself flinging them toward the innocent clock ticking quietly on the wall.

'Two fifty five' she replied helpfully transferring the ground coffee into the machine and pressed the on button. Within seconds the seductive smell filled the small space.

'And your watch?'

'Same'

'Mine too' she whirled around to face her friend. 'I take coffee at three o'clock Miss Spring. Where is my coffee?' She mimicked her boss's accent perfectly and pulled a funny face. 'One of these days I'm going to tell him exactly what he can do with his coffee.' She wagged a slender finger at her friend.

'Then you'll get fired.' Helpful as ever Toni set the tray as Mr. Reynolds insisted. Cup and saucer with spoon, sugar bowl with tongues, and small jug of cream. One individual pot filled with rich dark coffee.

'Oh but it would be worth it.' Aurora smiled at her friend. 'Thanks Toni.' Turning she walked carefully across the office and balancing the tray with one hand, knocked on the door.

Toni watched from the kitchen. She freely admitted she would have lost her job almost instantly if she had been foolish enough to apply for the position of personal assistant to Mr Reynolds. Thankfully she was very happy with her position as office secretary to two associates who shared the small space. Peter Reynolds was short, fat and fiftyish and had no personality whatsoever. He was now sole owner and senior associate of Reynolds and Reynolds, architects and surveyors. He was never wrong. He was not to be questioned regarding any decisions he made. His word was law and he ran through personal assistance like water through your fingers. Until Aurora. Four months had past since she had applied for and was given the position as PA to Mr. Reynolds. Miss Aurora Spring had sailed through the three-month probationary period with apparent ease. None of the others had lasted for more than a month. Rick and Martin, the two young men that worked in the office, placed bets on how long she would last. Both had lost out to their secretary. Never once was a file lost or misplaced. Not once were legal documents ever late for his signature at the end of the day. Billing was issued weekly and reminders sent in a timely fashion should payments fall outside of the agreed schedule. Drawings were numbered and registered on a daily basis. Alterations made in a timely and seamless fashion. Mr. Reynolds could never fault Miss Spring's work ethic. She was prompt, very efficient, presentable and even tempered. Mostly. As well as very beautiful in a naive sort of way. Not that she had been employed for that reason. Mr Reynolds didn't seem to notice her at all so long at the requested letters and documents were in a folder on his desk, along with his daily schedule, at the start of the day. Mail was placed on his desk at precisely 09:30 and at 10:00 Aurora went into the office to take dictation and came out promptly at 11:15 loaded with papers and a full steno pad. She had however negotiated an excellent salary and Mr. Reynolds made sure she earned every dime.

'Is he still breathing?' Toni enquired when Aurora came out of the office after delivering the coffee.

'I don't think he knows how' she whispered as she sat at her desk and turned to speak to Martin.

'Marty he wants the updated drawing for the Precinct job as soon as.'

'Yeah I got it' he reached behind him and opened a wide draw and pulled out the top drawing then rolled it carefully as he walked towards the office, knocked and went inside.

All was quiet for the next hour as all were busy with their allotted tasks. There was a continual stream of paper from Aurora's printer as she worked her way through her reams of shorthand. When Aurora had arrived in the city she was unemployed and had registered at a secretarial school as a full time student. Typing came easily to her as did the shorthand. She left after two months fully certified.

The phone rang at regular intervals on Toni's desk and calls past onto the correct associate. Any calls for Mr.

Reynolds were past to Aurora who in her efficient manner managed to deal with up to 80% of them. Calls from Mrs. Reynolds were to be put through immediately.

At 17:30 correspondence for approval and signature were taken into Mr. Reynolds. At precisely 17:55 Mr. Reynolds left his office placing a thick folder of signed correspondence and papers on Aurora's desk and left the office with a brisk 'Good evening'. Aurora was usually the last to leave, armed with mail for the post office. She set the alarm and locked up before she left. She handed Stephens, the security guard on the front desk, the office keys before Aurora signed out for the night.

'Night Mr. Stephens' she smiled and waved as she left.

'You be careful out there Miss Spring.' He returned the wave. Wishing he was thirty years younger.

'Always' she replied as the door clicked closed behind her.

Seven thirty had her kicking off her shoes in her apartment. Seven forty-five had her sipping on a small glass of white wine as she ate chicken salad as if it were going out of fashion. Nine o'clock and the drapes were drawn and the hard electric light switched off before she stripped off her clothes and sat naked, cross legged, on a thick rug in the centre of the living room, her hands resting gentle on her knees, her eyes closed. Her mind floated as she took in deep cleansing breaths. Several minutes past before a shudder ran the length of her slender body and her head fell forward until her chin rested on her chest. Her shoulders rounded as she rolled them forward and let out a deep sigh as her wings broke free from between her shoulder blades. Rising quickly to her feet the delicate wings unfurled. A gentle flick from her mind had them springing to life and shimmering a silvery light around the room.

'That's better' she sighed after flexing them for some minutes before she folded them down her back and walked carefully to her bathroom. Her living space was too small for her to attempt even the shortest of flights. From the gentle curves at the tip of her wings to the spear-like points at the base, her wings were seven feet in length. When fully extended they measured fourteen feet across.

In the tall bathroom mirror Aurora studied herself closely. She was tall, five feet ten inches. Her hair was a rich chestnut that fell in gentle waves to her waist. Her eyes were as blue as the summer sky and thickly lashed with dark high arched brows; cheekbones high and well defined. Her nose was straight and slender and sat atop a mouth that was made for kissing. It was beautifully sculptured with lips of deep pink. There was a stubborn set to the chin but even she could see there was nothing wrong with her general appearance. Her shoulders and arms were finely toned and needed to stay that way to enable her to fly. Turning slightly sideways she studied her general appearance. High full breasts that any woman, human or faerie would be proud of, ending in soft pink nipples. Her ribs were defined under smooth creamy skin. Her waist was slender by any standard and the gentle flare of her hips was not displeasing. She ran her hands over her smooth bottom and thought she could probably do with a little more padding in that area, not a lot just a little. Aurora was however proudest of all of her very long legs. In her homeland her legs were presentable, albeit, skinny. Flying did that and no one took any notice. Since coming to this world she had found it necessary to put in some serious exercise in order to promote muscle development. Now they were sleek and toned and she loved them. Her feet were nicely shaped and she had developed a liking for ruby red polish on her toenails.

'Not bad' she smiled. In her world she was considered a beauty. She was pleased that she held her own in this world.

In her bedroom she slipped on a pair of black panties. She preferred to fly naked but had discovered that it was a lot cooler at night here than back home. Even this one simple piece of clothing captured enough of her body heat to keep her warm on her twice-weekly flights. It was all she could allow herself with any safety. She dare not be discovered. She only ever flew at night whilst she was in the city. It took a great deal of concentration to dim the silvery glow from her wings so that she could step out onto her balcony, jump nimbly onto the safety rail and launch herself into the night. Her outspread wings caught the updraft from below as she glided over the city and out over the sea. There was no great effort in flying, not for her at least. Wings so fine and tissue thin belied the strength that was needed to lift her high into the darkened sky. It was glorious. She twisted and turned and gambolled across the heavens revelling in the freedom it gave her. But always careful to keep below three hundred feet to avoid the pesky radar system from a nearby airport. Before returning home she flew across the city hoping to hear the man she had been sent to find.

Her bedside mirror was shimmering when she returned. Without hesitation she ran her fingertips over the glass and her father appeared.

'Daughter' he sat in a high-backed chair covered with thick furs. His hands were resting on the padded arms.

'My father' she bowed politely, heedless of her naked state then closed her wings as she sat on her bed. He was as relaxed as she about their nakedness. He was a fine figure of a man and rightly proud of the fact. 'My mother is well?'

'Misses you of course. I have to keep carting her off to bed to take her mind of things.' He winked at his daughter. 'Works most of the time.'

'You are a rogue my father and no mistake.' She smiled broadly. He was one of her greatest loves.

'Truer words my daughter.' He lent forward. 'Any news?'

'I wish I could report success. I wish I could report something, anything.' She sighed. 'Is the oracle sure he is here?'

'I consulted with him only this hour past. Aaron is there, but he has no knowledge of what and who he is. He is coming to the end of the third cycle. He will be fully developed now; his wings will need to be released. Time grows short my lovely Aurora.'

'Should I call to him. Would he understand and come to me?'

'He may feel something. He was taken away so young, just days old. He knows nothing of his heritage.'

'What if, when I find him, he does not believe me. What if, when I find him, he believes me and still refuses to come back with me. What then?' she asked sincerely.

'Let us worry on that when you find him. He must spread his wings or he will die. Call him. Call with your heart. You know what must be done to ensure his good health. Blessings be upon you my daughter.' He looked on her lovely face. His only child. He missed her with all of his heart.

'I will honour your name and our house. Blessings be upon you my father. I will find him.' They reached through the glass and touched fingers before the image vanished and Aurora sat staring at her own reflection.

On the roof all was quiet. In a pair of silk pyjamas and a warm robe Aurora climbed to the highest point on top of an air conditioning vent and sat cross legged, eyes closed and hands resting lightly on her knees. She cleared her mind of everything but the one she sought. His father had named him Aaron the day before his mother had whisked him away. For what reason he knew not. Nobody knew why. It was only recently that Aaron's singing could be heard. His heart was singing to his people, to his heritage, and the oracle had received that signal. Aaron would know nothing of this. He may experience strange feelings, but he would not know the reason. This year he would be turning thirty. Thirty was the time when the males of her species grew their wings, a full decade behind the females. At home he would have been trained, would know what was happening, why his body was in such pain. The meditation his father would have taught him would alleviate much of his suffering. But here, in this strange world, he was alone. Aurora had to find him. Soon.

Still as a statue the young faerie filled her mind with her own song and sent it far across the city. It was midnight when she returned to her apartment and crawled into bed. She had a throbbing headache but knew that sleep would take it away and give her rest.

Aaron Summer woke from a weird dream, hot and sweaty. He could have sworn that he heard singing. A song so sweet it made his heart ache. There was a naked woman, that part of the dream he liked because she was truly lovely, that shimmered like sparkling silver in a cloud of wispy white and pearly grey. She held out her arms to him and as he reached for her his body was racked with pain. Unspeakable pain, as if fire burned the length of his spine. It was the dream of pain that woke him. He was also fully erect and throbbing for the first time in his life. It took some minutes for him to regain control. Although the pain from the dream was agonising he was at last relieved to have an erection. Maybe he wasn't impotent after all, just a late developer. His doctor had assured him there was no medical reason that he had been unable to perform sexually. He had suggested a visit to a psychiatrist to see if there was an emotional reason for his condition. Aaron had said he would think about it, but had, in fact, done nothing.

He swung his long legs out of bed and rose naked to walk to the bathroom. He splashed water on his face and towelled dry before he filled a glass and downed it in a couple of large swallows. His head was throbbing and between his shoulder blades ached like a rotten tooth. Back in his bedroom he looked at the clock.

'Four in the morning' he huffed out his cheeks. 'No more sleep for you pal.' Once his sleep was interrupted that was it for the night. So he fell back on an old remedy as he walked through to his second bedroom that he had transformed into a small home gym. On a thick exercise mat he sat and crossed his legs and rested his hands on his knees, closed his eyes, and drifted into his mediation. Within an hour he was free of pain. Within two he was showered and dressed for the day.

"I tell you Mike it was the weirdest thing.' Aaron sat across from his friend in a diner not far from their place of work. Steaming mugs of coffee sat between them along with plates of eggs and pancakes. They shared a stack of toast and butter.

'And you woke fully tooled up. That's gotta mean something.' Mike was a couple of years older than Aaron and happily married with a couple of kids.

'Yeah. Frustrating or what!' The fact that he had never before in his entire adult life had an erection he kept to himself. It would not do for his friend to realise he was still a virgin.

'Probably means you need to get your pipes cleaned buddy.' Mike waved his fork in Aaron's general direction. 'Frustration can lead to all sorts of problems both physical and mental.'

'Thanks for the advice Opray' Aaron smiled and shook his head. 'When was the last time you were frustrated and woke in the early hours with a hard on. Come on be honest.' He piled egg onto a piece of buttered toast and filled his mouth.

'Oh we married men are not immune my young apprentice. Twice as I recall and it was whilst my lovely Sophie was recovering from childbirth.' He was grinning however.

'Yes, and?'

'She has a terrific mouth.' Mike tossed bills on the table. It was his turn to pay.

'Can I borrow her for a couple of hours?' Aaron just avoided the punch that was coming his way, rose quickly from his chair and made a hasty retreat as Mike gave chase. By the time they reached the workplace Mike had Aaron in a headlock and they were laughing like a couple of kids.

'Needs a replacement boss.' An hour later Aaron rolled out from under the fire truck he was examining. 'I can put a temporary patch on for now. If I do a replacement it will take this baby out of service for the next several hours.' The crew of truck one three four had complained it was 'farting like some old man' on its way back to the station. It took Aaron a couple of minutes to discover the hole in the exhaust manifold.

Aaron's boss, Station Chief Spelling, scratched his bristled chin. 'Best do the replacement Aaron' he checked his watch. 'I'd like it back in service by fifteen hundred.'

'Can do' he pushed the trolley to one side then hoisted himself into the cab and drove it to repair bay two. Spelling watched the younger man very skilfully reverse the huge truck into the bay in one easy motion. He never even craned his neck out of the window to align the wheels onto the plate like most of the other drivers did. He was a natural. In an emergency Aaron could be relied on to drive a speeding truck towards a fire. Could manoeuvre the big engine into seemingly impossible spaces and man the gauges and controls. But he freely admitted he could no more go into a burning building than he could jump off a skyscraper. He was however an excellent mechanic. With Mike at his side and two young apprentices they kept the station fleet in top-notch condition. One three four was back in service at fourteen forty-five.

'You okay buddy?' Mike watched his friend roll his shoulders as if to alleviate some pain. They were on their lunch break the following day. Mike tucked into fresh sandwiches that his wife packed every day. Aaron rarely ate during the day. He drank water, lots of water, but rarely ate.

'Must have pulled something' he pushed his shoulder blades together and winced. 'I need a minute' and so saying went to sit in a quiet corner, crossed his legs and rested his hands on his knees and closed his eyes.

'Why doesn't he take a pain killer like everyone else' Billy Wainwright, one of the young apprentices asked in a whisper.

'Never, in all the time I've known him have I seen him take any sort of meds. He just sits and meditates the pain away.' Mike replied in a likewise manner.

'Ya think he's okay though 'cause he's been doing that a lot lately.' Billy's voice was full of concern. They were a close-knit group in the garage and they all looked out for one another.

As it happens Mike had noticed. 'We'll keep an eye on him. Discretely mind.'

Billy nodded. 'He should maybe eat something' and walked over to the other young apprentice and they went outside for a short game of one-on-one.

Three days later and Mike was getting seriously concerned for his friend. Aaron was having the same dream every night; the pain in his back was increasing daily and at one point he collapsed into unconsciousness at the end of his shift and was whisked to hospital.

He dreamed as he lay in the hospital bed. He saw her sitting in a cloud of blue mist, meditating as he often did. Her rich chestnut hair blew gently in the breeze. And she called to him. It was the only way he could describe it. 'Who are you?' he asked.

'I am your destiny' she replied. 'Find me, we have little time. Sing to me. Let me find you.'

'How?' he asked then started to come to wakefulness. He was totally disoriented with images of a beautiful naked woman and swirling silver clouds.

'Nice to have you back with us Mr. Summer' a doctor hovered close to his bed and took his pulse and then looked closely into his eyes. They were rolling around in his head. 'We're going to take you down for a scan in just a moment.'

'What happened?' A confused Aaron asked. He couldn't focus and felt nauseous.

'You collapsed at work. You've been unconscious for a good forty minutes. Your temperature is rather high. Your blood pressure however is perfect. Very unusual.' He studied the chart before continuing. 'Mr. Townsend says you've been experiencing some severe back pain. Is this correct?'

Aaron nodded. 'Between my shoulder blades.' He freely admitted and yawned behind a hand. He felt exhausted. Hospitals always made him sleepy.

'The scan will tell us if anything is wrong.' The door opened and two orderly's came in to take him for a scan. He was not allowed out of bed so they wheeled him away. He fell asleep again as he was pushed along the busy corridors.

Chapter Two

At last she felt him. Thankfully Aurora was alone in the elevator when she heard him call to her. She felt his disorientation and the residue of pain and confusion. There was no way she could concentrate on reaching out to him on the short ride to ground level. It took all of her skill and patience to sign out, mail the correspondence and rush home as quickly as possible. Ten minutes after entering her apartment she sat on her rug and reached out to him.

'I hear you.' He replied.

'Where are you?' she asked.

'The pain was worse today. I'm in hospital.'

'Where?'

'Morg….' And he was gone.

'No, no.' He couldn't possibly be dead, in the morgue! She would have known, have felt his passing. Aurora dashed across the room to her laptop and efficiently logged in to all the listings of hospitals in the area. 'Morgan Latchmann Hospital on 94th Street.' Her mouse clicked on the map attached and within a couple of minutes she had pushed some clothes and shoes into a small bag, unfurled and dimmed her wings and took to the sky. It was risky so early in the evening, but the light was poor and hopefully she could be across town in a few minutes. She landed on the far side of the parking lot deep in shadow and was dressed and making her way to the entrance within ten minutes. A gentle wave of her hand

and the visitors and staff were blinded to her presence. No one seemed to notice the admissions register lift and turn or a slender finger scan down the names of those recently admitted. With the information she wanted she eased back and lifted the spell and headed for the elevators and the fifth floor. She found his room easily and of course it was empty. A quick look at his chart informed her he was on his way for a scan. The information board at the end of the hall indicated the scanning equipment was on the ground floor east wing, which was thankfully directly below her. Rather than wait for the elevator she took the stairs and reached the ground floor in minutes and headed for the Xray and MRI suite of the hospital. It was packed. Occupied beds and wheelchairs lined the corridor; Outpatients filled every available chair, nurses and technicians hurried about. Dismissing all female patients and older men Aurora concentrated on the young men. She reached out with her mind and found him. On the far side of the room, three beds down from the head of the queue. Without hesitation she hurried over to his bed. The orderly's had long since left to see to other duties around the hospital.

'Aaron' she bent down and spoke softly to him. His eyes were closed, but a grimace crossed his face as if pain were causing him discomfort.

'Aaron can you hear me.' She took his hand and felt the jolt of recognition. His eyes flew open.

It took a moment or two to focus on the beautiful face looking down at him. 'You' was the first thing that came into his head.

'What have you done to me?' He pushed himself up and pain burst down his spine and he cried out in pain.

'I. Nothing. Lie still now.' She ran a gentle hand down his arm. He instinctively pulled it away even as the pain receded.

'There is nothing wrong with you. They will find nothing on the scan. The pain will go now. I will wait for you and we will talk.'

'You're damn right we will talk.' He snatched at her hand and felt the jolt again. 'Who are you?'

'Your destiny. Relax now.' She placed a hand over his. 'It's quite natural.' She stepped back as a couple of nurses came to get him and pushed his bed into one of the scanning rooms. He never took his eyes of her until the doors closed.

Aurora's attempts to get anywhere near Aaron were thwarted when he was wheeled back to his room. Mike and his wife and children all crowded in the room to visit with him.

Aaron had decided against speaking to Mike about the woman who had come to him and spoke of destiny and everything being natural. He'd think he was going crazy. Hell he thought he was going crazy. Best to keep this little episode to himself.

'Do you have to stay long Uncle Aaron?' young Philip Townsend, a strapping six year old sat at the foot of Aaron's bed. A look of deep concern on his chubby face.

'Nar, be out tomorrow. They have a machine that can see inside me and they didn't find anything wrong. They think it's some sort of muscle spasm.' He turned to Mike. 'Said I have to take a few days off and rest, fill myself up with pills' he grimaced. 'And no heavy lifting for a while.'

'Can you come home now?' Sophie asked as she sat close by with her daughter asleep in her arms.

'They want to keep me overnight, just to make sure I take the first lot of meds and don't have another episode.' He ran a large hand down the woman's arm. "I'm okay."

'I told them he never, and I emphasised *never* took medications of any description.' Mike grinned widely. 'So they are going to jab a needle in his ass every four hours.' His smile widened and he rubbed his hands together in glee at his friend's grimace. He wasn't going to mention the sheer heart stopping alarm he had felt when his friend simply cried out in pain and keeled over at his feet. It was all the harder to endure because as long as he had known him Aaron had never even had a cold, a simple headache, nothing. He probably scared ten years off his life.

'I'm hungry daddy. Can we have pizza?' Philip scooted off the bed.

'Sure tiger. We should go and let the guy rest.' Mike lifted his sleeping daughter into his arms. She stirred slightly. 'Daddy' she murmured.

'Yeah baby doll. You want pizza?' Mike settled her safely in his arms, her head on his shoulder.

'Okay' and was instantly asleep.

'We'd better get drive-thru honey, she needs to be in bed.' Sophie rose and went to give Aaron a kiss. 'Don't let them do too much damage to that sexy ass of yours.' She ruffled his hair like she would have done to her son.

'I wanna go home mom' Aaron pulled on her hand and made a funny face at Philip. 'Don't let them stick needles in me.'

Philip giggled and turned his face into his father's legs, but his shoulders were shacking. Mike was grinning.

'Arr poor baby' Sophie settled herself at Aaron's side enjoying their game. 'Now you know you have to stay here for tonight so that you can get better.'

'Yeah but can't I …..' Aaron milked it for all it was worth.

'Be a good little soldier' Sophie interrupted 'and tomorrow I'll buy you a big tub of your favourite ice cream.'

'With hot fudge sauce?' he licked his lips and winked at Philip.

'Only if you're good' she kissed his cheek again. 'Jerk' she whispered. 'Witch' he replied and kissed her in return.

'Enough all ready' Mike herded his family out of the door. 'I'll come get you after doctor's rounds tomorrow. You're going to stay with us for a few days. No arguing buddy. Later.' The door closed behind him.

He barely had time to settle down before the door opened again and Aurora stepped in.

'I thought I dreamt you' He pulled himself up and winced slightly with the effort.

'I'm real enough. We should talk.' She stood at the foot of his bed. Lord he was a handsome devil. Thick dark hair that fell in unruly waves to his shoulders. Eyes as green as freshly mown grass with long dark lashes and dark well shaped eyebrows. A sculptured face with high cheekbones, a slender, not over long nose and a mouth that would devastate any woman that he kissed. His chest was toned and well muscled without too much bulk and his arms were lean and finely toned. His hands at the moment were loosely fisted, but she knew his fingers were long and strong.

'I prefer face to face rather than invading my dreams and causing me pain. Who the hell are you?' Strangely he felt no fear of her. She meant him no harm of that he was certain.

'I am Aurora.' She held herself erect, her head tilted a little to one side.

'Aurora. As in sleeping beauty.' He shrugged. It took all sorts.

'I am Aurora, daughter of Salvax, King of what you people call faeries.' She had no idea who sleeping beauty was.

He didn't answer immediately. What he did do was press the alarm button on the hand set close to his left hand. He knew he wasn't crazy, so she must be.

'Yeah right. Faeries!' He kept one eye on her and one on the door. Security would come pouring in any moment and cart her away.

'Did your mother ever mention your home your father?' Aurora moved around the room, a practical demonstration may be called for. 'It does not work' she noticed Aaron pushing the red button again and again. 'I mean you no harm. None will enter whilst I am here.' She slipped off her light jacket and tossed it over the chair. 'Your father?' she repeated.

'I want you out of here. Now. I don't know you. I don't want to know you. Get out of my room and out of my head.' He did not raise his voice. He didn't feel it necessary. Her devastating beauty would not, he told himself, sway him.

'I have come a long way to find you. I have searched for many months. It was only recently you began to sing and I was able to link my song with yours.'

'Again. Yeah right.' Yet he had the strangest feeling creep over him. Something vaguely familiar.

'I do not lie. Listen.' She closed her eyes and let herself sing.

'Nothing happening here.' Aaron sang out.

'Listen with your heart, not your head. Close your eyes and listen.' She lifted a fine eyebrow at his sarcasm.

'What the heck' he settled back and closed his eyes. Little realising that Aurora hadn't spoken a word.

He found himself drifting in the nether world between awake and sleep when the body was relaxed and at peace. It was one of the reasons he was so adept at meditation. He could switch his busy brain off by simply closing his eyes and breathing deeply. In some ways he found it more relaxing than eight hours sleep. He heard the faintest sound. Music. A soft sound of pan pipes, or maybe it was a flute. It was so sweet he smiled and let it envelop him.

Across the room Aurora also smiled. Aaron may not realise it but he was singing loud and clear. Harp song, soft as the rain, gentle as a breeze.

'Your song is lovely' she said aloud and opened her eyes. He was staring at her. 'The doctor will come soon and release you. Is your home far from here?'

'Why should I tell you?' A deep frown wrinkled his forehead.

'Don't act the fool Aaron. There are things you need to know, and to do. Adjustments to be made. You are under no obligation to accept your heritage. But you need to make the adjustments or the pain will return and kill you. This is not a threat. It is the truth.' She looked toward the door. 'The doctor is coming, he will not see me.' She stood totally motionless against the far wall of his room.

'Well Mr Summer you'll be pleased to know we're not keeping you overnight.' He read the chart as he spoke. 'Your scan results were negative. We're putting it down to severe spasms. We've also decided to give you a course of oral medication rather than the injections. Be sure to complete the course.' He made notes on the chart. Aurora pushed herself away from the wall and stood at his elbow studying the chart as the doctor wrote. 'You can pick up your medication at any pharmacy but make sure you collect it this evening and take your first tablet soonest. Any questions.' He handed over the prescription. 'Don't mean to rush you but we could use the bed. Nasty accident on the interstate and we're to expect a number of casualties. We need the bed.'

'No problem. Thanks Doctor. I wasn't looking forward to those injections.' He swung his long legs out of bed and reached into the bedside cabinet for his clothes.

'Don't blame you. I'm not overly fond of them myself!' he smiled. 'Any problems come back and see me. Take care now.' He was out of the door in seconds.

'You going to stand there while I get dressed?' He looked over his shoulder at her. He was completely naked. He'd pulled off the hospital gown the second he was back in his room.

'Yes. Are you embarrassed?' She in turn came around the bed and stood before him.

He rested his hands on his knees as he looked at her. The bed sheet snarled over his hips. 'You give me erotic and painful dreams. Dreams in which I am naked and have a major hard-on. You visit me in hospital, tell me to relax, tell me you're a 'faerie'' he made speech marks with his fingers. 'So why the hell should anything you do or say embarrass me?'

'No reason at all. Hurry up.' Deliberately teasing, she sat close by in a vacant chair and watched him. He was absolutely gorgeous. His wings would be beautiful. She was truly sorry that he would have to endure some serious pain before the night was over.

'Do you live with your mother?' Her question was unexpected and caught him off guard.

'And if I did?' he pulled on his jeans and left them unstrapped whilst he pulled on his shirt and buttoned it over his chest.

'She would know me.' Was all Aurora said as she rose to her feet and Aaron tucked his shirt into his jeans and buckled his belt. Socks and boots followed before he picked up a denim jacket and pushed his arms into the sleeves.

Wallet and loose change went into his pockets along with his prescription.

'She died when I was two.' He had little recollection of her.

'Your father will be sorry to hear of it.' She preceded him to the door.

He slapped his hand on the panel before she could pull it open. 'If he knew of me why didn't he come and look for me?' There was such hurt in his voice. Hurt he didn't realise he carried with him.

Aurora placed a hand over his on the door. 'He had other responsibilities. You have a sister, two years older. She needed him when your mother left. He could not come.'

'This is bullshit!' he hissed and pushed her aside and hurried from the room.

'It's a lot to take in.' Aurora tried to engage him in conversation whilst they descended to the ground level. He pushed out of the elevator ahead of her and kept on walking without saying another word.

'Aaron wait. Wait damn it!' she snatched at his arm and managed to bring him to a halt. 'I know that you are angry and confused.'

'Ya think!" he snatched his arm away but didn't continue walking, just pushed his hands into his pockets and stared off into the distance.

'Two hours. Give me two hours. We'll take a cab to your home, we need to be private.' As if by magic a cab drew up to the curb and she opened the door. Amazed at himself he got in and gave the address to the driver. They said not another word until they were in his apartment.

Chapter Three

'Time starts now.' he closed his door behind them and tossed his jacket on a peg behind the door and walked down a short corridor to his living area.

'This will do nicely.' Aurora went over to look at the view from his windows. Like herself he was not overlooked. He too faced the sea. Her apartment was on the other side of the bay, although it could not be seen from here. All these months, so near and yet so far away.

'I take it that you do not believe me?' Aurora removed her own jacket and placed it carefully on a chair with her bag. She then pushed one of his armchairs a couple of feet out of the way and gauging the distance seemed satisfied.

'Sorry the positioning of my furniture isn't to your liking' his voice dripped with sarcasm as he stood with his arms folded on the other side of the room.

'Practicalities Aaron.' She snapped open the button on her tailored trousers and slid down the zip before they fell to her feet. 'This is best done naked. Take your clothes off.' She flipped a hand toward him.

'If you wanted a quick fuck we could have taken care of that at the hospital and I could get a little peace.' He did however appreciate her lovely long legs.

'I can assure you that fucking is the last thing on my mind.' Quick or otherwise she thought. 'Take your clothes off.' The rest of hers fell at her feet. 'You meditate, correct?'

she glanced over at him. He was not co-operating. 'I cannot help you if you are not prepared to help yourself. If I leave now you will be dead by morning, and your death will not be easy.' She sighed heavily. 'Please take your clothes off, down to the skin. You have nothing to be embarrassed or ashamed of.' She turned away and sat cross-legged on a rug in the centre of the room. From the corner of her eye she could see the young man reluctantly removing his clothes. 'Come sit across from me, cross your legs and rest your hands on your knees.'

'I know how it works.' He sat across from her and took up the position, thankful that, at the moment, his libido seemed to be asleep. He serious hoped he didn't have to dream to get a hard-on.

'The young men at home have been trained in meditation from birth to prepare themselves for this moment. Every man when they reach their thirtieth year learns how to fly. Females can fly when we reach the age of twenty, a full decade before the male. Why this is I have no idea. It simply is.'

He snorted in derision. 'You seriously expect me to believe I will be able to fly without…..'

'But of course. Watch carefully. Do not be alarmed.' She closed her eyes, breathed deeply for some minutes before her chin came to rest on her chest and her shoulders rolled forward. Within seconds her wings started to appear. They unfurled as she rose quickly to her feet. One mind flick and they spread out on either side and shimmered brightly in the late afternoon daylight.

'Holy shit.' He sat rigid at her feet looking up at her. 'Mother of God.' But somewhere deep inside he knew. He just knew. When he was a kid he used to dream of flying across the heavens with his arms spread wide. There was such a sense of freedom as he soared across the sky.

She flapped her wings gently distracting him; there was more than enough room. 'My apartment is too small for me to flap my wings. I do try to fly a couple of times a week to keep them healthy and I do love it so.' She smiled down at him.

'They are absolutely beautiful. I can see through them.' He felt a slight breeze as her wings swept back and forth before she closed them and tucked them away before resuming her place on the floor. He was curious enough to lean forward and look behind her. The wings had completely disappeared back into her body.

'Your wings have caused the pain that you have been experiencing. They are ready to break free for the first time. This first time' she reached out and took his hands 'will be agonising. But it is only this one time. Thereafter it is just a case of concentrating and they will appear.' She watched as he absorbed the information.

'Will mine be like yours?' he asked. Willing to believe just about anything now. It had been a very strange day. He was a faerie for crying out loud.

'Similar, but not exact. How tall are you?'

'Six five.'

'Then I would estimate each wing to be eight feet, span up to sixteen feet. Yours will be of a slightly heavier grade in order to take your weight. You are nicely muscled without being bulky. This will help. If you were to increase your weight, your wings would not be able to carry you. Weight is a problem for us. The slimmer the better.'

'I can't see you having a problem. You are all around beautiful.' He squeezed gently on her fingers. Relaxed. 'So what happens now? What do I do?' He puffed out an anxious breath.

'Right then. Now remember, the pain will be severe." She lifted both hands and pushed the air out toward the walls. "I've put a temporary soundproofing on this room only. If you wish to scream, then scream, believe me it will help. We all get through this.' She smiled at him. 'And you will also get one major erection.' Her gaze went to his loins where his manhood rested. She secretly couldn't wait to see his reaction.

'I'm amazed I don't have one now simply looking at you.' He freely admitted, thankful that his penis seemed to be asleep. 'My dreams of you were very erotic.' She smiled.

'Your body knows. It just waits.' She took a deep breath and let go his hands. 'Now close your eyes and take a minute to breathe deeply. Try not to think of anything. Calm thoughts.' She watched him closely; his heart song was filling her mind. 'Rest your chin on your chest. Breathe deeply. That's right. Now roll your shoulders forward. When the pain starts it will be mild. Get to your feet then and hold my hands. Think wings, just wings. Picture them in your mind at full spread. Think wings.' She watched as his head slowly lifted. His eyes were closed but his face was etched with pain. There was a slight 'pop' and he groaned. 'Stand up now' she sprang to her feet and caught hold of his hands and pulled him up. The tips of his wings started to appear above his shoulders. His entire body shock but he locked his knees as the pain ripped through him and he cried out, then he screamed and he screamed. Tears ran down his cheeks he was unable to stop them. He was shaking so badly he stumbled a number of paces to the side. Aurora kept a tight hold of his hands.

'Nearly done Aaron, one more minute.' It had taken ten agonising minutes for his wings to unfurl. 'Oh Aaron they are beautiful.' At last she felt his hand relax their bone-crushing grip on hers. Agony dulled to severe, to bad, to bearable, before he could even speak amidst his gasps for air. His entire body trembled from head to foot.

'Is it over?' His voice was a whisper of sound. He wanted desperately to sit down but didn't think he should. He didn't like to admit it, but he was afraid to open his eyes and look over his shoulder. He expected to be standing in pools of his own blood.

'Look at me' she said gently as he lifted his face. The tears had stopped but his face was wet and his eyes red rimmed and puffy. She placed a finger against his lips and once against let her thoughts talk to him. 'Can you hear me?'

'Yes' he blinked and answered with his mind. 'Perfectly.'

'Then spread your wings.' Aurora stepped away to get the full effect. It was rewarding to see the change happen. The shimmer was slow to form on this his first time. It appeared to be a pale pearly blue with flashes of rich sapphire thrown in for good measure. Then whoosh!

'Oh' Aurora said and stepped closer. 'Oh they are beautiful.' Many shades of blue would be his colour. Mingled with swirls of smoky grey and white. 'Magnificent.' She said with awe.

'Can I see?' Aaron was still facing forward. He thought himself a coward as he had his eyes closed.

Aurora placed both hands on his shoulders. 'Do not turn around. Open your eyes and look over your shoulder. I have seen many young men on their first opening. They pale in comparison to the magnificence of yours.' She looked up into his lovely red-rimmed green eyes. She didn't think he realised that he did have one major hard-on. It brushed gently against her hip. She thought it best not to mention it. For now.

The first thing he noticed with a bright pearly shimmer that ran the length of his wing on the right side. Turning, he discovered the same on the left.

'Wow' words failed him. No feathers, synonymous with wings on birds. No thick folds of skin as you would expect on a bat. Not even a delicate butterfly had wings as transparent as this. And they were huge. 'It's unbelievable' he reached out with his right hand to its fullest extent and gently touched his wing. He felt it. As if his fingers brushed his arm. Whereas he had expected to find a delicate network of membrane, easily broken, he felt the beginnings of strength and power.

'They are tender yet and easily damaged.' Aurora did not object when his arms came around her and held her close to his warm chest. Her head fit nicely under his chin.

'It's incredible. Awesome.' He took a deep breath. 'My heart is racing.' He looked down at her when she lifted her head.

'Perfectly natural. Your heart is pumping blood into your wings. It will slow in a moment. In a day or two I will teach you how to dim your shimmer. Flying at night is the safest time, but we cannot be seen.'

'Are they at their fullest extent?' he swung his head from side to side. He would have to get a huge mirror to fully see the effect.

Aurora giggled and pinked a little causing the young man to turn a quizzical eye on her. 'Not quite yet, in a little while.' Her eyebrows rose high on her forehead, there was a twinkle in her eyes as she stepped reluctantly out of his embrace and look down at his loins.

'What's so funny? Why are…you…oh shit.' He looked down at himself recalling her words earlier. 'Is this…natural….I mean…will it always be this ….big' he said for want of a better word. I mean he was six feet five inches tall and his anatomy coincided with his build. He had never been…well like….small, even without an erection, but surely there was a couple more inches in length and it seemed a little thicker around the circumference. From root to tip it had to be ten inches at least.

'Most men appreciate the increase in the size of their… equipment. Even in our world it is a cause of some pride and a maid needs to know what she is letting herself in for when she is betrothed. She would stand as witness to his first opening.' She tried to get her thoughts in order so as not to be too crude in the telling.

'She watches?' he looked at her askance.

'His family, her family.' She stepped close again. 'All the maidens in my world go naked even after their wings appear at aged twenty. When married a woman would then wear a loincloth of silk, then a shift of silk when she conceives a child. Males go naked until they are thirty. Thereafter they wear a loincloth of leather.' She licked her lips before continuing. His manhood twitched between his legs. 'At the first opening when his penis is at full arousal the maid has the option to approve or decline her betrothed. If she accepts him they mate immediately to seal the bargain. The marriage would take place after his first flight, usually within three days.' Her warm hands spread over his chest. 'Until his thirtieth birthday, until his first opening, the men are…unable to perform sexually. They may have an erection from time to time but are unable to sustain it for more than a moment or two. Until a maid accepts a mate she is also a virgin. It has been that way from the beginning. The men are unable and the females have no desires.'

'You're a virgin?' Aaron stepped away, his wings quivered and flapped gently. Something smashed but he wasn't sure what it was. The tip of his wing has brushed against something. He thought close and his wings furled and disappeared. It was second nature to him. There was a twinge of pain. Aurora noticed. 'So you're here to…so that I…bloody hell.' He pushed his hands through his thick dark hair and wished he had on a pair of trousers so he could push his hands into the pockets. 'You're telling me that you're my mate. That somehow we are betrothed?' His voice was incredulous. 'I don't know you. We met only hours ago. This is ridiculous.' His throbbing erection didn't think it was ridiculous at all.

'This is all very strange and new to you.' She reached out a hand to grip his wrist. 'My father sent me to find you. I am obliged to perform this service for you. You are under no obligation once the act is consummated. If you chose to remain in this world then you are free to do so. But until you mate with one of your own kind, and the only one available is myself, you will not be able to perform as a man. If you refuse me your penis will whither in due time and will never again bring you pleasure.' She kept her voice level and calm.

'Let me get this right.' He paced across the room and back. 'You were sent here to find me and assist with my opening. You then tell me that we have to have sex now, like now' he threw his hands in the air 'because if I don't I'll be impotent for the rest of my life.'

'Yes.'

'If I decide to stay here in this…world, I have sex with you, you fly off and I'm a normal healthy man except I have wings and can fly.' He shook his head in total frustration.

'In a nutshell.'

'Well that's just fucking brilliant.' He took a deep long breath and was silent for some minutes. 'I assume you know what to do? Because I sure as hell don't want to be a eunuch for the rest of my life.' He had visions of being just that before the accident that took him to hospital. Not even Mike knew he was still a virgin at thirty for God's sake.

Aurora nodded and started to move furniture around to give them more space. 'Your wings need to be spread. The blood rush will enhance the pleasure of the mating.' She stepped aside and drew the curtain to shut out the twilight. 'It is a simply procedure and normally doesn't last too long. I'm told the benefits are reward enough.' She held out a hand. 'Come.'

'I assume you know the female anatomy?' She would not blush she told herself, repeatedly. As she stepped to the rear of a hard-backed chair and let her wings unfurled and spread out as she bent over the chair. 'Step up behind me, take a firm grip on my hips and guide yourself into me. Do it quickly, the full length. Then do what comes naturally.'

'Sweet Lord above' he muttered. This was not how he envisaged his first sexual encounter. Just do it, he said to himself. Step up to the plate, slot A into slot B and enjoy the ride. If only it were that simple. He was terrified. He was thankful that she faced away from him as he was blushing to the roots of his hair. He took several deep breaths to calm his over hot blood. He spread his wings.

In the end he went with instinct. He did step up behind her and ran his arms over her warm soft flesh. The experience was new to him but he and Mike had sat through enough soft porn movies in their youth to know what was expected and what areas between a woman's legs gave her pleasure. No time like the present to find out if it was true. Searching fingers found her already warm and wet. Using her own juices he slicked his fingers toward the sensitive nub that nestled between the lips of her vagina. Within moments she erupted under him as her first orgasm washed over her.

'Well I'll be damned' he whispered. 'It works'. He replaced his fingers with his manhood slipping it gently across the nub until his penis was saturated with her when she came again and cried out. Her legs buckled and she would have fallen if the chair hadn't kept her upright. Her breathing was gasps; her wings blushed a bright pink. Her bottom was the same colour. For some minutes he was simply lost in the show she was providing. Her wings were truly beautiful. Silver merged with greys and white when she was at her ease. Now they changed from a pale pink after her first orgasm into a deeper richer pink with a silvery cast. Not only did her body tremble, but also her wings vibrated rapidly as her excitement grew.

He wanted the full experience. He needed to get his hands on her. It was difficult to touch anything other than her legs and buttocks. He wanted the feel of her breasts against his palm, the hard nipples in his mouth. He wanted to kiss her so badly his face grimaced as he kept up the gentle pressure between her legs. He pulled away quickly.

'Stand up. Close. Turn around.' She did it automatically.

'Is something wrong?' she couldn't focus properly. Her body was alive with feelings.

'Open.' He commanded, and she did. He pulled her arms around his neck and lifted her off her feet and clamped his lips down on her in a brutal, almost savage kiss. His large hands cupped her thighs and lifted her up so she could wind her legs around his hips. Tearing his mouth from hers some minutes later he lifted her higher and fastened his mouth, gently, over her breast and lathered his tongue across the pink hardened crest.

Her head fell forward and her cheek rested on the top of his head. 'More, give me more.' She did not say the words but he heard her clearly enough, and, with an unsteady hand lowered her and guided himself home, plunging deep.

'Don't stop, don't stop.' Aurora cried out this time and clung fast around his neck as his powerful arms and hands lifted and released until they were both spent with limbs as wobbly as jelly.

He had to put her down his strength was gone. They were forced to cling together when her feet touched the carpet, swaying together for several minutes catching their breath.

Aurora was the first to recover. 'Your wings are red.' They were vibrating strongly, sending out flashes of gold and sapphire. Truly beautiful.

Forcing his eyes to open was an effort. 'So are yours. Pretty great huh.'

'For a first time we did good I think.' She stepped away and looked down at his withered penis. 'Be more comfortable now.' She looked up into his eyes. 'You should close now. Just think close and picture your wings folding back under your skin. There will be no pain.' He did and there was not.

'I am sorry' he looked at the blood flecks on her thighs and also on his own.

'Don't be. I was well prepared. There was no pain just pleasure. Thank you.'

'My pleasure entirely' he took her hand and bought it to his lips. 'Lets take a shower and get something to eat. I'm starving.' They managed to wash in between passionate kisses and some heavy petting. Aurora then discovered he had a great fondness for chicken salad.

'So what happens now?' They stood at the sink washing dishes together. Both were still naked, it seemed perfectly natural.

'The first thing to do is call your friend.' she placed the plates back in the cupboard. Her six months in this world had taught her many things. 'We will need to go into the countryside for a few days so that you can practice flying where no one can see.' When she turned he was right behind her, she had to take a pace back to see into his eyes. 'What is it?'

'Will you go back….home wherever that it when I can fly?' his brows came together in concern.

'Not right away' a warm hand touched his chest. 'But eventually. I miss my family and have been away too long.' The hand moved up to cup his face. 'Do not concern your-self about me. There is no obligation between us. Even if you decided to come with me, you would be free to choose another if you so wish. Our laws would not bind you unless you decide to stay permanently.'

'Is your reputation compromised now? Will another man refuse you because another spilled your virgin's blood?' It only just occurred to him that this might be the case. Virginity wasn't as highly prized nowadays. Not in this world anyway.

'It was my choice to make.' She broke away and walked to the living room and began to dress. Being naked didn't bother either of them.

'That's not answering my question' he reached her in seconds and turned her to face him, his hands firmly on her shoulders.

'It is the only answer I can give you. I must go now. Call your friend. Be ready to leave in two days. I will come to collect you.'

'Did it mean nothing to you. Nothing at all. Just a job?' He let his hands fall to his side. He thought they had a connection.

She looked him in the eyes. She would not be weak now. The connection was made, for her anyway. 'It was never a job Aaron. I came to you in order to save your life. I care what happens to you.' She finished dressing. 'I'll pick you up at eight o'clock on Friday evening.' Then she fled his apartment.

Chapter Four

It took an hour for him to compose himself. He had never been one to pace, his mind in turmoil. Now he seemed capable of nothing else. Meditation was the thing, the thing that had always been able to calm him. It didn't help, so he paced.

'I'm a faerie' he said aloud. 'A honest to goodness faerie, complete with wings.' He paced back and forth. 'Bloody huge wings.' He spread his arms wide. 'Then I have sex, for the first time mind you' he said to the empty room 'with the most gorgeous creature I have ever set eyes on. And *she's* a faerie too.' He puffed out his breath. 'You're losing it Aaron. You've gone completely nuts.' He brushed his hands through his thick dark hair. 'What the hell am I going to tell Mike?'

He was pondering just that when the phone rang. It made him jump.

'Aaron Summer.' He answered.

'I know who you are. Why are you out of hospital and why aren't you here with us?' Mike's disgruntled voice blasted down the phone.

'Got waylaid by a sexy brunette.' Aaron tried to sound cheerful.

'That is not an explanation buddy.' The decibel level down the phone dropped a few degrees.

'There was an accident on the interstate and they needed my bed. You'd not long left and this absolutely beautiful creature offered to come home with me and see me settled in. We had a nice meal together then she very efficiently cleaned my pipes. I am beyond relaxed buddy of mine. I can almost fly. She's coming back tomorrow to do some….physiotherapy on me.' Aaron prayed his voice sounded dreamy and relaxed enough.

'Way to go buddy.' Mike's voice sounded remarkable cheerful suddenly. 'Okay your forgiven but if you need anything, anything at all, give me a call okay?'

'Sure thing, thanks. See you in a couple of days. Bye.' He hung up then went and got himself a beer. He downed half a bottle before he realised he was still naked so went to find an old pair of sweat pants and pulled them on and stepped out onto his balcony. It was a cool night and the breeze felt good on his warm skin.

'As you're out on the balcony half naked I hope you've a young lady similarly attired inside?' a soft voice chuckled.

Aaron turned to his left. 'She had to go home. You wanna come take her place?' he ambled over to the barrier that separated his property from hers. Iris Evans was a nice old lady well into her eighties and had lived next door for nearly four years now. She had to walk with the aid of a cane but everything else about her was as sharp as a new pin.

'You're not ready for someone as good as me yet. In a year or two maybe.' she smiled warmly at him and patted the chair next to her.

'I'll take you on any day.' Aaron vaulted over the railing and plonked himself down beside her. 'How are you keeping Iris?' he stretched out his very long legs and they both studied the stars.

'I'm just dandy.' She patted his hand. 'Off to my granddaughter's in a few days. She just had her second child and asked me to go stay for a little while. Chuck, her husband, is coming to get me on Friday.' They chatted about this and that for thirty minutes before he helped her rise and escorted her inside.

'You're one classy broad you know that.' Aaron kissed her soft wrinkled cheek.

'Without a doubt' she patted his cheek. 'You take care now.'

'Same goes. See you soon. Good night.'

He slept fitfully. There was no dream, no pain, just peaceful restorative sleep. When he woke it was seven in the morning and the start of a beautiful spring day. He lay on his back, closed his eyes and pushed his hands behind his head and thought of Aurora.

'Are you awake?' he thought.

'I am an early riser. I have work.' She had just stepped out of the shower when he 'called'.'

'What am I supposed to do with myself today?' He could feel himself getting hard just by thinking about her.

'Go swimming. It will help maintain your overall health. Keep your shoulders and upper arms in optimum condition.' She dressed as she linked with him. She smiled as she felt his manhood stirring, pleased that she had caused it. He was an exceptional specimen.

'Swimming' a smile crossed his face. 'Come with me. Play hooky?'

'Tempting as the offer is I have responsibilities. Now get out of my head or I will be late. We'll talk later.' Then she was gone. He went swimming.

He was not the only hardy soul out for a swim in the bay that morning. Couples strolled on the sand, browsed in shops along the wharf or like himself waded out into the gentle surf. Once past the icy chill of the water he plunged beneath the surface and stayed submerged for twenty feet before breaking the surface and striking out in a powerful crawl across the bay. Swimming, like meditation, cleared his mind and exercised his body. Things were changing in his life. Change was inevitable, whether good or bad. What he was going to do about this change was a problem for later. Now he simply glided through the water like some mystical sea creature enjoying the warmth of the sun on his back.

'Oh my God!' a young woman grabbed the arm of her friend and spun her around to face the sea. 'Tell me I'm not dreaming.'

'Oh my, oh my, oh my.' The friend whispered. 'Be still my heart.'

Aaron rose up out of the water and waded in the surf to shore. The seawater ran off him in rivulets down his skin. Long fingers ran through his hair as he pushed it back from his handsome face. He felt good. His heart was pumping heavily in his chest and air rushed into his lungs a little faster than the norm. The towel he had left casually on the sand was used briskly as he ran it across his wet skin before he slung it around his neck to catch the drips from his hair.

'Good morning ladies' he inclined his head briefly as he past the two young women who were openly staring at him.

'Oh it certainly is.' They sighed and kept watching as he strolled to his car and reached in for an old pair of sweat pants that he pulled over his wet shorts before getting in and driving away. An hour later he was showered and dressed and stuck for something else to do. Inactivity was not a normal part of his day. He opted for research. He could easily have sat at his computer and used the Internet, but this would not have eased his restlessness. So he locked his apartment and took a stroll to the library. In the myths and legends section he pulled out a number of books and started to read. There was very little in the way of information. Pages were dedicated to the likes of goblins, elves and trolls. Witches and sorcerers, dragons and mythical beasts filled one entire volume. The only mention of faeries that he found was a short column on pixies and the like. Small winged creatures, living in sun drenched forests, under toadstools. Nocturnal which was why they were rarely seen.

'What a load of rubbish' he muttered and replaced the books.

He checked his watch as he jogged down the steps of the library. Just after 3pm. He headed for the park. With his hands stuffed in the pockets of his jacket he ambled along doing a little window-shopping on the way. He was bored to distraction.

'How do you counteract the boredom?' he thought. 'I'm window shopping for Christ's sake.'

'I'm rarely bored.' He jolted as she came into his mind. 'I'm having a very busy day. What are you looking at?' Her fingers dashed across her keyboard as she completed the letter she was typing. All day she had resisted the urge to link with him.

'It's a dazzling display of the very best in cast iron cookware' he grinned. 'The very best on the market so it says. I ought to go and buy some immediately.' He turned away and continued walking.

'Too heavy. Even worse when food is cooking.' She replied easily.

'Arrrrgh now this is better.' He felt like a perv staring at the lingerie on the models in the window.

'It must be sexy underwear. I can almost feel your pulse racing.' The letter was printing out as another was started.

'If I buy it will you come over and model it for me?' He was smiling to himself as he pictured her in the black lacy bra and panties. It then turned to mild alarm as he began to get hard. He turned and walked away immediately. He felt her laughing. 'Give me a break here. I'm new at this.'

It was the excuse she needed. 'I'll come over if you cook me dinner.'

'Deal' he replied immediately. 'Seven okay?'

'Perfect' then she was gone.

She felt the tug low in her belly. Just the sound of his voice in her head was enough to make her ache with need. Her mother had assured her that the sacrifice of her virginity in no way tied her to the man involved. 'It takes weeks to become sexually mature. Once married when intercourse is an intimate and regular act, then your natural urges will kick in. There is much pleasure when your passions and lust are combined.' Her mother had informed her.

'What of love my mother?' she had asked in all innocence. She was then an immature female of eighteen years.

'Love will develop when you pick your mate; make a home together, as it did with your father. We love each other very much.'

Some years later she was asked to accompany her father to the opening of a young man who was betrothed to one of her closes friends. The young woman had accept the young man and the mating took place. Since that time she had seen many such ceremonies. Nothing however had prepared her for what had taken place with Aaron. He had wanted more than she was lead to believe was required. Break the maidenhead to seal the bond. A quick joining so the man could release his seed in order to be whole and able to perform as a man.

Aaron wanted much more. To feel and to touch. To kiss and caress. To run his tongue over her quivering flesh, to nibble at her shoulders and suckle on her breasts. To play havoc with the heat between her legs. It was never expected that a maiden would reach orgasm the first time. Yet she sat here as proof that it was possible, with the right lover, to have multiple orgasms. To lose her senses and tremble with need, to feel the rush of Aaron's seed fill her body as she convulsed around him. All whilst he stayed on his feet and manoeuvred her with his large beautiful hands as his wings flamed and flashed with gold's and reds the like of which she had never seen before. And she wanted more of the same.

It was her custom to take her holidays whenever Mr. Reynolds was out of the office. He took a weeks vacation at the start of Spring which was fortunate in this case as it coincided with Aurora's need to spend the time with Aaron to teach him to fly. A week in the mountains would do them both good. After the office was closed she booked a small cabin in the mountains with no immediate neighbours. She showered in the rest room before she left with the post and then took a cab to Aaron's.

Her knock was answered in seconds. An urgent pull took her into his arms. He kicked the door closed as his mouth found hers in a hungry hot kiss. He lifted her into his arms and carried her into his bedroom without breaking contact. They fell onto his bed together. 'I hope you're not hungry because I need you now.' Then he absolutely destroyed her. Never in all of his wildest dreams did he imagine a need so great, so overpowering, as to render him incapable of any other thought than his possession of Aurora.

It came over him the closer the time got to seven. He was preparing spaghetti and meatballs, another of his favourites, when the ache began in his loins. As it was not a normal occurrence for him he wasn't at all sure if it was normal. He was forced to hold onto the kitchen counter to steady himself. Within minutes he had yanked his jeans down over his hips to release his growing manhood and alleviate the discomfort.

'Must be a faerie thing.' He muttered when at last he was able to calm himself and restore his clothing.

But even now with all the urgency and need pumping through his veins he took time to savour the essence of her. His lips travelled over flesh warm and damp with desire as he carefully peeled off her clothes. He was more ruthless with his own. Of paramount importance was the feel of his flesh against hers. The spread of his hands over her long slender body. 'That's better, that's much better' he whispered in her ear.

Instinct guided him. Those long ago soft porn films had educated him in the ways of the female body. The experience itself however was beyond imagining. He had to taste everything from the top of her head to the soles of her feet and everything in between. She cried out with passion as his tongue probed between her legs and pushed gently into her. When he withdrew and found the sensitive nub with his tongue she was beyond delirious. The hands that were holding onto his hair slipped limply to the bed, her back arched and her head rolled listlessly from side to side. She mumbled unintelligent words; coherent thoughts were lost to her. Never like this. Never like this.

Before her system had time to recover Aaron was between her legs, lifted her hips high and wide and drove himself home, his full length. She took a huge breath then plunged into the mad ride towards the finish line.

There wasn't enough air to fill her lungs, panting seemed to be the only way to get enough oxygen. Her vision was blurred and her head spinning. Every few seconds a spasm ran the length of her body, centring at her core. Her heart was pounding so hard and fast within her chest she thought it might stall at any moment. And she was being crushed.

Hot breath caressed her neck. Strong hands held her shoulders down. The same hands that had pushed under her body and clamped down on her shoulders to keep her in place as he thrust energetically into her. His heartbeat was as wild and erratic as her own. She felt amazing. Thoroughly ravished.

'Aaron' her voice was a harsh whisper.

'Ummm' was all he could muster. There wasn't an ounce of strength left in his entire body. He was totally drained.

'Please. Can't breathe. Heavy.' Her hands slapped ineffectively against his back. She had to get him to move.

'What?' he managed to lift his head and looked into her flushed face. Her eyes were rolling back in her head. 'Oh shit' he pulled himself free of her and rolled onto his back. 'Sorry.' Silence reigned for some minutes as breathing and heartbeats returned to normal.

Aaron turned on his side to look at her. She was a mess, a lovely mess, but nonetheless a mess. Her face was very flushed. Her hair was mussed and her lips swollen. Those lovely nipples on her full breasts were deep pink and looked as hard as pebbles. Her arms and legs were spread and limp. Signs of their lovemaking were clearly visible on her thighs and belly and dampened the sheet beneath her. He could still taste her on his lips. He hadn't given her any choice had he? He simply took what he wanted. It wasn't all one sided. He knew she had reached orgasm at least twice. Selfish bastard that he named himself he wanted to do it all over again.

He ran warm knuckles down her soft cheek. 'I'm sorry Aurora. Forgive me.' He positioned himself between her limp legs and guided himself inside her. 'I just have to have you again.' His trusts were gentle however and he took most of his considerable weight on his elbows.

Aurora came to her senses slowly. She had very nearly fallen asleep when she felt his hand on her cheek. She was amazed that he could perform again so soon when he filled her only seconds later. But what did he have to be sorry about? Why did he need forgiveness? Instinctively her arms went around him and she lifted her legs high around his waist as he rocked them gently towards completion. She did not have the devastating orgasm of earlier, but a gentle pop and warmth spread through her as she felt his seed leave his body and fill her own. It was she who turned her lips to his and kissed him long and softly.

'Better now?' she brushed his hair from his face as he looked down at her. God he was beautiful.

He nodded. 'I think I'm empty for a while.' He started to pull away but she tightened her legs around him.

'You said you were sorry. Why would you be sorry?' She looked carefully into his eyes.

'For not giving you a choice.' Again he ran his knuckles down her cheek. 'Twice.'

'Do you hear me complaining?' she began to run her hands slowly up and down his back. Enjoying the feel of long powerful muscles under her fingers. He would be a good flyer.

'No but that's not the point. I should have more control. Considered your feelings.' As he spoke he ran his thumb across her lips and then gently over her tongue when she opened for him. It disappeared into her mouth when she lifted her head slightly and sucked intimately on the long digit. He got hard instantly. Filled her completely. When her hips began to lift beneath him he thrust gently to meet her. Her teeth nipped his thumb when he tried to pull it out of her mouth. She sucked hard on his thumb in unison with his thrusts. It was the most erotic thing he had every experienced.

'You're a good cook.' She filled her mouth with spaghetti and meatballs in a spicy tomato sauce. 'I'm ravenous.' Chicken salad would not suffice for occasions such as this when she would need all her strength to keep up with the man opposite her at the table.

'Dinner was supposed to be at seven. It's ten now.' Aaron also filled his mouth and ate with as much enjoyment as his partner. Not even a cleansing shower could stop their passion from running amok. 'Is it always like this. So intense, so …..mind boggling.'

'As you are my first experience with such things I have no idea.' She absolutely refused to tell him that it was considered 'honeymoon fever' back home. When appetites ran to the extreme in all things.

'Can I ask you something?' He was busy rinsing dishes and pans before putting them in the dishwater.

'Of course.' She wiped down the table with a sheet of kitchen towel.

'Could I visit your world. To see for myself.' He closed the dishwasher and set it to start.

'I would need to ask permission of my father. To be honest I have never heard of such a thing.'

'But you came here.' He insisted.

'I did.' She stepped to his side. 'For a specific purpose. I believe I am the first female to be given the task. Circumstances being what they were it was imperative that a female come through this time. I do not regret it.' She took his face in her hands. 'Not for one minute do I regret it. Should you decide to stay in your world then there will be no regrets on my part. None whatsoever.' She kissed him softly.

'I must go now as I have things to do. You should go and see your friend tomorrow and tell him you plan to be away for a week. Cell phones do not work in the mountains.'

He called for a cab and put on sufficient clothing to walk with her down to the street.

'Bring what food you have with you tomorrow. You won't need many clothes, just a few toiletries.'

'I like the naked part' he patted her bottom as they stepped from his building.

'Stop that.' She scolded gently. 'It restricts your movements when flying.' She kissed him quickly as the cab pulled up to the curb. 'If I can get away sooner I'll be in touch.'

'I'll be ready.' He waved her off before going indoors. He went straight to bed and slept like a baby.

Chapter Five

He did his duty call the next morning, calling in at the garage at ten in the morning. Chief Spelling was delighted to see him and fully agreed that he should take a week off and complete the full course of medication he had been given and to fully regain his strength. Aaron felt guilty as hell as he had picked up his prescription but hadn't taken a single capsule.

Mike was of a likewise mind. 'Rest up buddy 'cause I can't afford to lose any more years you scared off my life.' They were having coffee together in the break room before Aaron left.

'And I don't want that sort of pain ever again. Be by to see you when I get back. Love to Sophie and the kids.' He jumped into his truck and was home by noon.

Aurora linked with him at two and told him she would be able to get away at four that afternoon and to expect her around five.

He had already packed and bagged his groceries; so to pass the time he went to the basement and did his laundry. He had a smile on his face when he was folding the dried sheet when he thought of the activity that had taken place on it the night before.

At his door he stopped to say hi to Iris and Chuck as they were leaving her apartment for the expected visit to her granddaughter.

'Have a good time. See you when you get back.' He kissed her cheek and shook hands with Chuck. They were soon gone.

He took his truck through the car wash and gassed up and was waiting at the entrance of his building at five. Her cab pulled up at ten past the hour. They were soon on their way. They kept to the main highway out of the city and headed up to the mountains. After two hours Aaron pulled onto a single dirt track and following Aurora instructions kept to the track for a further hour, winding through thick brush and tall trees. The cabin was set in a small clearing high on a ridge overlooking the sea.

'Hey this is great.' Aaron stepped from his truck and walked to the edge of the ridge and gazed down at the rolling sea below.

'Beautiful spot. Very secluded.' Aurora took his hand and they watched the sunset together. 'Do you want to try your wings?'

'Now!' he asked, stunned. They had come here so he could learn. That was the point. He didn't think he was quite ready.

'Nothing to it. Come on. Strip down to your shorts.' Aurora moved away from the edge and peeled off her clothes down to a skimpy bit of lace that covered hardly anything at all. She tucked her socks inside her shoes.

'I can do this.' Aaron muttered to himself and stripped down to his boxers. The butterflies in his stomach were doing everything in their power to escape.

'Take my hands.' She reached for him. 'Remain on your feet. Spread your wings.' They did so in unison. The clearing filled with light. 'Have you ever studied how birds fly?' she asked.

'I've watched a number of wild life programs on the tv. Slow motion photography.' It had been some years but he recalled it clearly.

'To take off from a standing position like this takes a little more effort. If you jumped from your balcony for instance you would simply spread your wings and ride the updraft. But for now watch me. Wings fully extended.' He stepped back a pace or two and copied her movements. 'Draw your wings in at the elbow, the reinforced ridge in the centre. Do you see?' He nodded and tried it. 'Now lift your wing tips high into the air, level out the wing from elbow to tip then pull them down sharply to the ground. Like this.' Aaron watched closely as Aurora rose silently into the air a couple of feet off the ground, lift her wings slightly and touched down.

It took Aaron five frustrating minutes before he managed to lift himself more than an inch off the ground. He was so astonished at this accomplishment that when he looked towards the ground his left wing tipped lower than the right and he hit the ground with a thud and staggered a couple of paces to the side.

'It's harder than it looks.' He folded his wings down his back. 'Show me.'

'All right.' She turned quickly and ran to the edge and literally threw herself into the wind. A couple of quick flaps and she soared into the air. For ten wonderful minutes she glided, twisted and tumbled through the darkening skies before gliding back to the clearing. Aaron had a wide smile over his face as he watched her soaring across the sky and couldn't wait to get airborne. He paid close attention and watched carefully the way she landed.

'They're like a rudder, your legs. You lower them when you come into land, curve your wings to fill with air to slow your descent. Fascinating.' He looked over the edge of the ridge. 'I'd like to try that.' The waves were crashing against the base of the cliff below.

'No, no, not tonight. You need more practice.' Aurora snatched at his hand. Concern written all over her face. 'You must promise me that you will not try that until I think you are ready.'

'Be great though. Just leap off the ledge and fly into the night.' He was looking out over the sea.

'Aaron you're scaring me.' She pulled him away from the edge.

'I don't plan on killing myself Aurora. I'm not stupid.' He smiled at her. 'But I will do it before the week is out. That's a promise. Come on I'm hungry.'

'A week should do it if you follow my instructions to the letter!' She wagged a finger under his nose. 'No funny business Aaron Summer.'

'Who me!' The look of total indignation that crossed his face had her laughing. 'I'll get the bags and you get the groceries, and we'll see what we have.'

Aurora had thoughtfully picked up a crusty loaf and several tins of soup. Salad and fruit, pasta, cold meats, eggs and bacon. A whole chicken and some sausages, two boxes of cereal and a gallon of milk, tea, coffee and sugar found their way into the fridge or cupboards. Enough to keep them going for a while. They had ham sandwiches and soup for their supper. Conversation was primarily on the techniques of flying. How to take off and land being the main topic.

The cabin consisted of one living area, kitchen, bathroom and two bedrooms. None of them overly large rooms, but all had modern conveniences that thankfully included electricity, plumbing and sanitation. They closed their wings and fell into bed at eleven. It was three in the morning before Aaron allowed her to sleep. The cries of her passion soaring out of control spurred him to greater efforts to satisfy them both.

Aurora opened her eyes to the first rays of dawn, lying face down on the bed. An arm and her long dark hair spilled over the side and touched the floor. The other arm was tucked under her pillow. Her feet hung over the other side of the bed. She was totally naked and practically glowing with heat. Raising herself to awareness took a few minutes by which time she managed to lift herself up on her elbows and turn over onto her back. Aaron was nowhere in sight.

She recalled being carried to bed. Remembered the long drugging kisses, the rough texture of his hands as he took her on a journey of sensual pleasures. Until she cried his name over and over as one orgasm followed another until he joined with her and drove her close to madness.

She thought she'd had some sleep. A few hours at least. Her last coherent memory was of her being turned onto her stomach, Aaron's large hands lifting her hips as he took her deeply from behind. She was the barred gate set against his battering ram and had little in the way of defence against the inevitable breach of her defences. Whether that had happened during the night or at first light she couldn't recall.

She stumbled her way into the shower and was fully awake when she stepped out twenty minutes later and towelled herself dry. From her bag she took a large pot of cream that she had brought from home and rubbed it lavishly over her skin, all areas she could reach. Her hair was left to dry naturally after she brushed out the tangles. Her only clothing was a pair of white lace panties.

Coffee was still hot on the stove so she helped herself to a cup before going in search of Aaron. He was outside, with a full spread, practising. Keeping within the shadow of the doorway Aurora watched him closely. Never in all of her life had she seen wings so magnificent. From the back, and out in the open, she had a better view than the confines of his apartment. Every shade of blue could be seen, with the darkest colour around the edges. This was mingled with silvers and greys and the occasional flashes of red and gold as they flapped when he tried to rise off the ground. His shimmer was brilliant.

Having no idea how long he had been outside Aurora was surprised that he could now manage to raise himself at least six feet into the air. The only problem that she could see was that his legs where hanging straight down beneath him. This was fine for hovering. He needed to learn how to straighten out in order to gain some forward momentum. But for now he was simply keeping himself airborne and turning himself in slow circles. His wings working independently so that he turned first one way and then the other. He landed with remarkable grace.

He furled his wings as he turned towards the cabin and saw her watching from the doorway.

'Sorry. Did I wake you?' She shook her head.

'I was watching your display. Very impressive.' She wondered if he realised he was naked. She felt the heat from his body a good two feet away.

'Restless, couldn't sleep.' He took her mouth under his as soon as he was close enough. Pulling her warm body close to his heat. The coffee mug slipped from her fingers and bounced on the ground when her arms went around his neck. She was amazed that she wanted him again. His large hands hoisted her up so her legs wrapped around his hips as he carried her indoors. The first available surface on which to lay her was the small table in the kitchen. He pulled her panties down her long legs and threw then aside then used his mouth on her as he knelt on the floor and pushed her legs high and wide. He thought she would be dry and unprepared to take him, but he was mistaken. She was already wet and had her first orgasm before he rose and penetrated deep, lifting her legs high about his neck. Her hands gripped the edge of the table by her hips as he lent over her and gripped the opposite side of the table, locking his arms so as not to crush her and let himself go. His wings started to spread and vibrate but some internal warning bell went off in his head and he managed to keep them just slightly short of half open. Wing tips touched the counter and the door jam but didn't spread any further. They were bright red and vibrating strongly. As his seed left his body his arms buckled and he came down on his elbows and kissed her softly as they shuddered and vibrated in unison.

'I haven't woken up to anything so precious since…. forever.' He pulled her to a sitting position and wrapped his arms around her for a long minute. Aurora watched his wings return to their normal colour and furl down his back. How he had managed that degree of control was a miracle as far as she was concerned.

'It was a wonderful start to the day.' She whispered and kissed his shoulder. The heat from his body seeped into hers and she let it fill her. It was a mistake. She knew it was, but her feelings for this young man were very strong. At home they would be married by now. The honeymoon fever would be upon them and they would make love for hours of the day and night. But this was not home. He was not her husband. He may never be her husband.

'Are you hungry?' She lifted her head to look into his handsome face.

'Yeah' he kissed the top of her head before he released her and she unwrapped her legs from his hips so he could withdraw, all magnificent ten inches of him, as he took a small step back. It was almost clear when he stepped close to her again and embedded himself back in the warm nest.

Aurora gasped. 'I thought you were hungry?' Her eyes were huge pools of blue as she looked into his handsome face.

'I am. Starving in fact.' And plunged.

Aurora found her panties hooked on the sink tap when Aaron allowed her off the table so she could wash. She rinsed out the cloth and turned to face him thinking to provide the same service for her man. The look in his eyes changed her mind so she thrust the dripping cloth at him and hastily pulled on her panties.

They had an apple each and a bowl of cereal before they went outside to continue Aaron's training. After brief instructions and a demonstration Aaron was soon able to fly around the clearing with little difficulty. Aurora kept him below the tree line, as his shimmer would clearly be seen even in the daylight

'So how do I stop it?' They were indoors and having lunch when he asked. He usually skipped lunch but to ensure his partner ate he sat at the table so they could share a meal.

'Dimming your shimmer isn't difficult. It just takes a degree of concentration. A young flyer is usually too excited and unable to gain the control needed. At home there is no need for such a precaution. On this world it is imperative.'

'Is there a reason for the shimmer, other than in the throws of passion?' he asked. Apparently his was brilliant.

'All of our kind have a shimmer. Those in the highest authority are usually the brightest, colours more defined. The leaders of the council, village elders and the like often develop a brighter shimmer so that the people can rally to their side for instructions during times of conflict or crisis.'

Aaron absorbed this information. It was foolish, he had to admit, to think that her world was any different from his own. Crime and war were universal.

'You tell me my shimmer is very bright. Where would that put me?' He filled his mouth with crusty bread and cheese.

'You are from a noble house Aaron. Your father is second minister to the King. You would naturally hold a position of importance.' She did not tell him that he would automatically have an important role to play. People would look up to him. Especially if he were to be married to the King's daughter.

He got to the feet and paced the small kitchen. 'That can't be right. I have absolutely no idea of who I am or where I come from. Up until a week ago I was Aaron Summer, mechanic. Living alone and impotent. Now here I am, with wings, and a stunningly beautiful woman, telling me I'm a nobleman. An important nobleman.' He pushed his hands through his hair as he paced. 'Talk to your King. I want to see for myself. I need to learn about my heritage. If I don't fit in then I'll come back.' He noticed the look of sorrow on her face before she could mask it. What else could he do? Everything in his life was upside down, turned inside out. He would be an alien in his own world. He went to kneel by her chair and took her hands in his.

'You mean a great deal to me. You are the first for me in so many ways and I would hate to lose you. But it must be this way Aurora. It would be impossible for me to stay if I am not accepted or if I feel an outcast. Going with you means giving up everything here. Right?' How he knew this he wasn't sure, just another of those strange feelings. Hadn't she said 'from her world' not this world. Not his world.

She nodded. Wetness filled her eyes, but no tears fell. He was only speaking the truth. The truth she herself would probably say if their positions were reversed. After all she didn't want to stay in his world. Did she?

'How do you reach him?' He released her hands and cupped her face, the thumb of his right hand automatically brushed over her full pink lips.

'I have a mirror. Come with me.' She rose quickly and headed for their bedroom. He followed in her wake. From her bag she took the dressing table mirror from the folds of a thick towel and set it upright on top of a chest of drawers.

'Please stand to one side for a moment. He may be with others at this time of day and this conversation should be held in private.' She sat on the side of the bed and reached out for his hand. 'It may take a few moments.'

'I understand.' He bent and kissed her softly before stepping out of line of sight.

With her right hand she reached over and brushed her fingers gently over the mirrored glass. It shimmered and swirled for some minutes before it cleared and a group of people could be seen. All eyes in the mirror turned in her direction.

'Forgive the interruption my father.' She bowed her head and waited.

'Is something wrong my daughter?' the King asked.

'A private matter my father.' She did not raise her head.

Although Aaron could not see into the mirror, he could clearly hear the exchange of words.

'Leave us.' The command was given; footsteps heard receding and a door closed. 'We are alone my daughter. Lift your head my lovely Aurora.' There was much affection in his voice now that they were alone.

'It is good to see you my father.' Her smile was full of love and respect. 'Contact was made and the ritual observed. Aaron is whole.' Aaron could see her eyes lower for a moment.

'You have done well Aurora. Tell me how he progresses.'

'We are in an isolated spot up in the mountains where I am training him in the art of flying. Even after less than a day he has mastered flight at treetop level. Later today I think we could take to the open water. It comes to him naturally.'

'This is good. His father will be pleased.' He sensed something more. He waited for his daughter to continue.

'Aaron is undecided about his future. There is obvious confusion in his thoughts.' She lifted her eyes to Aaron. 'He is here with me now and wishes an audience.' To Aurora's absolute amazement her father smiled.

'Well let me have a look at the boy then.' He sat back relaxed in his high-backed chair as his daughter moved aside and Aaron took her place. The King noticed immediately that he was naked. He may not have realised, and he was sure his daughter would not have mentioned it, but it was customary for a man to be naked when first presented to his King. Aaron bowed his head with respect.

'So you're the lad all this fuss has been about.' It was not a question, just a statement of fact.

'So I'm told Your Majesty.' Aaron saw a man of perhaps fifty years of age sitting lean and powerful on a throne like chair wearing just a loincloth. He was a very handsome man.

'Speak your mind lad. Let me hear what you have to say.'

'Firstly I want to thank you for sending Aurora to find me. From what I understand I would have perished on my thirtieth birthday, in three days time, had she not found me.' The King simply nodded.

Aaron went on to explain what Aurora had told him about her world and his father. His nobility and his place in the hierarchy.

'She speaks the truth.' The King responded.

'I've no doubt about it. But that doesn't help me. Tell me Your Majesty what would happen if I returned with Aurora and found I didn't fit in, didn't like it in fact. Hated your world, my father, everything. What then?' He did not look away. He spoke honestly, man to man.

'A fool is what you would be.' He lent forward in his chair. 'A life of privilege awaits you lad.'

'I care naught for privilege. I have little in this world. I work for a living. I'm a mechanic; I fix things that are broken. Wealth and power mean nothing to me.' He said sincerely.

'Whether you want it or not it shall be yours when you come home.' King Salvax insisted.

'If' Aaron interrupted. 'I want to visit initially. A few days, a week possibly, to see the lay of the land. If I don't like the set up I want to come home, back to my world. Those are my terms.' Out of the corner of his eye she saw Aurora's eyes widened and her mouth dropped open.

'You dare dictate to *ME*!' The King's voice roared and filled the small bedroom. Aurora gasped and looked with horror from one man to the other. No one spoke to the King with such disrespect.

Aaron remained calm. 'I dare. This is *MY* life we're talking about. I don't know you but from what your daughter has told me you are a good and honest man much loved and respected by your family and people. *YOUR* family. *YOUR* people. You give me your word that I can return to my world before a week is out and I will gladly travel with Aurora and see for myself.' He too lent forward and rested his hands on his knees. They exchanged stare for stare for some minutes. Neither blinked.

'My father.' Aurora pushed Aaron aside so that she might speak with her father. 'The situation is unprecedented in recent history. Are there no entries in the ledgers to indicate that something like this ever happened in the past?' She kept her eyes respectfully lowered as she spoke.

'The scribes would know or be able to find out. Until then you are to continue his training.' He turned his head to consult a clock on the walk. 'Call again in eight hours.' His voice was sharp with annoyance.

'Yes my father.' She reached up to touch the screen.

'A moment' Aaron lent over so he could see the King. 'What happens to Aurora if I decide not to stay? I had her virginity. What does that mean?' His eyes did not leave those of the King's.

'What concern is it of yours if you do not stay?' he did not flinch when his daughter winced and coloured hotly.

'I care for her. I would take it much amiss if she were to suffer because of me.' His voice held an unmistakable threat. Aurora was horrified

The King looked closely into the eyes of the younger man and chose to ignore the threat. He smiled to himself. This Aaron Summer loved his daughter. He may not know it yet, but he was well on his way. 'She is my only child, my lovely Aurora. She will be safe with me.'

Aaron nodded. 'Thank you.' He stepped aside.

'Blessings be upon you my father.' Aurora lifted her hand to the mirror and her fingers slipped through the silvery swirls.

'Blessings be upon you my daughter. Eight hours.' Then he was gone.

Chapter Six

'You insulted my father!' she sprang to her feet and turned on him. 'How dare you show such contempt toward my King. How dare you!' She screeched as her wings unfurled and vibrated with her anger. The bedroom was just wide enough to allow her wings their full spread. Brilliant silver and greys sparked from her shimmer.

Under her stormy glare Aaron remained reasonably calm. 'He is *YOUR* father, *YOUR* King not mine. I will do everything in my power to safeguard *MY* life and see that *YOUR* life isn't harmed in any way. You don't like it then tough.' He did no more than turn his back and walked away. Aurora's shriek of anger followed in his wake.

'To hell with it' he muttered when he was outside. 'I'll stay right were I am.' He spread his wings without hesitation and flapped them angrily. The sky had turned an angry grey as the clouds rushed across the sky. A storm was coming. It suited his mood perfectly. 'Ready or not, here I come.' He ran towards the ledge full out and flung himself into the abyss.

'Noooo.' Aurora came outside just as he disappeared over the edge. 'Aaron!' she screamed and dashed towards the edge. It was dangerous to fly in stormy weather the currents of air were too unpredictable. A sudden turbulent could throw you into a tailspin or smash you against cliffs or trees. Wings could easily be ripped asunder in such weather.

She was just in time to see him fold his wings down his back, his body arrow straight as he hurtled towards the sea. She was braced to follow him, to spread her wings and fly to his rescue, when he spread his wings and caught the wind, skimmed the surface of the rolling sea and rose swiftly into the air with a almost lazy flap of his wings. She had never seen the like before. He rode the angry wind with apparent ease, twisted and turned, furled his wings to plummet towards the earth only to spread them wide and ride the wind.

It was instinct Aaron told himself. How else could he have known how to ride the wind like this? This was true freedom. This was truly living. As he flew in a lazy circle he spied Aurora standing on the edge watching him. He turned and dived toward her. As he approached he held out his arms, she raised hers and he scooped her up on his fly by. His wings were powerful enough to carry them both. Instinctively she wrapped her legs around his hips; her arms around his neck as his powerful wings took them out over the sea and the upward current of air.

'Take me in for God's sake take me in.' He cried and wrapped his powerful arms around her. When she was safely secured in his embrace she reached down between their bodies and took his ridge manhood into her warm wet nest. When he was securely embedded her arm return to his neck and his lips found hers. It was lucky that her wings were closed inside her or this manoeuvre would be impossible. A couple of lazy flaps of his wings took them horizontal. Then she started to move against him. One hand came down her warm slender body to cup her buttocks and hold her securely. With her legs locked tightly around him her hips rocked gently back and forth as they rode the wind. His wings went red, like volcanic lava. She saw the glow behind her eyelids. When she began to climax she pulled free of his lips and tongue and begged. 'Hold on to me Aaron' and erupted under him. Arms and legs went limp. His fuzzy brain registered the need and held her close as he flapped his wings vigorously to allow his own body to rock gently within hers and his own completion followed. He turned smoothly and glided back down to the clearing just as heavy rain fell from the sky. Aurora was snuggled close to his body when they landed. His legs buckled shortly after touchdown and he collapsed over her in seconds. He closed his wings and tucked them away and took full advantage of the fact that they were still joined and he was rock hard. By the time they had their second orgasm they were rolling around in the mud and laughing like children.

They had a shower together before lighting the fire in the living area and enjoyed a glass of wine. They sat together on the floor with their backs to the sofa and watched the flames.

'I won't apologise for earlier.' He had his arm around her shoulders. 'I meant what I said.' He felt her tense slightly.

'It is difficult for me.' She turned and looked into his eyes. 'I have much love for my father. He is a good man, a good father and good King. I am his only child much as my parents would have wanted more. For anyone to dare make demands of him in contradiction of our rules is unheard of. To question his honour or integrity. It's like blasphemy.' She hoped he understood.

'Sounds like a dictatorship to me.' Aaron did not look away from her worried expression. 'That nobody is allowed to question the King. To put forward ideas or suggestions. We would not get along.' He was absolutely sure of it.

Unexpectedly she laughed softly. 'We are a democracy Aaron. Although the title of monarch is hereditary we have councils and voting. Rules and legal matters are discussed at regular monthly meetings. My father votes just like everyone else. When he addresses the people with the results of such meetings his word is then law. Nothing is passed unless it has been debated in a full council.'

'He wasn't addressing his council, but talking to me. I need to know where I stand if I agree to go back with you.' He was determined not to give in on this matter. 'I don't want his decision to be formed around your needs.'

'He wouldn't do that.' She turned and knelt at his side. 'He wouldn't.'

'My lovely Aurora' he ran his thumb over her lips. 'Your King would not. Your father on the other hand may be swayed.' He hadn't meant to hurt her, but he could see hurt in her eyes. She got swiftly to her feet.

'In all honesty I hadn't thought of that.' She paced and worried her bottom lip. 'He wouldn't force you to stay. He wouldn't. I know him.' Her fingers tapped repeatedly against her thighs as she paced.

'Aurora' Aaron lifted his hand and snagged hers as she paced back and forth. 'I apologise for putting doubt in your mind. Let's wait until we speak with him again.'

Aurora looked down at him. He was such a good man. Just perfect for her. She would be heartbroken if he decided not to stay. 'Your right of course. Come on' she tugged on his hand 'let's get something to eat.'

The atmosphere was a little tense in the kitchen, but as they worked together they started to relax again and chatted together happily as they ate. Aaron asked her how she thought he did today with his flying.

'Honestly I didn't expect you to be able to control your flight over the sea so easily. It normally takes three or four days and certainly never in a storm. That was reckless.'

'I was pissed off' he freely admitted 'and thought what the heck in for a penny.' And shrugged. 'But when I was airborne man it was so exhilarating. I just knew what to do. It was amazing.'

'I have never, and I mean never, heard of a man with wings strong enough to carry another into the air, let alone be able to…….' She was suddenly embarrassed.

'I think its called having sex. I'm sure you've heard of it. When a man wants a woman he has to …..' Aurora slapped him on the shoulder. He grinned wickedly.

'Oh shut up you idiot. I know what sex is. Haven't we had it often enough already.' For some unknown reason her cheeks flamed.

'Hell yes. I'm making up for lost time.' He saluted her with his wineglass then took a healthy swallow. His lovely green eyes positively sparkled with amusement.

'Yes well' she rose and started to clear the table. It was then that he recalled she had worn lace panties when she spoke with her father. He didn't recall her wiggling out of them when they were up in the air.

'What happened to your lacy things?' He indicated her nether regions with his long fingers.

'In the bedroom somewhere. I tore them off in temper after I shouted at you.' She was busy at the sink filling a bowl with hot water. Aaron came up and stood behind her and slipped his arms around her waist and started to nibble her neck. She squirmed.

'Stop it I'm washing dishes here.' She lifted her shoulder up to stop his tongue from probing into her ear. She giggled.

'Well you just carry on with the dishes and I'll amuse myself back here for a while.' His large hands cupped her breasts and kneaded the flesh gently. They filled his palms nicely. The gentle brushing of his thumbs over the nipples had them hard as pebbles in an instant. Aurora gasps and clung to the counter for support. The dishes were forgotten.

With infinite care his hands travelled down her body as his lips kissed and nibbled the back of her neck. As his fingers probed gently between her thighs her legs began to buckle. He bit into her neck with his sharp teeth, not to hurt or draw blood, just enough so that she locked her knees and remained on her feet.

'That's my girl' he whispered and worked his fingers deep inside her. She came in a rush and soaked his fingers.

'More' he whispered in her ear.

'Yes' she gasped 'more, give me more, give me everything. Oh, oh, ohhh' and again she came. Twice, three times and then four.

'Take more' he gasped 'take more of me' he pulled his fingers from her body and spun her around and crushed her lips under his. His arms banded her close to his chest as her hands dug into his hair and did likewise. He would have stopped then and turned her towards the table but she would have none of that and pushed with all her strength until his back hit the wall. Then she went to work on him. She nipped at his bottom lip and then his tongue until he moaned with pleasure. Her hands blazed a trail everywhere they touched and like her lips travelled down his long powerful body. She took as much of him into her mouth as was possible. He was huge and hard and as thick as her wrist. She managed two of his ten inches. As one hand held him in place and set the rhythm, the other gently scored the heavy sack between in legs with her fingernails.

'Oh Christ' he moaned and had to lock his knees in order to stay on his feet. He thrust gently with his hips to keep up her steady rhythm, careful not to thrust too deeply and choke her. 'You have to stop now.' He begged. 'You really have to stop now. Please.' A shudder ran the length of his body from the top of his head to the soles of his feet.

She pulled herself free of him, but her hands still worked him. 'Come, it's okay' and opened her mouth again to take him in.

'No. Inside you, please. Inside you.' His hands fisted in her hair. 'Please.' He begged unashamedly.

Immediately she released him and turned onto her knees and elbows, thrusting her hips high into the air. His knees buckled and took him to the floor and inside her in seconds.

'Hard and fast Aaron, hard and fast.' Her forehead touched the floor as he drove himself deeply into her. It was hard. He grunted with each thrust of his hips as flesh slapped against flesh. It was fast. His hips were like pistons working at full power. He pulled her urgently towards him as he emptied himself into her after a short ninety seconds. They collapsed onto the kitchen floor and slept for two hours.

Aurora's internal clock woke her fifteen minutes before they were due to call her father. It would not do to be late.

'Aaron' she shook his arm gently.

'Ummm' he blinked rapidly until her face came into focus.

'Wake up now. We need to call my father in fifteen min-utes. Are you awake?' She nudged him again.

'Yeah I'm good' and to prove it he sat up and ran his fingers through his hair. 'That was quite a rush sweetheart.' Her heart leaped at the endearment.

'The feeling is mutual.' She looked down at herself. 'I need to clean up. You should too.' She rose to her feet in steady stages. 'My legs don't seem to want to work properly.' She gripped the kitchen table and managed to stand erect.

'I'll be right behind you' he still sat on the floor.

'Okay' she staggered to the bathroom.

They managed to look respectable in ten minutes. They sat close together on the bed as Aurora called her father.

'My father' she bowed her head respectfully when he appeared in the mirror.

'Your Majesty' Aaron simply nodded his head.

There was silence for some minutes. The King would speak first. Aaron never lost eye contact.

'There is nothing documented in the ledgers to help guide us in this matter.' He sat relaxed in his chair. 'My senior councillors have been advised of the situation regarding the son of Parlax. They have agreed that he may come for a short visit. Four days only. Then he must decide if he wishes to stay or return to his world. This has been entered into the ledger. There will be no further negotiations. Aaron Summer do you agree?'

'A question first if it is permitted.' He would ask it anyway but felt it wise to abide by certain protocols. The King simply nodded.

'Should I decide to stay what happens back in this world?' He lent forward and rested his forearms on his knees.

'Nothing, you will simply have disappeared.' The King shrugged both shoulders and eyebrows.

'Not acceptable. I have friends here. Good friends who do not deserve that kind of heartache. What options are there?' He would set matters to right first.

'Should you decide to stay with us permanently. I will grant you a day, 24 hours, to set your house in order. There will be no going back thereafter. You must be absolutely sure of your commitment to this new life.' The King watched the young man mull if over. Aaron then rose and walked out of his eye line.

'What is he doing my daughter?' The King lent forward and tried to peer around the edge of the mirror. He had expected the young man to agree immediately to his terms.

'He paces my father' Aaron was out on the landing between the bedrooms pacing back and forth. 'His best of friends is a man called Michael Townsend. Michael's mother adopted Aaron when he was twelve years old. She died only recently. He loves them very much. I think it will be a terrible wrench for him to leave them. He will want to be certain he is doing the right thing. For all concerned. He is a good man my father.' She looked up as Aaron came back into the room and sat next to her on the bed.

'The terms are acceptable.' He took Aurora's hand. 'When should we leave?'

'Midnight tomorrow. I shall open a portal next to the cabin.' The King looked at his daughter. 'It will be good to hold you in my arms again my daughter.'

'Until tomorrow my father.' Tears ran unhindered down her cheeks. 'Blessings be upon you.'

'Blessings be upon you also.' His fingers touched the mirror and he disappeared.

'Open a portal?' He was thinking of some form of transport. A space ship. He shook his head. He should have realised the foolishness of his thoughts.

'The Oracle will open a portal between our worlds.' Aurora answered easily. 'We will just step through.'

'So what happens now?' Aaron didn't want to think about portals and different worlds. It would drive him crazy. He used his fingertips to wipe the tears from her cheeks. She was smiling however.

'Are your affairs in order?' She asked with all seriousness.

'I made a Will when I took out a mortgage on my apartment five years ago. My lawyer has the necessary papers and authority to deal with my estate should anything happen to me.' He felt sick to his stomach. Mike and his family would benefit financially. He had a little equity in his property, some savings, a few shares in various utility companies. He was far from being a rich man. What he did have were people who loved him. And he them.

'How is it done? My disappearing?'

'I thought that perhaps an accident. Something that would destroy our bodies entirely. It would be cruel to leave those you love in turmoil should you simply disappear.'

'Our bodies?'

'Of course. I have been here some months. We are together so naturally I would be….involved in the accident with you.' Aurora reached for his hand. 'None of this will be necessary if you decide to come home. I know it seems mercenary, but in the end it will be a clean break and less stressful on all concerned should you decide to stay.' Her heart bled for him. His face was a picture of misery. Suddenly he got up and walked quickly from the room. She did not follow.

It was late into the night when Aaron came to bed. Aurora was still awake waiting for him. He put his arms around her and pulled her close to his chest as they lay like spoons. He kissed her shoulder. 'Good night sweetheart.'

'Good night my love.' She pulled his hands to her lips. 'Sleep well'. They slept.

It was late the next morning when he woke alone in their bed. The rain had stopped in the night and a weak sun filtered through the grey clouds crossing the sky. His mind turned to Aurora.

'Where are you' he thought.

'In the kitchen. Coffee?' Her thoughts were happy.

'Please.' After a few moments he heard her climb the stairs then enter the bedroom.

'I don't think you moved a muscle all night. You okay?' she came to his side and sat on the edge as he pulled himself to a sitting position.

'Better. Got things settled in my head. Thanks.' He took the mug she held out for him. Drank some coffee.

'Do you want to talk?' She sat with her hands in her lap, waiting.

He shook his head. Drank more coffee.

'Breakfast?'

He shook his head. Put the mug aside.

'Are you sure you're all right?' He was behaving strangely this morning.

'Perfectly' he took her hand. 'Do you want to make love here in bed or have sex on the kitchen floor?' His face was totally serious. His eyes were intense; there wasn't a hint of a grin anywhere on his face.

She rose to her feet, he released her hand. Then she pulled back the single sheet that covered his lower body. His magnificent penis sprang to attention.

'I think here will do nicely.' She went willingly into his arms. They spent most of the day flying, eating and having really good sex in many and varied places and positions.

Chapter Seven

'What do I need to take with me?' Aaron had his bag open on the bed.

'Nothing' Aurora dug into her own bag and pulled out what Aaron thought was a piece of leather made up of various shapes and colours sewn together. 'Put this on' she held it out to him.

'And this is?' He took it between his thumb and forefinger of his left hand, his nose wrinkled as he took a sniff. At least it smelled new.

'Your loincloth' she smiled at the look on his face. 'The pouch goes at the front.' Aurora then knelt down at his feet.

'Why is there a pouch on the.....inside?' He cringed and screwed up his face. 'You can't be serious.' He looked down into her smiling face.

'Being of a more....healthy specimen than the normal males in this world. The men in my world find it beneficial to have a sheath sewn into their loincloths to forestall any injury should they partake in physical activity outside of their bedroom. Running would be a painful experience.' The look of pure innocence on her face intensified the irritation on his. 'Step into it please so that we can try it for comfort. I have two others of various sizes if this does not fit,' she lowered her head so Aaron could not see the wide smile on her face. He looked so embarrassed.

'If you're laughing down there this could turn nasty.' He dropped the loincloth next to his feet and with Aurora's help stepped into the leather. Then with a free hand loosely grabbed a handful of her hair and pulled her head back so that her face was raised toward him. Her eyes were sparkling and there was an unmistakable smile on her face. 'I thought as much.' He tweaked the end of her nose, which she then rubbed with a free hand.

'Let's get this done Aaron' she sat back on her heels as he pulled the leather up his body. His penis slid into the pouch easily and snugly, the waistband was secured with a leather strap and silver buckle on his right side.

'It looks good on you.' Aurora rose to her feet and did a turn around him. 'Very sexy' she gave him a gentle pat on the butt.

'I feel like Tarzan' he looked at himself in the mirror. The leather came to a point between his legs. This was long enough to cover the bulge of his manhood. In fact the design concealed it altogether. When he twisted to see the back there was an identical vee. 'All the men wear these?'

'All mature males wear them.' Her meaning was clear. Everyone would know that he had taken her virginity and they were not yet wed. They would have been married by now if this had happened back in her world. Her mature state would mean that a silk loincloth would be worn to indicate she was no longer innocent. That she belonged to a man and he to her.

His concerns were verified when he saw her pull on a pair of white panties that just came to her hips.

'Do you have to wear those. Can't you go naked?' He looked at her reflection through the mirror.

'No' she came to his side. 'There are no other females here. Your wings have spread. I do not lie, not for any reason.' She took his hand. 'Come it is nearly time.' They hid all of their valuables, his wallet and keys to the truck, his watch. Her purse and some jewellery, under a lose floorboard before stepping outside.

'When the portal opens I will step through first. Wait a few seconds then follow. As soon as you reach the other side spread your wings as wide and full as you can. I want my father and the members of the council to see how magnificent you are.' Aaron was amazed at the pride he heard in her voice.

'Will my father be there?' Suddenly he felt quite nervous. What would he say to the man? How would he feel?

'Without a doubt.' She kissed him softly on the lips. 'It is customary for one to go down on one knee before the King upon their first audience. Thereafter a bow is sufficient.' They stepped outside into the cool night. A full moon gave light to the arena. Within moments a bright swirling light started to appear and grew larger within seconds. 'Are you ready?' She squeezed his hand.

'As I'll ever be.' He puffed out his cheeks. His heart was pounding heavily in his chest as he watched the blue light shimmering a few feet away.

'Just a few seconds, then follow. I will be waiting.' She stepped into the light and disappeared.

Aaron counted to five, took a huge breath, and followed her.

He had expected swirling lights, a revolving vortex, a long tunnel and popping out on the other side. All the television programmes he had seen seemed to favour this approach. In reality he simply stepped through a doorway. It took less time than a blink of his eyes. When he looked over his shoulder he was in the centre of a large hall crowded with people. All eyes turned in his direction.

'Your wings Aaron' Aurora whispered from behind and to his left.

'Oh right.' He did not look in her direction, but straight ahead as he spread his wings to their full impressive size. All colours of blue could clearly be seen. There was an audible gasp from the audience present. On a raised dais at the end of the chamber sat Aurora's father, flanked by his most senior ministers and noblemen. Aaron had never seen so many near naked people in one place before. Women were amongst the gathering and he found this to be a little disconcerting. Fascinating, but disconcerting.

Those in the room saw a magnificent specimen of manhood. A handsome face, broad shoulders and well-muscled chest, slim waist, narrow hips and long well muscled legs. But many had never seen wings the like of his before. There was no mistaking his house.

Aaron stood tall and relaxed and awaited the King's pleasure. There was utter silence for 5 minutes.

'My daughter' King Salvax spoke at last. 'Bring him forward.'

'Would you come with me Aaron Summer' she swept an arm toward the dais. As they walked Aaron notice a number of heads go together and one or two women shook their heads and turned away to speak to others around them. He could well imagine they had noticed her attire. Aaron stopped and turned in their direction and made eye contact that stopped the whispered conversation instantly. Aurora felt his tension. 'Not now Aaron please' she whispered. 'My father waits.'

King Salvax saw the exchange and the tension fill Aaron's wings before they were subdued. He had little doubt that Aaron was Parlax's son. Their shimmer was the same.

'My King' Aurora bowed respectfully. 'It is my pleasure to introduce to you Aaron, Son of Parlax.' She stepped aside as the King rose and Aaron took a step closer. He went down on one knee, bowed his head and to everyone's amazement did the royal salute with his wings. They shimmered red as they swept forward until their tips touched and a gold spark shot from the contact. Aaron himself was just as amazed as everyone else that he even knew what he was doing. The King and his ministers had taken a step back in alarm. Palace guards hurried forward until the King lifted a hand to stop them.

'I'm not quite sure what happened there.' Aaron rose swiftly to his feet. 'I apologise if it was an insult. It just happened.'

'You were not tutored?' Salvax asked, looking quickly at his daughter. She shook her head.

'No Your Majesty' Aaron looked from father to daughter. 'It seemed the right thing to do.' There was a rustle of movement around him as he focused all his attention on the King.

'As it was. Welcome to Fayland.' He stepped from his dais and came down the three steps to stand beside Aaron and clasped his hand in a friendly greeting. He was perhaps four inches shorter in stature. 'The hour grows late and my wife would see her daughter before too long. Your father has requested that you take lodgings in his house during your stay. We will take breakfast together tomorrow. Come daughter I cannot keep you from your mother any longer.' He walked through the now empty chamber.

'Aaron may I introduce you to your father Parlax, Second Minister to King Salvax.' She squeezed his hand. 'I will see you at breakfast.' She released him and hurried after her father as a tall man came to stand at Aaron's side.

Aaron's eyes lingered on her departing figure. 'She is lovely is she not?' A deep baritone voice sounded behind his left shoulder.

'I owe her my life.' Aaron pulled his eyes from the now empty hall, furled his wings down his back and turned to look, for the first time, upon his father. The recognition, from both parties, was instantaneous. It was a shock to Aaron to see himself in thirty years. There was just a little silver running through his thick dark hair, the same colour as his own, at his temples. A few laughter lines at the eyes but the skin was wrinkle free and clear. They were eye to eye with the same tall strong build. The only difference was in the colour of his eyes. Parlax had clear blue eyes.

'Like peas in a pod' Parlax observed. 'You have your mother's eyes. Your sister's eyes are blue like mine.' Large warm hands came to rest on Aaron's shoulders. 'I never gave up, not for one moment.' His wings were furled, but the tips were blue.

'I don't know what to say. I can see clearly that you must be my father, the resemblance is amazing. But I don't know you.' He felt at odds with himself. For some unknown reason he wanted to fling his arms around this man and hold him close. Then on the other hand he wanted to run away and hide. The turmoil was clear in his eyes.

'We will talk my son' he had wanted to say those words for so long that moisture filled his eyes. 'Come, I'll take you home. It's just a short flight.' They walked in silence out into a wide courtyard. 'Just follow me' and with that Parlax took to the darkened sky. Aaron was a wing span behind him.

There was the shimmer of other pairs of wings as father and son glided effortlessly through the silent night. No rumbling of cars or trains on tracks. No planes flew overhead disturbing the stillness. It was weird. The flight was indeed short, barely five minutes. Parlax dipped his left wing and began to descend. Aaron saw a wide courtyard below and followed his father into land. Whereas Parlax landed easily. Aaron stumbled and took several steps to the side.

'Take offs are fine, but I haven't mastered the landings quite yet.' He brushed back his wildly tossed hair, much as his father did.

'From what I have been told you have made remarkable progress in a very short space of time.' Both men closed and folded their wings away.

'I get irritated with myself when things go wrong. It really pisses me off.' He followed his father across the courtyard and through a set of wide double doors into what must be the family room. There was a fireplace with stone mantle. Sitting in the hearth in place of a fire was an enormous piece of multicoloured crystal. It sparkled all manner of colours when the light from two tall candles flickered over it. Wooden floors with occasional rugs scattered around. Long leather sofas with wide colourful cushions, occasional tables on which stood vases of strange looking flowers, nik naks and family photos. Tucked into one corner was a grand piano.

'Are you ready to retire or would you like to have a drink and talk?'

'Water please. I don't drink much.' Aaron wondered the room as he father disappeared around a corner. He found himself at the piano. It had been years since he ran his fingers over ivory keys. Like a lot of things it came back naturally. A soft melody filled the room. Aaron didn't even know the name of the piece he was playing. It was in the back of his mind just waiting to break free.

Parlax stood at the entrance to the room listening to his son playing. He had no talent himself. Crystal, his daughter, played, as did Aaron's mother. He had been told that his wife was now dead. Although it had been many years he mourned for her. He had loved her so completely. Then she was gone. He had no idea why and for many years had no idea where she was. It took a great deal of skill to open a portal. To his knowledge she did not have that particular talent. So therefore his search was centred here, in this world. Yet somehow she must have mastered it and fled taking his only son with her. Then the oracle had picked up a feint signal, Aaron's song. His heart was singing, reaching out to those who loved him, and the search had begun.

The only regret he had about the entire affair was for Aurora. If his son decided to go back to his world Aurora would stay. But her life would be one of duty. Being the King's only child she would need to marry and produce an heir for the next generation of leaders. From what he had himself observed the only young man available was Thorn, son of Clen, First Minister to the King. Thorn was only twenty-nine and not yet ready to open. If he should reject her as being 'used' and he was well within his rights to do so, it would add to her humiliation. A further complication would be if the young woman conceived a child outside of wedlock. It was a well documented fact that ninety percent of woman conceived at the opening with their betrothed. The honeymoon fever took care of the remaining ten percent.

'Best not to mention this to my son' Parlax muttered to himself before he stepped fully into the room.

Much like Aaron, Aurora was too energised to sleep. She spoke extensively with her parents. Nothing had ever been taboo between them. Every intimate detail of her and Aaron's joinings was discussed. Her father paced, nothing unusual in that. Her mother, on the other hand, gasped and blushed often.

'You reached orgasm the first time?' she placed a hand over her pounding heart.

'Twice' Aurora said earnestly. 'When he opened I was prepared to do what was necessary. You understand?' she looked from mother to father. Both nodded. 'It wasn't enough for him. He wanted to touch me to feel me to kiss me. I was facing him when he took me, lifting me off the floor.'

'His wings' her father interrupted. 'What colour his wings at this time?'

'Red. Volcanic red, flashes of red and gold. They are huge when he is excited. In the hall you did not see the full intensity. He is an amazing specimen father. I have never seen the like of him before.'

'Tell us everything my daughter. It is best we are prepared.' Father and mother then sat together as Aurora told them every detail that she could remember. When she finished she was hot and itchy; this too was transmitted to her parents. 'He destroys me every time. The need is too great to be denied.'

'You must resist my daughter' her mother reached over and took her hand. 'Do you love him?'

Aurora nodded. 'I fear that I do.'

'Why do you fear my daughter?' Salvax asked.

'I fear that he will not stay. I fear that he will leave me. I fear that he does not love me in return.' A single tear escaped to roll down her cheek.

'Nonsense!' her father snapped 'You only have to look into his eyes to see his true feelings. The man loves you.' He rose to his feet. 'He will stay and you will be married.'

'No. No father you cannot. You gave your word.' Aurora sprang to her feet. 'Your word, as my father, as my King. You cannot force this.' She spun around to look at her mother. 'Do not allow this mother. I would be too ashamed to look either of you in the face again. I will refuse Aaron under these circumstances.' She rushed from the room, the door slammed behind her. Through the hall she ran and out into the courtyard. Her wings spread and within seconds she took to the sky.

'Why are men such fools' Aurora's mother, the lovely Pearl, snatched at her husband's pacing figure. 'She loves him, you think that he loves her.' She relented and touched his beloved face. 'Let nature take its course.'

'I cannot bear to see her unhappy. I would do anything within my power to see her happily married to the man she loves.' His strong arms went around her slender body. 'She could well be with child, what then?'

'My love, you know that should the worst happen and he leaves that Parlax will take her. It is not an ideal solution, but she would have a good home with people around her who love her. She would have a well respect name and can raise her child with its grandfather.' She lifted her head. 'You made a decision to send her. It was the only choice you could have made. No other father would have sent his daughter for someone else's betrothed. And can you honestly tell me that one of the widows would have been suitable to the task. You only have to see them together to know that none other but Aurora would have been acceptable. When Aaron was born you and Parlax made an agreement that our first-born daughter would be his betrothed. You did not go back on your word, even after he was taken away. Your word is your bond. You must keep it.' Pearl look into the eyes of the only man she had ever loved.

'I hate it when you're right.' He smiled at her upturned face. 'I do love you so my lovely Pearl' he took his lips to hers and kissed her so thoroughly she moaned. 'You up for an orgasm or two my love?' he winked at her.

'You should link with Aurora and speak with her.'

He shook his head. 'Tomorrow is time enough. She will be flying now and I doubt she will want to talk with me until she has calmed down.' He swept his wife into his arms and headed to their bedroom. He could do with an orgasm right now himself. As he lay his wife on their bed his thoughts turned to his daughter. 'I'm sorry Aurora. My word is my bond I will not break it.'

She had cried long and hard and was miles away when she heard his thoughts. 'You are a good man my father and I have much love for you. Good night.' Then she turned her mind to the simple enjoyment of flying. Her heart was full of sorrow however.

'So many colours.' Aaron looked up into the night sky. There was some traffic flying high over his head.

'Simple things like going to and from places of work, a night out, secret assignation, romance, postal deliveries.' There was laughter in Parlax's voice.

'Why the different colours?' his son asked.

'All members of the royal household are primarily silver. Our house, the house of Summer, is blue and so on. In time you will come to recognise each house.'

'What if a green marries a blue?' he raised a quizzical eye to his father. It seemed impossible but they had clicked after a few minutes when they each realised they had the same wicked sense of humour.

'The female takes the male colour once they are officially married.' He leant forward in his chair to rest his elbows on his knees to face his son, who was doing likewise. 'The royal salute that you gave to the King this evening.'

'I recall'

'Well at a marriage ceremony the female steps into her husband's arms and pins back her wings until the tips are touching. The male then folds her into his embrace and draws his wings around her until his wing tips touch hers and his colour sparks and is taken into hers. The colour change is immediate. The marriage is then confirmed.'

'Sounds like a lovely ceremony.' He looked up at the sky. His attention was immediately caught. He stood and walked to the centre of the courtyard. Parlax followed his gaze.

'Is something wrong?' Both pairs of eyes focused on the night sky.

'Aurora' he pointed to the silver shimmer that swirled and tumbled above their heads.

'She's upset. Excuse me.' He was in the air within seconds and shot straight up like a rocket.

The pride in Parlax's eyes was evident as he smiled. Aaron's wings were bigger then even his own, and his were nothing to be ashamed of. He was like a blue streak crossing the sky.

'Must put him forward for the games' he thought as he watched the blue and the silver merge into one brilliant glow in the sky and watched the display.

Aaron came underneath her as she glided across the sky. 'What's the matter?' he called to her. She jolted and looked down.

'What! How are you doing that?' she was astonished. He was flying upside down; his wings were beneath him. She was looking into his handsome face. He was barely a foot away.

'Doing what?' He looked around him. 'You taught me how to fly remember.'

'Yes but not upside down!' she cried and made a grab for his arm. 'You'll fall!'

'Nar, not a chance' she was pulled against his chest within seconds. 'Close' he ordered. She complied and instinctively wrapped her arms and legs around him. 'Hold on tight.' Then he simply threw his body backward and fell a couple of feet. Aurora screamed in panic. He was up for it however and continued to fall for some minutes before he took them in a complete circle, not once but twice. His huge wings sweeping gently back and forth to carry them safely across the sky.

From the ground Parlax watched as his son's wings turned red and sparked gold and red as he turned the full circle in the sky. He could almost feel his son's exhilaration. He vaguely wondered where Aurora had disappeared to.

'You know of course you are insane.' Aurora was smiling however as she accepted another drugging kiss as they slowly spun in slow circles across the sky.

'But you're crazy about me anyway.' He nuzzled her neck and therefore didn't see the anguish cross her face.

'Without a doubt. I must go now, I need a little sleep.' She kissed his cheek.

'Tell me first why you were upset. I felt it.' He insisted.

'My father and I had an argument. But it is resolved and all is well. No worries.' She smiled at him.

'He was going to make me stay wasn't he?' He wanted the truth.

'Yes. We argued. I ran off. My mother has spoken with him and he is resolved to keep his word. I would never forgive him if he betrayed you. Never.' She cuddled close to the heat of his skin.

'He loves you very much.' Not a question, just a statement. 'I'll speak with him at breakfast, man to man.' He kissed the top of her head. 'There's no way you can come to my bed tonight is there?' He felt her anguish and sorrow, the wet tears on his skin.

He felt her head shake. 'Sorry.'

'I want my hands on you so badly. I want the feel of you underneath me, over me, beside me. I want to bury myself inside you, to lose myself in you. It hurts.' There must be something on the loincloth because he did not have an erection.

'Don't Aaron, please don't. It hurts so when I am not with you.' Tears wet his chest as he held her close, his arms a hot band around her. 'I must go. Release me.' She pushed away from him as her wings spread. Then sped away from him across the sky.

Parlax watched his son hover for a moment as Aurora streaked away. The fact that Aaron was able to hold her when her wings were closed was unheard of. Then he jumped to his feet as his son shot straight up in the air his wings flashing red and gold in high temper or more than likely in deep frustration. The smile on his face turned to a gasp when Aaron dropped like a stone. He was like a red comet plunging to earth. His wings drawn tight down his back.

'Pull up, pull up!' Parlax's strangled cry filled the courtyard. 'I've only just found you. I can't lose you now.' He whispered. 'Pull up.'

As if hearing his father's silent prayer Aaron slowly opened his wings as he dropped his legs and put on the brakes. Bending his wings at the elbow he cushioned the air around him and landed gracefully in the courtyard. No stumbling this time. His wings were still vividly red and vibrated with irritation.

'Is Aurora all right?' his father dare ask. He kept his distance however. Aaron could do a lot of damage with those strong powerful wings.

'He made her cry the bastard.' His reply with a hiss and a snarl. 'Does his word mean nothing. Does it take a threat from his family to make him acquiesce?' Is this the kind of rule I'm expected to live with.' He was livid. His wings were red and vibrating so quickly he rose a foot from the ground without him realising.

Parlax had heard of this reaction of course but had never seen it in his lifetime until now. Red and gold sparks flashed and looked like flames shooting from his son's wings.

'Aaron my son. Look at me.' He did not raise his voice but stepped into the hot wind caused by his son's anger. 'Look at me son, look now.'

Aaron's eyes might have been green, but when he turned them on his father, they took on the hue of his wings. The green was clouded with red and gold. It was then that he realised he was off the ground. From the corner of her eyes he caught sight of his wings.

'Christ' he gasped and thudded to the ground and crashed down on his hands and knees. In that position his wings calmed, turned to blue. He folded them away when he could breathe with some normalcy.

'Are you calm now my son?' Parlax came and helped Aaron to his feet. His skin was on fire.

'What the hell happened to me. What is this?'

'We call it red rage. In our kind it is a very powerful and destructive weapon. In that state you are very unpredictable. Dangerous in fact. Come inside and we'll get you in the pool to cool off. Come now.' He lead the way indoors. Heat was pouring off his son in waves. The sooner he was in the pool the better. They past through the house into an inner courtyard, crossed this and into a huge indoor pool. Aaron didn't hesitate. He unbuckled his loincloth and allowed it to drop to his feet. He stepped out of it and dived into the blessed coolness of the water. It hissed and bubbled around him for a few seconds, as he remained motionless beneath the ripples. He rose to the surface a short time later and struck out for the far side of the pool. He was an excellent swimmer. He calmed. His mind emptied, he relaxed. His angry strokes became a smooth motion propelling him through the water with apparent ease. For thirty minutes he did just that. When he climbed out he took the thick towel his father handed him and dried off.

'I'd be a medical miracle back home.' He pulled on his loincloth.

'You must have noticed that you rarely, if ever, feel the cold. We run at about one hundred twenty degrees. In red rage it can make one hundred sixty.' He rested his hand on his son's arm. 'You really should sleep now for a few hours. It can be draining.'

Aaron simply nodded and followed his father to the room made ready for him. He dropped into sleep as soon as he collapsed face down on the bed. He did not dream.

Chapter Eight

At seven the next morning a young woman came to get him. He was already awake. He had showered and pulled on a clean loincloth that he found at the foot of his bed when he woke.

'Come in.' he called at the knock on his door and turned to see who it might be, expecting his father. She was tall and slender and wear a simple silk loincloth, denoting her married state. He recalled seeing pictures of her around the house, along with a number of his mother. She was his sister.

'You would be Crystal?' He stepped toward her and held out his hands.

She smiled widely. 'Aaron, my brother. At last.' And flung herself into his arms. 'It has been so long.' She hugged him tightly for some minutes. 'You were such a tiny little thing when mother took you away.' She pushed herself away from his chest so she could look into his face. 'You don't know me at all do you?'

'I'd like to. From the pictures I've seen you look a lot like her.' He pulled her again into his strong arms. 'Mother died before I had a chance to know her. Before I had a chance to ask the usual questions asked of a one-parent family. But you know' it was he this time that pushed her gently away 'I always felt there was something missing. Some part of me that was gone. I never had a chance to find out what that was, until now. I'm mighty pleased to meet you sister.' He lent forward and kissed her forehead.

'And I you my brother. Come meet the rest of the family. You are an uncle by the way.' They left his room hand in hand and by the time they reached the main room they were laughing together. Parlax's heart did one massive leap in his chest when they came in.

Another man and two young children were already there and the children rushed to their mother when she hurried in.

'Aaron, these are my children. Toms, who is six and Jewel who is four. Children this is your Uncle Aaron.' He crouched down to their level to make eye contact. 'Hi kids. How's it going?' He held out a hand formally to the young boy who smiled timidly and shook two fingers of his large hand. The little girl who was indeed a jewel flashed him a smile and shook a single finger. 'You look like grandfather Parlax' she whispered in his ear.

'So I'm told' he then lent forward to whisper in her ear. 'You look a lot like your mother. A real beauty.' He winked at her and she giggled. He turned to Toms and did likewise. 'You going to be a good looking guy like your father over there?' They both turned to look at the other man in the room who smiled indulgently at his son. 'I guess' he whispered back, his young face totally serious.

'Aaron this is my husband Mar' they reached out their hands simultaneously, when Aaron rose to his feet, and exchanged a warm handshake. He was older than Aaron by a few years, with a mass of thick blond hair and wide brown eyes. His smile was infectious.

'Welcome home Aaron.' He said sincerely.

'Thank you. Are we all going to the palace for breakfast because I could eat a horse.' He turned a questioning face to his father.

'We are. I just need to call for a carrier then we can leave.'

'A carrier?' Aaron looked from one adult to another.

'It's a lightweight cradle sort of thing. The children and Crystal will ride in it. Parlax and I will take the weight between us and fly to the Palace.' Mar answered.

'Can't you fly?' he turned to his sister.

'Yes of course, but I don't like the children to travel alone.'

'No need for all of that. I've got this.' He turned to the children. 'Come on kids let get airborne.' They didn't hesitate; they raced out of the room after their uncle.

'No Aaron I can't allow it, it just isn't possible.' Crystal charged after her children. Mar was not far behind.

'They don't weigh anything at all.' He looked over at his father who seemed totally unconcerned. 'Tell 'um dad. I'll race you.' With a child under each arm to shot up into the air where he did a quick figure of eight then hovered over the astonished parents in the courtyard. Toms and Jewel were screaming with delight. 'Again, again Uncle Aaron, again.'

'He is extraordinary Crystal. Have no fear.' He called up to his son. 'Go ahead we will be right behind you.'

'Hurry up I'm so hungry I could eat one of these kids.' He made a growling noise and nuzzled each neck to their absolute delight.

'How long did you say he's been flying?' Mar asked as he spread his wings of russet brown tinged with gold. Crystal's were the same.

'About three days. I'm going to enter him into the games.' Parlax replied as he rose into the air.

'Three days!' Crystal's cry of alarm was clearly audible. 'My children.' She flashed by the men and zoomed after her brother.

He had slowed a little to allow the rest of the family to catch up. In that short space of time young Toms was sitting on his shoulders and secured his position by holding onto chunks of Aaron's hair. Little Jewel was safely in his arms with her back to him her arms spread out and her legs close together and flat against his body. She was having the time of her life.

When Crystal flew alongside Toms called to her. 'Look mother I'm flying' then let out a loud. 'Wooooooooooooooooooooow' of excitement. Not to be out-done little Jewel cried. 'Look mother. No hands' and waved them wildly about and cried 'Weeeeeeeeeeeee' Aaron was laughing like a loon.

'Aaron don't you dare hurt my children' Crystal scolded. 'Not one scratch do you hear me?'

'Do you have any scratches kids?' he looked down and then up and both young faces shook from side to side. 'We're just having a bit of fun sis. No problems here. We're going into land now.' Instead of dropping like a stone to give the kids a bit of a rush he controlled his decent and saved his sister and brother-in-law from a heart attack. Thirty feet from the ground he adjusted Jewels position to under an arm as he reached up and plucked Toms from around his neck and touched down with a child in each arm. They were safely on the ground and clapping with excitement when their parents landed.

'Did you see mother, father, did you see. Can we do it again?' both eager faces beamed with delight and excitement.

'Not today children. Uncle Aaron has important busi-ness to attend to after breakfast. You must be on your best behaviour is this understood.' Mar looked sternly at his children.

'Yes father.' They said in unison. Mar looked up at Aaron, an eyebrow raised.

'Yes sir' He spoiled his serious face by winking at the children. Who giggled. He cleared his throat when his father jabbed him in the ribs. 'Behave' he said and had to bit his tongue to stop the laughter that was bubbling. It was a good start to the day. Parlax kept his thoughts to himself concerning the remainder of the morning.

Aaron was more relaxed than he thought he could be. His family was great, the kids especially. He was an uncle for goodness sake. Didn't that beat all.

They were shown into the King's private quarters where breakfast would be served. Once the formalities had been taken care off, everyone sat down at the table and helped themselves from an array of dishes set out along the length of the polished wood. The King sat at the head of the table his wife to his right next to her was Aaron, then Jewel and his father on the end. Mar sat next to the King on his left side with Aurora next to him, then Toms and finally Crystal. Conversation was light and included everyone. There was much laughter and many smiles to accompany the meal. Aaron touched Aurora's long legs under the table in silent communication.

'You look rested. Did you sleep well?' She asked.

'Dad has a pool so I took a swim then slept like a baby.' Aaron for one didn't like the 'my father' or 'my mother' endearment. His father was his dad, end of story and he would call him that. He liked the man.

'What are your plans for the day Aaron' the King asked from the head of the table.

'Nothing specific. I'd hoped to visit some of the people. Get to know a little of the surrounding countryside. See what work I might be able to do should I decide to stay. As I've mentioned before I am not a man of leisure. I work for a living. With nothing to do I would become bored very easily.'

The King simply nodded then continued with his meal.

'What is it that you do in your world son?' Parlax had felt the tension rise a few degrees around the table.

'Mechanic. I fix engines that are broken. I'm good at it.' He filled his mouth with some sort of bread. He was sure he'd never tasted anything like it before, but the flavour seemed vaguely familiar.

'I head the Department for Public Works and Construction. I could show you some of the work in progress there may well be an area that could use your expertise.'

'Could you fix my kite?' Jewel asked from her place beside him, before he could answer his father. 'It got caught up in a tree and broke. My father bought me a new one but it doesn't fly the same.'

'If your father doesn't mind I can certainly take a look at it' he used his napkin to wipe a bit of egg yoke from her chin. He was fast falling in love with his little pretty niece.

'Take a look by all means. Perhaps it will stop her nagging at me.' He screwed up his face and waved his fork at her and she giggled and screwed up her nose in return. Aaron was a gonna.

Pearl and her daughter escorted the family outside after the first meal of the day when her husband and Aaron went into his private office to talk.

'I thought you might like to see your family history.' Salvax indicated a wide desk on which a role of paper had been opened out. 'The Noble House of Valspec the Blue Knight, of which the house of Summer is a direct descendent. This scroll goes back four hundred years. There are others in the archives should you wish to look further.' He watched as the young man studied the scroll, with his hands resting either side of the desk.

'A very impressive history' he tapped his finger on the scroll. 'A lot of deaths here. Entire families wiped out.' He looked up at the King. 'Was there a war, disease?'

'A lot of both. When war comes to our shores we fight and die like every mortal. Disease usually follows. Taking the weak, the old and the very young. We are fortunate that war has not visited our shores for many generations. We are not without enemies. What Kingdom ever is? But for the most part we live in harmony with our neighbours.' He drew Aaron's attention to a huge map spread over an entire wall.

'This here is Fayland. As you see we are landlocked on only a quarter of our territory. The remainder we face the sea. To the south some three hundred and forty eight miles over open ocean lies the lands of King Ruscul. He holds sway over land approximately three quarters that of Fayland. He covets more. His kingdom shares a boarder with three other countries and the talk is there are often disputes over territory. For the most part we share nothing but a trade agreement. Our ships carry merchandise back and forth and so far there has been no trouble. To the east and west' he slashed his hand from left to right 'across the ocean lie vast ranges of mountains. What lies beyond them I do not know. Men have volunteered to make the journey but after the second expedition did not return I refused to allow others to die simply to see what lies on the other side. To the north, our closest neighbours are the Elfin people. Their King is Dard. A good man. A man I have dealt with for many years. But I fear his time is short now. He was King long before I attained the position upon my father's death. He is well into his hundred's now and if the rumours I am hearing are true his great grandson will be crowned King when the time comes. In-fighting amongst the King's male descendants is rife, hence his great grandson, Nall, will become King in due time. When this happens I fear for the Fayland people closest to the border.' He left Aaron studying the map. 'Some months ago Nall sent an emissary to our Court and announced, if you please, that he would take Aurora to his wife so that peace would be secured. On the understanding that Fayland would then fall under his rule upon my death.'

'And he still lives?' Aaron turned his attention back to the King. For the first time that day the King smiled.

'He is a worm of a man. The elfin people are short in stature. Their females are surprisingly delicate looking and standing barely four feet tall. The males are thick set with pointed ears and long hooked noses. They stand only inches taller than their women. Needless to say I declined his offer. Since then I have received reports of mysterious fires breaking out in fields of wheat. Indiscriminate slaughter of farm animals. People's livelihoods wiped out in a single night. No evidence has been found that points directly to Nall, or even the elfin people. It is however too much of a coincidence.'

'He feels insulted.' Aaron came back to the desk. 'What is it that you are telling me?' He rested a hip on the corner and faced the King.

'Fayland is a beautiful country. Our soil is rich, our people hard working and honest. Should you stay, and I sincerely hope that you do, you may find yourself embroiled in a war not of your making. Should this catastrophe fall upon our land every able-bodied man will be required to defend it. You may find, should this happen, that the only part of it that you will ever have is your grave.'

'It is written somewhere that war is hell.' Aaron countered. 'Should I decide to stay then the commitment to this land and its people will already have been made.' He had more respect for the man now after this frank and honest discussion. 'Do you have weapons?' That was at least something he may be able to help with.

'Cannons, slingshot, bows and arrows.'

'No guns, grenades, bombs?'

'When we fight, we fight face to face, not from a distance. We find the war less prolonged this way. Anyway, this is all for the future and hopefully will never happen.' Salvax indicated the map on his wall. 'Any advice you might see fit to impart regarding our defences we would consider.'

'I came here today' he got to his feet and walked to where the King now stood looking out of the window onto the courtyard below where his breakfast guests were assembled. 'to rip your head off.' He still wished for pocket so he could shove his hands into them. 'I find I have little in the way of control of my temper where Aurora is concerned.' His gaze fixed on the woman he was thinking about. 'You made her cry. I was so angry I could have committed murder.'

The King simply nodded at his side. He said nothing. He was not a stupid man. It was one of the reasons he wanted this alone time with Aaron. To show him that being a King has great responsibilities. Responsibilities that can sometimes sway the father to rash decisions. He wanted the best for his daughter after all.

'It took my father some time to calm me down. He said I had something that is called 'red rage'. I very nearly burst into flames. I had no control whatsoever.'

'Your father looks in fine health so I would consider that statement far from truthful.' The King replied and smiled as he turned to the younger man. 'I do not mock you young Aaron' he quickly said as Aaron's back stiffened and his hands went into fists. 'I simply state a fact. Red rage is rare amongst my people. Those whom it affects usually also have immense self-control.' Laughter outside distracted both men. 'I love my daughter very much Aaron Summer.'

Aaron very nearly said 'so do I' but managed to bit his tongue. 'She is….very special to me.' He turned away from the window and walked across the room, then turned. 'I miss her in my arms, in my bed. Hell I just miss her.' He said honestly, looking her father straight in the eyes.

'It would be most unwise to pursue that avenue, as enjoyable as I am sure it would be for both of you. Until you decide what it is that you want from your life, whether here or there.' The King headed for the door, Aaron followed. He rested his hand on the doorknob and held it there. 'She misses you very much. Some of the sparkle has gone from her eyes.' He paused, studying the young man. He could read nothing in his stern face. 'Stay away Aaron. Do not seek her out. Not for myself or her mother. For Aurora.' He pulled the door open and strode through. Aaron watched him depart then closed the door and turned in the opposite direction.

Chapter Nine

He flew over the sprawling city. Over homes, shops and businesses. There were fields of grain and vegetables. He saw horses, pigs and sheep. What he didn't see were cows. In fact cattle of any description. What he did see were herds of antelope type animals. They grazed on the lush grasses and drank from troughs lining the fences. As he watched, a young man walked over the field and dropped large scoops of grain at various points. The animals headed for the treat as soon as it hit the ground. As the young man was naked Aaron realised he had yet to reach maturity. A sprawling house and large outbuildings sat on a high rise in the next field. Men and women worked in the gardens and three naked young women were churning butter close to the house. As he flew closer many hands were raised in a wave. He returned the gesture. Further from the city limits was what he could only assume was a business park. There was a lot of activity on the ground. A slaughterhouse was set to the far left; the tannery was next door. Some sort of smelting factory was also set on the perimeter. Smoke streamed steadily from a tall chimney. Next to this was a smaller factory for pottery. Four kilns were busy with people bustling around. Crates were being loaded on a high-sided wagon. Four huge Shires stood in harness ready to hail the heavy conveyance. There was a timber merchants and a large building with a yard that was filled with building bricks. The last building was multi-storied with wide windows. On flying closer he saw men and women working with ledgers. He recalled Aurora mentioning they had limited technology, confined to an electrical power station and radio station. There was only one power point in his father's house. This was used for the radio. As he headed north passed the business park it was primarily farmland. Houses and buildings were scattered about, but for the most part it was acres and acres of fields. In the very far distance he could see another sizeable community. He veered west and crossed a wide tumbling stream. On its bank a mill stood with the huge mill wheel turning steadily as the water flowed over it. Everywhere he was spotted they waved. He felt very much at ease.

He turned back to the city and landed on a busy street. He folded his wings down his back as he walked along window-shopping. It was not unlike a street in the city back home. There were a number of restaurants, a very large glass fronted shop displaying household lines, grocers, butchers and hardware. Side streets branched off to other shops he had yet to investigate. He did notice a lack of baby strollers. Mothers carried their children. There appeared to be no dogs at all. He didn't recall seeing any pets at all on his travels.

He stopped at a window displaying some beautiful jewellery. A fine gold chain with a diamond-encrusted emerald caught his eye. He was about to go inside to make some enquiries as to the price when he realised he had no funds, no money whatsoever.

'Got to get a job' he muttered and started to walk away, desperately wishing for pockets.

'Something take your fancy young man?'

Aaron turned and came face to face with a short wrinkled old man with a stock of white curly hair and deep-set blue eyes. The door to the shop was open.

'A number of things sir, but I am without funds' he shrugged and began to turn away.

'You look strong enough. Are you open for barter young man? I could use a strong back today.'

'I might be.' Said Aaron cautiously.

'Come on in then. Let's deal.'

Aaron closed his wings and followed the old man into the shop.

'Where is he?' Parlax looked up into the sky hoping to see his son come home. It was past the dinner hour and getting dark. He had not been seen since breakfast.

'Relax father. He is a grown man. He does not have a curfew.' Crystal came to his side. 'We must go now the children need their beds, they have school tomorrow.'

'Just worried my daughter' he caught her in a tight embrace. 'He is new to this world, this life, if anything…..'

'He's coming.' Mar stepped toward his wife as a blue streak plummeted to earth.

'Oh I wish he wouldn't do that.' Crystal's face wrinkled in a frown just moments before Aaron touched down. He was filthy.

'Are you hurt?' she rushed forward to lend whatever assistance was called for.

'Don't!' Aaron's smiling face stopped her short. 'Don't touch me yet I need to wash up.' He held up his hands palms facing her as he closed his wings. They thankfully were clean. 'I've no idea what I've been wading through this afternoon.' He was still smiling however. 'It really stinks doesn't it?'

'Where the hell have you been. We've been worried sick?' Crystal stood with her legs apart hands on her hips. Both father and husband knew that stance. They each firmed their lips to stop the smile that threatened.

'I helped an old man dig some sort of draining ditch.' He sniffed at his hands. 'I really think I should wash this off.' The stench was awful. Whilst he looked down at himself he thought he had better find a hosepipe first. He'd definitely clog up the drains if he tried to shower with all this muck over him.

'Oh I think I can help you with that brother.' When he lifted his head a jet of water hit him full in the face. The pressure was such that he staggered a pace backward before he steadied himself.

The initial curses turned to laughter as sister soaked brother in the warm night air out in the courtyard. Father and husband retreated into the safety of the house to escape the cold spray. Toms and Jewel watched from the window and cheered on their mother. 'Father, father' Jewel cried out 'Uncle Aaron has the hose pipe now!' her small face was alight was excitement as her mother's playful screams filled the air.

Moments later the soaked young woman dashed into the house to escape her brother's playful bent. Thankfully Aaron did not give chase into the house with the hosepipe. Instead he stood dripping in the doorway smiling. 'I think I'm clean but I'm going to take a shower with soap and shampoo. Later.' Then he jogged around the house to get to his room off the inner courtyard.

'I think' Aaron said an hour later when he sat at the table and had a late dinner. His father had a glass of wine to keep him company 'that the guy next door raises some sort of animals. The smell was seriously intense.' He didn't know exactly what he was eating, but it tasted good so he ate heartily. 'Anyway, the ground was like a mud wallow, clogged up all of Linnel's drains and was seeping into his kitchen at the rear of the shop. It was seriously disgusting.'

'Linnel, the goldsmith?' His father asked.

'Little guy, looked about two hundred years old. Bright blue eyes?' Aaron filled his mouth again.

'Arrrr that would be Linnel. ' Parlax grinned. 'He is a canny old man and very experienced in the art of the bargain. He'll skin you alive son beware.'

'You're telling me. I never worked so hard in my entire life. Felt good though, to actually be doing something. We worked out a deal. I'll finish tomorrow afternoon. We still on for the tour in the morning?'

'Yes of course. I leave at eight.' He was pleased his son hadn't forgotten the invitation. 'Do you require more food?' Aaron's plate was empty. He even used the heel of the bread to wipe up the remains of the gravy. He refused wine, but had a tall glass of iced water.

'No thank you. That was great. I was famished.' He took his place setting into the kitchen, rinsed and washed what he had used and left them to drain. Living alone had at least taught him not to be a slob.

'I have an extensive library should you wish to read.' There was no television in this world. Something Aaron was pleased about. He rarely watched the one he had at home. They did have radio however. Like back home there were hourly news reports, a selection of music channels, a children's reading channel, and audio books for anyone who wished to just sit and listen to a book rather than read and turn the pages.

'I'm going to meditate for a couple of hours. Do you mind if I use the courtyard, it's a nice night.'

'It isn't necessary once you've had your opening son. Not necessary at all.' Parlax wondered if he was suffering some discomfort.

'I've done it for most of my life. It relaxes me. It's normal for me. Good night dad.'

'Good night son.' Parlax watched him walk outside. He saw his son's loincloth fall to his feet then he stepped out of it and simply sat cross-legged on the hard stone his hands resting on his knees, palms upward. In less than twenty-four hours there had developed a unity between the two men. A closeness had formed. Physical contact was rare but this was to be expected. After all they were virtual strangers. They had talked at length that first night, mostly about Aaron's history in his world. Parlax showed him photographs and portraits of his late mother, his sister and her family. For the most part Aaron wanted to know the world he was now in, the people that were his own kind, what was expected of him. Parlax had said that nothing was expected of him. The choice was his to make. Stay or leave. No pressure would be placed upon him. That was of course before the red rage episode, but that thankfully had been resolved.

As the older man watched the younger he saw the moment Aaron linked with Aurora. His head fell back on his shoulders and a smile crossed his face. Parlax could imagine his body heat would increase a degree or two. They may not be together physically, but they would certainly never be apart emotionally. He turned and left his son in peace.

'Where have you been all day. I looked for you' Aurora was soaking in a warm scented bath when he linked.

'Digging a rather smelly ditch for Linnel, the goldsmith.' He could almost smell the scent of her bath. He got hard immediately. 'Your father thought it best that we not be seen together.'

'Yes he told me' she whispered. 'I don't like it.' Her sadness was easily transmitted.

'Me neither' he smiled however and it made her jolt in the tub. His thoughts were anything but sad. 'He didn't say anything about link sex though did he.' In his mind he did all the things he would like to do if he got his hands on her, and any other part of his anatomy for that matter. Aurora couldn't believe she had an orgasm simply thinking the same thoughts.

'Oh goodness.' The bath water rippled as she shuddered in the tub. Aaron felt the ache in his loins recede. This sort of sex would never replace the physical act, but it was enough for now. It made Aaron's heart pound and his blood heat.

'Meet me tomorrow night. Come fly with me' he urged as his blood cooled and his heartbeat returned to normal.

'I have duties tomorrow until a late hour. There is to be a private dinner with some visiting dignitaries and I am expected to attend.' Her mind sighed. 'I have to attend Aaron, I cannot disappoint my father or his guests.' She stroked her hands over her breasts as Aaron's thoughts transmitted his desire. 'Don't do this to me' she begged 'I cannot bear it.' Her hands were already travelling to her centre, driven by his desire to possess her.

'I'm sorry sweetheart. I'll see you tomorrow, somehow. Sweet dreams.' Then he was gone.

He sat in the cooling night air for another hour. The skill that he had learned over the years cleared his mind and gave him ease. As midnight approached he rose and stretched his sluggish muscles before snatching up his loincloth and headed for bed. Unfortunately it was his body that betrayed him in the hours of endless tossing and turning. He managed a fitful hour before dawn, but this did nothing to calm his racing blood, his pounding heart. So henceforth, on the morning of his thirtieth birthday, which he had completely forgotten about, he was irritable and restless. The tour that he had agreed to go on with his father held little in the way of appeal.

At the breakfast table he sat with his father and ate a bowl of oatmeal, at least he thought it was oatmeal, loaded with pieces of apple and green grapes.

'Something troubles you Aaron?' Parlax asked as silence spread over the room. His son seemed unusually quiet this morning. There was the usual 'hi dad' and then nothing. He ate with a determination of a man with his mind on something else other than eating. A frown covered his face.

'Stuff, nothing important.' He pushed his empty bowl aside and picked up a glass of purple juice. Again he wasn't sure what it was, but he liked it.

'I would have thought that on the morning of your birthday you would at least be pleased at the day.'

'What?' Aaron asked, distracted.

'Your birthday son. It is today. Your thirtieth birthday' he picked up a small box from the chair beside him and handed it to Aaron. 'A small token in honour of the day.'

'Lost track of the days. Thanks. Are you sure it's today?' he turned the box over and over in his hands.

'Absolutely. I was there when you rushed into this world kicking and screaming in total annoyance.' Parlax smiled at the memory. 'I loved you instantly.' He was not ashamed to admit.

'How old was I when my mother took me from here?' He hadn't asked before now, refused to even speak of it. But today seemed the right time.

'Six days old, just six precious days old.'

'Was she an outsider. I mean from my world?' Aaron pulled the ribbon from the box.

'No. I had known your mother all of her life. We were betrothed not long after she was born.' He saw his son's frown but continued. 'It is our way here. That is why every opportunity for the young people to interact is made available to them. Sex isn't a problem in our young. Should your mother have decided, long before my opening, that she preferred another, then it would have been accepted. The same would go for myself, should I have found someone else. She was very willing to take me for her husband. There was never another for me. I loved her with all that I am.' He sighed heavily. 'That is why her leaving was such a shock. I was called to the office to solve some problem and told her I would be gone less than an hour. She kissed me goodbye and stood and waved me off with you in her arms and Crystal at her side. When I returned she was gone and taken you with her. She left Crystal alone in this house. That is something I will never forgive her for. She was barely two years old.'

'And you searched for me ever since.' Aaron looked down at the box he had yet to open.

'Every hour of every day. I hired a small army of men to search for your mother. Forgive me but you were so very young, growing so fast. Trying to find your mother meant finding you eventually. Fayland was searched. Men were sent over the oceans and neighbouring states. I think the entire planet was searched. She was never found, so hence neither were you my son.'

'What made you search off planet?' Aaron's gaze was still fixed on the box.

'The oracle heard you. Well not precisely you, but a male song. Harp song, much like mine. It was very feint.' He reached across the table and laid a large hand over his son's. 'I do not fully understand how the oracle works his magic. But he is able to listen to many worlds. The children of our world sing at birth for a month and then do not sing again until they approach their maturity. It's a call to those they love, an indication that their opening is approaching. That preparations need to be made. The oracle informed King Salvax who came personnel to see me with the news.'

'Aurora's my betrothed isn't she' he raised his head now and looked into his father's eyes. He knew this of course, from what Aurora herself had told him, or hinted at. But he needed the truth now.

'Yes my son. Long ago when you were born Salvax, he wasn't yet King, came to me in order to arrange an alliance between our houses. We have been friends from childhood. The House of Valspec is a loyal and true friend of the crown. I agreed immediately. Even years after you went missing he honoured our agreement and pledged Aurora to you. That is why she was sent to find you. Your song became stronger, recognised as being from the House of Valspec. I can only assume you must have been in some pain.' Aaron got up to pace, the box still unopened in his hand. 'Aurora was asked, not commanded, to go and find you. Her primary objective was to ensure you had your opening and a joining with one of your own kind and trained how to fly.' Parlax rose and went to join Aaron by the cold hearth. 'I would have come myself son, I could have supervised your opening, taught you how to fly. The joining however, to ensure your sexual needs are secure, is beyond me.'

'I wouldn't have believed you. In my world a 'faerie' is another name for homosexual, a gay man, a man who likes other men. I wouldn't have thanked you for telling me I was one.' He smiled at the thought and turned to his father. 'On the other hand confronted with a beautiful naked woman, you tend to pay attention.'

Parlax nodded. 'Open your present Aaron, we should be going soon.' He stepped back as Aaron lifted the lid and put it aside.

'Oh wow.' He looked up at his father. Inside was a heavy silver chain on which a blue stone hung. Inside the stone was the Valspec symbol. A silver V with swirls of blue and silver in vivid relieve. Aaron lifted it from the box.

'Each young man, on reaching his maturity receives one of these. It denotes his house. In your case Valspec. And on the reverse his name.'

Aaron turned it over and in simple silver lettering was written Aaron son of Parlax. 'I don't know what to say.' He throat was constricted.

'Here let me put it on for you' Parlax hooked the chain around his son's neck and fastened the clip. 'The chain is never too long in length in case it gets caught on something that you may be carrying at the time.' The blue stone rested just below the hollow in his throat. 'You should wear it always so that people will know your house.' He wear one similar to his son. 'Happy birthday my son.' He stepped away so that they could both compose themselves. Aaron on the other hand eventually gave into the need to hug his father close to his heart, and did so. He was a man now but he put all the lost years into this one hug and they both knew it.

'I think I've missed you all of my life.' Aaron said at last. He hadn't shed tears but it was a close call. They were walking out into the early morning sunlight.

'I thought of you every day. Maybe we got connected over space and time. I hope so.' Parlax spread his wings. 'My office is in the palace. I'll race you.' And he shot into the air.

'Nicely done old man' he called after him before he spread his wings and gave chase.

Aaron had landed and folded his wings, on what he assumed was the main concourse leading to the palace, before his father touched down. People were taking off and landing at regular intervals. It was much like a busy station.

'I cannot believe you have only been flying for less than a week.' Parlax slapped him on the shoulder as they walked side by side into the palace outer courtyard. People branched off left and right and hurried about their business. They walked through the courtyard and into the main hall then turned left and up a flight of stairs. There were fewer people now. Parlax kept up a steady stream of conversation indicating various portraits of Kings and Queens past until they reached another flight of stairs that lead up to the top level. 'My office is down the hall the last door on the left. I have a short meeting to attend before I can give you my full attention.' He turned Aaron around and pointed to the right. 'Refreshments are always available in the first room on the left. I've left the Valspec historical ledger for you to brows through. I shouldn't be more than thirty to forty minutes.' With those words he turned and hurried toward his office.

'You could have mentioned his earlier dad!' he called after him. Parlax simply waved a hand over his head and disappeared into his office. 'So now I twiddle my thumbs for half an hour.' Deploring the lack of pockets yet again he folded his arms across his wide chest and debated simply finding the nearest balcony and flying away. Then he had to smile to himself. 'The nearest balcony and flying away. For Christ's sake!' Maybe they had coffee he thought as he headed in the direction of the refreshments. He didn't drink it often, just a mug in the morning with Mike when they had breakfast. That thought pulled him up short. He hadn't thought about Mike for days. Or Sophie and the kids. Strangely however he didn't feel the loss. He had good memories of the years they had spent together. They were the only reason that he had requested additional time if he decided to stay. He wouldn't leave them with uncertainty or doubt about what happened to him. His thoughts relaxed as he pushed open the door and there she was.

'Aurora' he breathed her name, she turned, and then ran into his arms.

'Lock the door' she begged 'lock the door.' Her fingers were unbuckling his loincloth as the key turned in the lock. She was already naked.

His hands couldn't find enough of her, his lips couldn't quench his thirst for her and his manhood couldn't go deep enough to fill all of her. She came the second his lips touched hers and his hand cupped her then his fingers invaded her centre. She was already hot and wet and flooded his fingers. Aaron only just remembered to close his wings as they wrestled each other to the floor.

'Take me, take me now. Inside me.' She unashamedly begged and spread her legs wide before he simply drove himself home. They remained perfectly still for a brief second or two.

'At last' he moaned and started to move. Slow hard thrusts, pushing himself deeply into her. He had most of his weight on his elbows as he rested his forehead on the cool wooden floor beneath them. Her legs found themselves high around his waist and her hips rose up to meet him in eager response.

'This is so good' she moaned. 'I can feel it building again. Oh Aaron its….' She gasped and arched her back when he increased his pace just a little, just enough to throw her over the edge, but not enough to take him along with her. For fifteen glorious minutes he did it over and over again until he felt his own release building. She was as limp as warm wax beneath him, barely holding onto her senses, when the gentle thrusts of his engorged penis turned into a battering ram. He wanted more, to go deeper, to touch her very soul with the love that poured out of him. He pushed himself up and dragged her ankles high over his shoulders as he lowered his hot body over hers bending her almost in half. Then he took more. She gave more. Hips like pistons she thrust up as best she could to meet him.

'Deeper, I need deeper.' He begged and was amazed when her knees folded over his shoulders lifting her hips high off the floor. 'Oh God' he clenched his teeth together as he hammered into her. Just a little more, just a little more.

'Now Aaron, now' she cried out as her muscles fisted around him and he exploded inside her. How long he shuddered his release he wasn't sure. The minutes ticked by until eventually he realised he was probably crushing her so he pulled himself free and collapsed at her side. His breath had evened out but his heart was still hammering in his chest. He felt amazing. He rolled to his side to face her.

'You are a very lovely shade of red. It's a sure give away' he inched closer and kissed the nearest breast. 'I didn't give these nearly enough attention. You must feel neglected.' He grinned however when she turned a happily smiling face toward him.

'We'll save them for next time.' She stretched lazily then sat up. 'Come with me.' She got easily to her feet and only stumbled a little before she wiggled her hips as if to set them in the right position then lead the way to a small anti-chamber. She delighted in washing him thoroughly then stood meekly when he returned the favour. When they were dried and dressed, her panties were on a hook in the anti-chamber, she took a dry cloth and proceeded to wipe up the signs of their intimacy from the floor. 'Don't want someone to come in and slip and hurt themselves do we.'

Aaron simply smiled at her comical face before she took the cloth back into the anti-chamber and he unlocked the door. When she returned and he reached for the door handle he stopped. 'You planned this. You and my father?' he looked both astonished and grateful at the same time.

'Of course we did. Happy birthday Aaron.' She kissed him softly on the lips.

He pulled back eventually and simply looked at her beautiful face. He ran his hands down her arms and captured her fingers with his. 'I've decided to stay. I think I knew I would even before we came here.'

'Oh I'm so pleased.' Unexpectedly tears ran down her cheeks. 'I'm so happy for you.'

'I feel so at home here. Like some part of me has always known I didn't quite fit in the other world. I feel whole here. The only thing missing in my life is you Aurora. I love you. I want to marry you.' He watched her face carefully. More tears gushed from her eyes. They streamed down her cheeks and plopped gently on her breasts before completing their descent to the floor.

'Let go of my hands.' She almost shouted and caused him to step back a pace.

'I'm sorry I didn't mean to upset you. I apologise.' Then his arms were filled with her. Her lips covered his face with kissed. 'Yes, oh yes I will marry you. I love you!' she shouted and her words filled the room.

'Well that's good to know. You had me worried there for a moment.' He crushed her close to his chest. 'I should speak with your father as soon as possible.' He eased her to her feet. 'If I leave tomorrow morning to speak with Mike and arrange…..things, we could be married as soon as I return. Tomorrow, late afternoon.' Words just poured out of his mouth. 'What day is it?'

'Friday'

'Friday! Really!' he had completely lost track of the days of the week. 'We don't work Saturdays on our rotation.' He thought carefully. 'He's off tomorrow and Sunday so that works well.' He grabbed her hand and opened the door and came face to face with his father.

'Is everything all right son?' He noted Aurora's tear stained face and hoped their plans hadn't come to naught.

'Everything is great. I'm getting married. Got to go find the King.' He gave his father a one armed hug as he refused to let go of Aurora's hand. 'Thanks dad' he whispered and received a 'my pleasure son.' They were disturbed by voices coming from the floor below.

'That would be my father and the council just finished their meeting.' Aurora looked over the balcony to the many heads below and recognised her father. 'We should speak privately.' Then opened her wings and folded them down her back as she lent over the balcony and called 'My father!'

He turned and looked towards the sound. 'My daughter. Is all well?' He turned automatically towards the stairs as Aurora, Aaron and Parlax headed for the top of the flight.

Aaron bowed deeply when the King reached the top of the stairs. 'I'd like permission to marry your daughter' He came straight to the point.

'Is that so' Salvax's face gave nothing away. He looked from one eager face to the other. He did wink at his old friend before he turned to the young couple.

'It is.' Aaron could play this game as well.

'Do you love her?' he asked Aaron.

'Very much.'

'And you daughter. Will you have this blue comet!' he laughed uproariously. 'Don't think I haven't seen you flashing across the sky young man.' He wagged a long finger at the young man.

'I love him very much my father.'

'Very well. Your mother and I will arrange it.' He held his hand out to Aaron. 'I'm delighted that you have decided to stay amongst us. To become part of my family.'

'I'll take my twenty-four hours tomorrow Your Majesty. Perhaps the wedding could be arranged for later that afternoon. I am most eager.' He hadn't released Aurora's hand yet.

'You should go and finish your work for Linnel, which I understand is completely repugnant.'

'My sister hosed me down in the courtyard last evening, before she would allow me into the house.'

'I always did like that young woman. So Parlax our Houses shall be unity after all. It pleases me greatly.'

'No more than I Your Majesty.' They shook hands.

'Come daughter, Parlax. We have much to do.' He took his daughter's hand and tugged her away from Aaron and proceeded down the stairs. Parlax bought up the rear. 'You should enter him into the games my friend. I've never seen the likes of his flying. He would beat that arrogant Arno for sure and perhaps I could recoup some of my loses.'

'My thoughts exactly Your Majesty.'

'What games?' Aaron called from the top of the stairs before he followed them down.

'Later son' Parlax hurried after his King.

The tour with his father forgotten Aaron flew to Linnel to complete his ditch and lay bricks and slate along the sides and bottom so that water, and whatever else there might be, could flow easily to the main drain at the bottom of Linnel's back yard. Using a garden implement similar to a lawn rake, he raked the surface of the yard to clear away any unsightly residue. Already signs of greenery could clearly be seen. What Linnel decided to do with the pile of muck at the end of his yard was his problem. A quick spray of water over the grass removed more of the smelly mud. Aaron then turned the hose on himself until he was clean again.

'That's a fine job you've done young Aaron. Come inside and we'll complete the deal.' He gave the young man a wide berth as he dripped his way into his kitchen.

Dry and with his treasure tucked safely inside his loincloth, he arrived home in time for his dinner.

In the main hall of the palace, with the portal open, Aaron took his leave of his father and family. The King arrived with his wife and daughter and no amount of insistence could keep the young woman from flying to Aaron's side for a farewell kiss. He nuzzled her neck shortly afterwards and made her laugh.

'Hurry home my love.' She clutched his hands tightly.

'I have something for you.' He pushed his fingers into the top of his loincloth and pulled out a small cloth pouch. 'In my world it is customary for the man to give his betrothed a small token to celebrate their forthcoming union. I'm not sure of the custom here, but I rather like the idea of everyone knowing that you will belong to me.' He opened the pouch and poured the contents into the palm of his hand.

'I Love you' He lifted her hand and pushed the ring down the third finger of her left hand. A twisted gold band crowned with an oval of tiny diamonds and a pale blue sapphire nestled in the centre. 'I will be back.' He kissed the palms of both her hands, stepped through the portal and was gone. She burst into tears before her parents hurried to her side.

Chapter Ten

It felt weird to wear clothes again and to drive his truck. He had stripped the cabin of their belongings and retrieved their hidden valuables and was on his way within thirty minutes. He reached Mike's' just after eleven that morning. The family were taking their ease on the back porch. Remnants of their first meal of the day still on the table. The kid's backpacks were by the door.

'Hi guys.' He called as he rounded the corner onto the porch. 'Uncle Aaron' the kids ran to greet him and he scooped them up in his arms and whirled them around and around for a few minutes. 'Jeez you're getting heavy.' He puffed his cheeks out as he placed them on their feet.

'We're off to grandma's. Can you come too?' Little Julia asked.

'Not this time baby doll. I have something for you.' He dropped his own backpack and dug down inside for a small package. 'Got something for you too big guy.' He handed a small gift to each child. They ignored the adults as they sat on the grass whilst they opened their presents.

'It's so pretty. Can I show mom and dad.' Julia threw her arms around his neck and kissed his cheek before running to her parents.

'Pretty neat uncle Aaron' Phillip lifted the gold medal from its box. 'What is it exactly?'

'A Saint Christopher. The patron saint of travelers. You want to be a pilot don't you?'

'I got to grow a bit first.' Phillip said in all seriousness.

'Well you wear this all the time and it will keep you save. See what it says on the back. 'Go where the spirit moves you.'

'What does it mean uncle Aaron?' He lifted the chain over his head.

'It means follow your dreams. Don't let anyone tell you its wrong.' Aaron patted his cheek. 'Plant one on me big guy.'

'Do I have to?' It was a game they always played.

'Wanna hug to.' Aaron opened his arms and Phillip giggled and gave him a kiss and a hug. Then charged off to show his parents.

'It's got words on the back uncle Aaron. What does it say.' Julia held up her gift. A silver faerie on a silver chain. Pretty and delicate.

'It says 'spread your wings and fly away' baby doll. It's a big world out there and you should see as much of it as possible when you're all grown up.' He slipped the chain over her head just as a horn sounded from the front of the house.

'That's the cab' Sophie said and picked up the backpacks. 'Say good-bye now kids. Come along.'

'Bye uncle Aaron.' They called in unison as they rushed around the house.

'Looking good buddy. How you feeling?' Mike lounged in his chair. He knew Aaron well enough to realise he had something on his mind.

'Feel terrific. Never better.' He sat on the porch steps and looked across the lawn.

It was silent until Sophie returned to join the men.

'Can we go inside we need to talk?' Aaron rose to his feet easily.

'Is something wrong sweetie?' Sophie took his hand.

'Not exactly, but it's important.' He followed them inside. He asked for the main parlour. It was wider by far than the kitchen where they normally talked.

'Spit it out Aaron.' Mike sat next to his wife on the sofa.

'I have to tell you something and I have to show you something. Something that you must never tell anyone about. I need a promise from both of you. Your word that this stays inside these four walls.' Mike and Sophie exchanged looks of deep concern.

'We promise. Aaron please what is it?' Mike asked.

'Okay' he puffed out his cheeks. 'I need to draw the curtains.' Which he did, all three windows in the large room were covered.

'Please don't be alarmed.' He held up his hands palms outward, before beginning to remove his clothes, down to his boxers.

'Your scaring me buddy.' Mike whispered and held Sophie's hand. She simply looked pale and afraid.

'You know those pains I was getting between my shoulder blades.' Both nodded.

'This was the reason.' He thought wings and out they spread.

'Holy Cow' Mike scrambled to his feet. Sophie just sat open mouthed. 'Are they for real?' He was gawking, open mouthed like his wife.

'I can fly too. The brunette I spoke to you about. She was sent to find me.' He closed his wings and got dressed as he told them what had happened to him and why he was visiting.

'You're never coming back are you?' Sophie held his hand.

'No I'm not honey. In a day or two the police will notify you of an accident. They'll find my badly burned out truck at the bottom of the cliff in the sea, near the cabin. It will simply look like I lost control and went over the edge. I have Aurora's and my things in the truck. You will probably be asked to identify them because no bodies will be found.' He went to his backpack and took out Aurora's ring and his watch. 'I'll make sure these are left in the truck to be found. Aurora's name is Aurora Spring. I don't know her address but she works for Reynolds and Reynolds the architects in the city.' He also handed over a thick manila envelope. 'In here are copies of all of my legal documents. My lawyer has power of attorney to deal with my estate. You get everything.'

'You're positively sure you want to do this?' Mike also took a hand and squeezed it tightly. He'd rather have his best friend than his money.

'I met my father Mike. He looks exactly like me, given the age difference. I have a sister, nephew and niece. They are the something that has been missing my entire life. I would be dead now if not for Aurora. If our wings haven't been opened before our thirtieth birthday we die. The males of my species die. I can't have a sex live in this world, because I am physically not able to mate outside my own species. Mike I was a virgin up until a week ago.' He said earnestly.

'What!' Why didn't you say something for Christ's sake.' Now Mike paced the room.

'It wouldn't have made any difference. I'm whole now. Look at this.' He lifted the chain and blue stone from around his neck. 'This is the symbol for the House of Valspec of which I am one.' He turned it over so they could both read the inscription. 'I want a family of my own. I don't want to live off yours for the rest of my life. I love you two very much and I absolutely adore your kids. But they are yours not mine. I want my own to love and watch grow. This is the only way for me. I'm a god damn faerie, with wings and everything.'

Mike cleared his throat as he paced and Sophie wiped away tears.

'How much you worth anyway?' Mike punched him in the arm and gave him a tight hug.

'Not sure, but I reckon about thirty grand and change.' He smiled at Sophie over Mike's shoulder. 'You can finally get your hands on that oak chest in my bedroom.' She simply burst into tears and fell into his arms.

'We really don't want your money Aaron.' Sophie and Mike walked with him to his truck an hour later. 'Hey speak for yourself' Mike had Aaron in a playful headlock and ran his knuckles over his head before he released him.

'Blow it in Vegas, take a holiday, put it towards the college funds. I can't take it with me.'

'There's no chance you can ever come back. To visit maybe?' Sophie asked. She missed him already. He shook his head.

'I only got these few hours because I wouldn't leave you without setting the records straight.' He kissed Sophie softly on the mouth and punched Mike on the arm as he swung into his truck. 'I'll miss you. Bye.' He didn't hesitate but drove quickly away.

He set everything the best he could. Picked the spot carefully that would give him the best drop onto rocks to create a fireball and that would eventually send most of his truck into the sea. Both bags were just tossed into the flat bed, so they would be thrown far enough away to be located and identified. Clothes from the skin upwards, along with shoes he placed on either seat. His watch and her ring he placed with the clothes. If they were lost in the fire or lost in the sea so be it. It was all he could do.

Wearing just his loincloth he set the truck in motion and headed for the bend in the road and leaped out of the moving vehicle just before it hit the barrier and disappeared from sight. There was an almighty crash, followed by a huge explosion as his truck crashed and bounced down the cliff and landed partly, on its roof, in the sea. There was hardly anything left. With a leafy branch he brushed away his naked footprints as he headed back to the cabin. It was just three o'clock in the afternoon. Standing close to where the portal would open he clutched the crystal around his neck and thought of Aurora. Three o'clock was the designated time for the portal to open. He only had to wait an additional five minutes before he turned his back on his old life and stepped through to start another.

Chapter Eleven

Their marriage was quite a public affair. She was the King's daughter after all. It appeared that the dancing and merrymaking took place before the actual marriage ceremony. They sat together on the high table and ate a hearty meal and drank from the same cup of wine. He took part in some form of tradition dancing and made a right fool of himself. Nobody seemed to mind over much as he laughed at his own ineptitude. Before the ceremony commenced he was treated to a set of formation flying that had him cheering and applauding along with everyone else. At seven p.m. sharp a bell sounded and the young couple were lead to the raised altar where a council elder stood ready to perform the ritual of marriage. Aaron wear a silk loincloth for the ceremony, Aurora was naked. It was basically a binding ceremony. His name was entered into a ledger along with Aurora's. They spoke of their love for one another as their wrists were bound in gold silk ribbon. The bride's mother then stepped forward and laid a silk loincloth over their joined wrist. To seal the union. 'They are wed.' the elder announced. 'We will now perform the wing ceremony.' He removed the golden binding and placed it in the ledger.

'A moment please' Aaron once again pulled a small pouch from his loincloth and took a simple gold band from within. 'I want everyone to know that you belong to me.' He lifted her left hand and removed the engagement ring and slipped on the gold band then raised her hand to his lips where he kissed the ring. Then he replaced the engagement ring. 'Let these rings stand as a symbol of our union. I will love you until my last dying breath.' His wings unfurled and spread to their fullest extent. His shimmer this day was blinding. Aurora opened her own wings and folded them back so that the tips touched. Aaron took her in his arms, lowered his lips for a kiss and enveloped them both in his wings. Nothing happened. His wings were far too long and missed her tips be several feet.

'My love' Aurora whispered beneath his lips. 'Bend your wings, our tips much touch for the change to happen.'

It took all of his concentration to bend his wings at the elbow and draw the tips down to touch hers. When they did it was a light show the likes of which had never been seen before. Flashes of blue, silver and gold burst from their union. They were locked together in a loving embrace and did not hear the loud cheering and thunderous applause from the crowds. When his wings began to turn red however his father intervened.

'Time for that later my son. Let her don the loincloth so that she may be presented to the crowds in her new colours.' He jabbed his elbow into Aaron's side.

Gradually his wings returned to their normal shades of blue. Those nearest to the newly weds could hear much soft laughter and female giggles as Aurora tried to don her new loincloth behind his vibrating wings.

'Will you stop that?' She could clearly be heard saying. Before first one foot and then the other was raised and the silk drawn up her long shapely legs.

'They will have amazing children.' Salvax whispered to his wife.

'I long to be a grandmother, many times over.' Pearl took her husband's hand.

They were interrupted when Aaron throw back his head and cried into the night. 'God I love this woman.' And opened his wings and stepped to the side before folding them down his back as Aurora stepped forward and opened her newly coloured wings of every shade of blue. The cheers were deafening. She raised her hands and waved to the people as her husband came and stood behind her and spread his impressive wings. What he wanted now most of all was to get away from here. To find a quiet place and spend hours making love to his wife. As if reading his thoughts his father stepped up behind him.

'Take this.' He handed over a large key. 'The King has graciously given you the summer palace on the lake to the north for your honeymoon. Stay as long as you will. It is permitted to leave now.' He stepped back to his place beside his family.

'Are you ready to go my love' he dangled the key before her eyes. 'The summer palace awaits.'

She turned a stunning face toward her parents. 'Thank you.' Then back to Aaron 'I am ready.'

Aaron turned to the crowds and lifted his hands for silence. Another first for the audience.

'I thank you most sincerely for a truly memorable wedding day. It will long hold affection in our hearts.' He held Aurora's hand. 'But now my wife and I must leave as we have other pleasures to attend to.' More cheers and much laughter followed as Aaron rose gracefully into the air followed shortly by his wife and they headed north together.

'I don't.….'Aurora tried again. 'I don't think I can take any more of you' she was spread eagle on the wide bed. 'I'm exhausted.' It was close to dawn of the morning after their marriage. Neither had slept.

'You forget sweetheart' Aaron lay face down across the foot of the bed. His head hung over the side. 'I have years of abstinence to make up for.' His mind was drifting into sleep.

'But not all in one night my love.' She yawned hugely and then was instantly asleep. Neither woke until well past the noon hour.

Washing, eating, making love and simple hot sex were the order of the day and night. Honeymoon fever was in full swung. Occasionally they snatched a few hours of exhausted sleep. Aaron ate like a starved man at every meal, putting away huge amounts of food. Aurora's appetite was keen, but she ate with more moderation. She did confess however to eating sugary snacks at any given time of the day. They indulged their every fantasy. Laughter rang out through the small palace when they played simple childhood games like hide and seek. When they took to the skies to exercise their wings it usually ended up with Aurora being wrapped around him so they could simple mate together in the air. Swimming in the lake had the same result. They just couldn't get enough of one another.

'Where do we live' Aaron asked after three wonderful weeks at the summer palace. 'When we go back. What is the custom?' His wife was curled up on his lap as they sat together in a large chair before the fire in their bedroom. There was a chill in the air today.

'We have a number of options.' She snuggled close to his warm chest. They were both naked and had been for the entire duration of their honeymoon.

'Which are?' he hand moved gently up and down her thigh.

'My quarters at the palace are situated in the east wing. My parents have the west wing. We could move into the east wing with little difficulty. It is a vast space that I have for myself.' She ran a small hand over his wide chest as she spoke. 'We could, if you prefer, move into your father's home. It matters not which you chose just so long as we are together.'

'I'd like us to have a place of our own. I want children with you Aurora. I want to build a life here.' His cheek rested on the top of her head. 'How do we go about buying land, building a house?' His mind wondered to builders and architects.

She struggled to sit up so she could look into his face. 'My darling husband' she began 'I want all of those things to. I want so much to have your child growing inside me. But one day I will be Queen, you King, and we will live in the palace as is fitting.' She lent forward and kissed his lips softly. 'My father is yet a young man of fifty-two years. I pray he will remain fit and healthy and live for many more years before the burden of the monarchy falls to us.' She smiled. 'He is also very wise my father. Do you recall seeing the orchard to the east of the palace.'

Aaron nodded.

'There is a plot of land hidden from view behind the trees. On this land a house stands. It is perhaps a shade larger than that of your father's. It has mature gardens surrounding it, along with a wall that runs the entire perimeter. It is private, yet not isolated from family and friends. The palace guards patrol regularly around the grounds and will continue to do so should we move in. They will not be seen unless you wish them to be. Entrance to the property can be made through the orchard or from the main entrance to the north. Both entrances are gated. Although there are no locks no one will enter if the gates are closed. It is the rule here in Fayland.'

She adjusted her position to straddle him. 'But understand me Aaron, there is no pressure for us to accept this property as our home. You will be master in whatever place we chose to live.' She watched him closely as he considered his options. He was such a handsome man and all hers.

It would save them considerable time and money if they moved into the palace grounds. King Salvax had spoken to him at length, upon his return, about his future responsibilities. Aurora would one day be Queen. It was her wish that he become King at her side. To share the responsibilities and rule Fayland together. It was a huge responsibility. One he would willing accept simply to have Aurora at his side. On reflection he considered it a boon that he could be within walking distance of the many books and ledgers he would need to study over the next several decades.

'We will stay here another week as I'm not willing to let you out of my sight just yet. Then we will move into the house behind the orchard.' He lifted her easily so that she could guide his rigid manhood into her warm wet nest. He lowered her slowly and she shuddered, and then began to ride.

When her system had returned to normal she linked with her father and gave him the news. He assured her that everything would be ready for their return. Aaron linked with his father and told him what had been decided. Everyone seemed pleased by the decision.

It was however one week and three days before they left the summer palace. Aaron simply wasn't ready to go home. He had to love her just once more, then again and again until his system was saturated with her. Saturated enough to hold him for several days.

'You've lost weight Aurora.' Her mother did a quick circle around the young woman. 'Are you well?' Her voice was soft with concern.

'I am truly wonderful mother.' They sat together in her solarium whilst Aaron and her father talked in another room. 'I have eaten more since my marriage than ever before. I'm surprised I could lift off the ground.' She sipped on a tall glass of iced water. 'My husband.' She thrilled at the words 'is a very physical man. We had plenty of exercise.'

Her mother laughed aloud and slapped her hands on her thighs. 'He looks the sort. Is he as good as he looks?' she was not embarrassed to ask.

'Oh yes mother mine. There were days when I couldn't even walk.' They laughed together and spoke of many things until the men joined them. Each went to his own.

'Your father, keen negotiator that he is, has convinced me to enter the games later in the year.' Aaron hooked an arm around Aurora's neck and drew her in for a kiss. 'He seems to have some idea that I am a good flier.' He settled down beside his wife.

'And so you are' Aurora agreed. 'I've not seen any better.' She was proud of the fact.

'He should talk to Gen tomorrow and decide what he wants to enter.' The King handed out small glasses of wine to each family member. Aaron had noticed that small amounts of wine were evident, but he had not seen a bar or inn where beer might be served. Maybe like himself faeries didn't drink much. He was also pleased to realise there wasn't a single cigar or cigarette in sight. The air was clean and fresh.

'And Gen would be?' the young man asked.

'Gen is our Games Master. He sets the training schedules, allots men to various teams according to their ability and sets the scale for those who do individual games.' Pearl replied. 'We have not won a games in five years. This must be remedied as soon as possible.'

'No pressure then.' But he was grinning. 'In which case we should go home and get some rest.' He bowed to the King. 'Your Majesty.' Then to his mother-in-law. 'My lady.' Then to his wife. 'Wanna lift cutie?' he wriggles his eyebrows and made her giggle.

'Sure handsome. My place isn't far' all four walked to the balcony. The King and his lady were not prepared however for their daughter to wrap her arms and legs around her husband and turn a smiling face toward them. 'See you tomorrow.' Then to her husband. 'Come on big boy, show them what you're made off.'

Aaron made a show of trying to lift off with his wife in his arms and kept thudding to the floor. Salvax and his wife looked on in concern. Surely he wasn't planning to fly the both of them. It was unheard of.

'Will you behave?' Aurora laughed in amusement. 'Now take me home.' She nuzzled his neck and whispered. 'I need to rest, I really need to rest.' She bit gently into his neck.

'Never satisfied are you?' He laughed and took a firm grip on her sexy bottom.

'Uh, uh.' She kissed him softly. Aaron moaned.

'Okay, okay. See you tomorrow.' He called as he shot into the air with such speed the King and Pearl took a step back and collided with one another. Their gasps of fright were in unison when Aaron stopped high in the sky, turned, and then dropped like a stone toward the earth as if his burden were too heavy. The King and his lady were not the only ones to look up in horror. They recognised the blue of the wings and knew them to be Aaron, newly married to their prin-cess. Salvax had already called to his guards to order them to rescue the young couple when Aaron curved his wings and slowed his descent to hover just above the balcony.

'Your daughter is safe with me. Have no fears.' He hovered with apparent ease, his massive wings curving back and forth.

'You young fool!' The King barked and raised a fist in the air. 'Put her down at once.' He couldn't quite hide the grin that crossed his face when his daughter smiled and waved at him.

'I will when I get her home. Until tomorrow.' He levelled out and flew swiftly toward the orchard.

'Did you see that, did you?' he asked his wife as he waved his guards away.

'I did. We'll definitely win the games this year.' And she turned and went inside, leaving her husband speechless on the balcony.

Chapter Twelve

Aaron thought it wise to remove himself from the King for a few days. Over the next two weeks he found Gen and started his training. Already sleek and toned muscles began to bulge, so much so that Aaron objected stating he was carrying too much weight and felt sluggish. Gen considered this and finally agreed. Aaron's performance in the air was so impressive that Gen turned over the training of the fliers to him. His team began to slim down after a short time. Bulging muscles were not the normal for his species. What he did do was to get them jogging to tone their leg muscles. In secret session they discussed strategy, complex manoeuvres, set patterns.

'I was thinking about a uniform.' Aaron was sharing a bath with his wife. It was one of the pleasures they often shared at the end of each day.

'What for?' she yawned sleepily. Her husband's energy never failed to amaze and exhaust her. He appeared to need very little sleep. It was the norm for him to wake her in the night to make love to her for hours at a time. Then he was usually up and breakfasted before she even lifted her head from her pillow.

'For the games. Something that will distinguish us from the other teams.' He had discovered that teams were arriving from all over the planet. It was like an Olympic games only everyone had wings that were used in certain events.

'What do you think?' There was no reply. 'Sweetheart.' She was asleep.

She did not stir when he lifted her from the bath or when he wrapped her in a thick towel and lay her on their bed and patted her dry. He unpinned her hair and pulled a quilt over her warm body and tucked her in. Knowing his preference for waking her in the night to love her all over again, he kissed her forehead and stretched out on the long sofa across from their bed and pulled a throw over his hips. He fell sleep after a few minutes a martyr to his wife's exhaustion.

When he checked on her the following morning she still lay in exactly the same position as when he left her the night before. 'Poor baby' he smiled and kissed her forehead and left quietly so as not to wake her.

It was noon when she finally stirred and stretched lazily reaching out for Aaron at the same time. The bed was empty and the sheets cold to the touch. 'Aaron?' she called out and sat up. No reply. Searching the room with her eyes she saw the throw from the sofa still rumbled on the floor. Rushing from the bed she pulled on a clean loincloth and fled the room, her hair flying behind her in a tangled mess. In the kitchen she could see where he had eaten breakfast. His plate, knife and fork were still in the sink.

'My lady?' one of the serving women who came to serve breakfast and see to the household entered the kitchen.

'Have you seen Lord Aaron this morning?' his wife asked, concerned.

'Lord Aaron left early this morning and gave strict instructions that you were not to be disturbed' she lifted a piece of paper from the counter, that Aurora hadn't noticed. 'He left a note my lady.'

'Thank you' she clutched at the note and returned to her room.

'Good morning sweetheart. Didn't want
to wake you. You fell asleep in the tub.
Knowing my habit of waking you at
ridiculous times in the night for some hot
sweaty sex, I was a good boy and slept on
the sofa. I'm amazed that you didn't wake
up when I cursed rather loudly when I
rolled off the damn thing in the night.
No problems. Have a lazy day. Love you.
Aaron.'

She folded the note carefully and put it away for safe-keeping. She had a smile on her face for the rest of the day.

'I slept on the sofa.' Aaron told his father when they met in the library and Aaron was reading through some Fayland law books.

'No problem I hope?' Parlax was sure no two people were more ideally suited.

'No, no. She was just exhausted. I don't allow her much sleep. I don't seem to need much, never have. But my appetite for her hasn't abated at all. It's like a fever I can't shake off, not that I want it to you understand.' He shrugged. 'But she needs more sleep obviously.' He closed the book and pushed it aside.

'People have been talking Aaron, saying she is much too thin, has lost some weight. Sleep depredation can do that.' He rested a hand on his son's shoulder. 'I assume you don't like sleeping apart from your wife.'

'Hell no. I like the feel of her in my arms, then one thing leads to another, and hey presto another disturbed night for the love of my life.' He shrugged his wide shoulders.

'Buy a sleeping pouch son.'

'A what?'

'Sleeping pouch. A lot of the soldiers have them for when they go off on boarder patrols and are away for extended periods of time. It is difficult for some as they still have painful urges in the night. You must have noticed that you don't get an erection when you wear your loincloth?' Parlax watched a grimace cover his son's face. He hid a grin.

"I wondered about that." He had noticed almost from the beginning when he first pulled on his loincloth back in the cabin.

'It's something in the hide that suppresses your natural urges. It was discovered many years ago and it was for that reason that the leather is used for the loincloths of mature males.' He rested a large hand on his son's warm shoulder. 'See the quartermaster at the barracks. Do you know your size at rest?'

Aaron nodded.

'Good. Make love when first you go to bed, or wherever you happen to be at the time.' Parlax said tongue in cheek. 'Then slip it on when you are at rest and get a good nights sleep. You will see the difference in your lovely wife in a very short space of time.'

'Sounds like you've been there?' His son asked.

'In my youth my son.' He rose and went about his business.

Aaron made haste to the quartermaster.

At first Aurora was upset to think that her husband needed to take action to prevent him from making love with her. Initially she hadn't noticed the change. Aaron was just as passionate and loving as any husband could be. He never failed to be intimate with her at least twice in the same day. Always at first light. The sex was hot, fast and devastating, leaving her weak, flushed and drained. She loved this time of the day. Then later when he returned from his training he would whisk her off to bed sometimes as early as eight o'clock and make love to her for hours. She loved this time of the day as well. It was only when she was allowed to sleep through the nights that she became concerned. Naturally she felt the benefits of a good night's sleep but this did not alleviate the nagging superstition that perhaps she was not satisfying him. He didn't seem unsatisfied, in fact just the opposite. So why the sudden change in his habits. The first two nights that this happened, she woke briefly in the night as Aaron was restless. There was a tension in his body that kept him awake. When she turned into his arms and placed her head on his shoulder he settled almost at once and slept. Now after a week, he slept soundly throughout the night. It was then that she found the sleep pouch when, after a particularly energetic bout of sex that morning, a sheet had become torn. They laughed about it in the shower together before he went down for breakfast and she stripped the bed. It was tucked down between the mattress and the headboard.

He was just finishing his first meal of the day when she came into the kitchen. As Aaron preferred to eat there instead of the formal dining room it was now the normal habit at the start of the day. He served her himself and watched her eat a healthy breakfast as he drank his juice.

'I should be finished at the foundry at two. Do you want to go to the lake? Do some swimming?' he sipped on his drink.

'I thought you finished the repairs yesterday?' He had been volunteered to have a look at a faulty piece of machinery at the foundry. Apparently there had been a breakdown, lots of grinding metals and sparks. The foundry manager had sent someone to seek him out and ask for advice. The current maintenance man had simply stood back and scratched his head.

'They're doing a test run on that machine this morning. I just want to be there in case it fails again. It shouldn't now that we've installed a better stabilising bracket and repaired a leak in the filtering system.' He drained his glass. 'Old Mr. Prez has asked me to set up a school of sorts to teach his maintenance crew, and anyone else who is interest, basic repair skills and so on. Like an apprenticeship back in the US.'

'Will you have time, with your training schedule as well?' She ate everything on her plate as her husband was watching every mouthful disappear. She started on her own glass of purple juice.

'The games won't last forever so I will need something to do sweetheart. I get bored very quickly.' He rose and took her plate and his glass to the sink. She drained her glass and followed.

Bored! Could he possibly be bored with her? Her heart lurched in her chest. But she would have this out now. She would face her fears and resolve them.

Taking a deep breath she said. "Is that why you wear a sleep pouch? Are you bored with me? Do I not satisfy you?' Her words came out in a rush, then she gasped when he spun around to face her. She was sheet white, her eyes wet and enormous in her beautiful face.

'No sweetheart, no, never.' He caught her in his arms realising that his intent to see her health return to normal had caused her such distress. 'Not for one single second. I love you.'

'Then why' she asked, her face pressed into his chest. She felt a deep sigh before he spoke.

'I spoke with my father after your mother and a number of others had mentioned to him that you looked too thin. Looked ill. To be honest I hadn't noticed. I was too busy enjoying myself. My greatest pleasure' he lifted her face up so that he could see into her tear drenched eyes 'is burying myself inside your hot little body. I feel so good, great in fact, even standing here like this with you in my arms. I'm energised. It takes every ounce of willpower I possess to go out the front door every day and leave you behind.' He lifted her chin with his hand. 'Behind where I can't reach out and touch you, where I can't see your beautiful face.' He used his thumbs to brush away tears. 'The sleep pouch takes away the urge to wake you. I can see for myself that in just a short week you look better, gained a few pounds. You look terrific. I want to keep you that way. If wearing a sleep pouch during the night it what it takes, then that's the price I am more than willing to pay.' He kissed her softly. 'Please don't be sad.'

'You should have told me. I would have objected. But I would have understood. I told my mother I feel fine, good in fact. I didn't realise that others had noticed the change in me. I didn't see it myself.' She ran her warm hands over his wide hard chest. 'But if I get the urge in the night would you object if I get my hands on you and toss the thing across the room?' She smiled seductively up at him as she licked her lips.

'Hell no' he grinned. 'But seriously. I need to see you healthy and well.' He hoisted her up into his arms and cupped her soft buttocks in his large hands. 'When can we have babies around here? I want lots of children.' He surprised her by saying as he sat her on the counter and pulled her legs around his waist.

'Soon I hope' she blushed. 'I'm not sure just yet. My woman's time is not due for another few days. Unlike women from your old world, we do not have morning sickness as such. We have veins.'

'Veins?' he seemed alarmed.

'Nothing serious. Veins appear within a few days of conception along' she ran her fingers from under her arm to her nipple 'on both breasts. Vivid red for a day or two then they fade and are barely seen. Veins also appear down here' she tucked her hands down the front of her loincloth and pulled them up to her navel 'again just for a day or two. We gestate for about seven months, no more.'

'Wow I can hardly wait.' He kissed her soundly. 'I do have to go now. Will you be okay?'

'I'm fine now. See you later.' He lifted her onto her feet and she walked with him to the door and watched as he shot off into the sky and waved until he was out of sight.

Four days later Aurora took lunch with her parents on the wide balcony overlooking the orchard. 'What is he doing?' Pearl stood at the railing and watched as Aaron took off for another circuit of the orchard.

'Jogging mother.' Aurora came to stand at her side, as did her father.

'What for?' her father asked.

'In his old world he took good care of his overall health by swimming, jogging' she swept an arm towards the orchard 'weight training and of course meditation.' She lent on the balcony wall with her elbows. She knew his heart would be pounding, his skin slick with sweat, and his breath coming in gasps. 'I'm so glad he belongs to me.' She wasn't aware that she had spoken out loud. Her parents exchanged contented smiles. They were both pleased that she seemed to have regained the weight she had lost during the first weeks of her marriage. She looked radiant.

'Are the preparations completed my daughter.' The King returned to his seat. A large contingent of delegates from across the world was due later today and tomorrow in readiness for the games that started in three days. The palace would be bursting at the seams. A luxurious tent city was assembled on the west lawn to accommodate those of lesser importance. But as with everything, luxury was in evidence everywhere.

'Yes my father' Aurora turned away from the orchard as Aaron disappeared around the side of the palace. He would shower and join them shortly. 'The quartermaster has assured me that all delegates will be comfortably housed and that the stadium has been marked out and the seating erected. It looks amazing.' She returned to her seat. 'Aaron has arranged for an opening ceremony.'

'Pardon me. I open the games.' Her father replied tersely.

'And so you shall, but he has arranged something in addition to the formal speech and greeting.' She had never seen an Olympic games so had no idea what her husband intended. 'He was very excited about it.' She coloured hotly as she recalled the excitement of their love making after the telling.

'Sounds fascinating.' Pearl said. 'Aaron has certainly taken his responsibilities seriously.' The young man in question landed on the balcony just them, a towel around his neck that he used to continually mop the beads of sweat from his brow. He dropped a scroll by the balcony wall.

He bowed politely. 'Your Majesty, My Lady.' He turned to Aurora. 'Hello sweetheart.' He kissed her softly. 'I could eat a horse' he took his seat at the table. A meal appeared as if by magic and he started to eat. Heartily.

'Where do you put it all?' Pearl shook her head and laughed at the amount of food that disappeared from his plate. Since coming home to this planet he never skipped a meal.

'All the exercise he does' Aurora replied on his behave. 'He never stops.' She pushed a tall glass of pale green liquid toward him. 'Apple juice' she said at his raised eyebrows. 'Father was asking about the opening ceremony you have planned for the games.'

He rose and snatched up the scroll. 'I've drawn up a plan for your consideration.' Aurora was already clearing the table when he turned around. He spread the paper out before the King.

'This is the entire stadium.' He swept his hand across the paper. 'I'm informed that all of the eight countries that make up this world will be sending delegates. I've arranged to have each country's standard flown from strategic points around the stadium. In the centre the dais will be raised where you will make the opening address and welcome the visitors. Once that part of the ceremony is completed, the delegates will then enter the stadium, in their teams, carrying their country's flag and do a circumference of the stadium. Once this is done they will file out and the games will start.'

The King nodded. It was a good idea. 'A united games.' He liked it.

The women left as the men got down to serious talks and finger pointing around the plans.

'Do all the delegates have wings?' Aaron never thought to ask before. He just assumed.

'Yes. To some degree. Not all of them are capable of sustained flight. We are a mixture of peoples in our world.'

Another thought crossed Aaron's mind. 'What is this world called. This country is Fayland not the world as a whole.' He was so happy here he never thought to ask.

'We are Earth my boy. Not your Earth but another in a different dimension.'

'The second I stepped through the portal, despite the confusion and being surrounded by strangers, all of them mostly naked, I said to myself 'Home, I'm home.' It was the strangest feeling I've ever experienced. I can't envisage myself living anywhere else now.'

'It's all in the blood son' the King reached across the table to his son in law and rested a large hand over his. 'When the time comes you will be a fitting King to stand alongside my daughter.' They rose together and took the scroll to join the woman. 'On a personal note' the King added as they crossed the wide chamber. 'Why is my daughter not pregnant? I had hoped to announce something at the games.' A hand slapped Aaron on the shoulder. 'A man needs children. A wife needs her belly filled with them. My dear wife demands a good number of grandchildren so don't let us down lad.' Aaron prayed to all the Gods that he wasn't blushing.

'Working on that.' He gave his father-in-law a curious look. Salvax was just grinning.

Taking his father-in-law's wishes to heart he took Aurora to bed that afternoon and there they stayed for the rest of the day. Such love and passion he released on her she was helpless to resist. She climaxed again and again. She cried out in her pleasure, said his name over and over as he sent her up again. He finally released his straining control as he plunged into her. She sheathed him completely, fisted her muscles around him, and sucked every ounce of his need from his body until it was he, this time that cried out her name as he poured himself into her.

They ate a very late supper and shared a quick bath before they tumbled into bed and slept like babies. Not even the sleep pouch was needed.

Aurora woke to her husband's soft kisses on her shoulder. 'Is it morning already?' The sun was up so she assumed it must be at least seven o'clock.

'Ummmm' he pushed her gently to her back. They had slept like spoons, close together, with his arms around her. 'Must be, sun's up.' He nuzzled her neck.

She laughed as she reached down to her husband's loins. 'So are you.' He was ready. Thick and hard and hot to the touch. 'Good morning my love.'

'Oh Yeah' he grinned and through back the covers so he could see his hands as they ran over her long slender body. His mouth found her breasts, nipples hard as pebbles. He smiled secretly as he continued down her body to the apex of her legs. 'Open for me sweetheart.' She did without hesitation, and then his mouth found her and drove every coherent thought from her mind. All that was left was feelings, intense feelings, and sensations beyond imagining. She gained purchase with her feet and lifted her hips higher in open invitation for him to take more, take everything. He did not disappoint.

She could taste herself on his lips when at last he settled himself between her spread thighs and eased rather gently into her. His kisses were unusually soft for this time of the day. Infinitely more stirring in there depth of feeling. Normally it was hot and fast in the morning leaving her dazed and dizzy in the aftermath. Today it was soft and gentle. When she came he was not far behind her and shuddered slowly and with great care until he was empty.

He rolled with her so that she rested over his body until her breath returned to normal. His heart galloped against her ear as her head rested on his chest. Out of character they drifted of to sleep once more. They woke an hour later.

Aurora raised her head and looked into his handsome face. His eyes seemed unusually green this morning. 'You have beautiful eyes' she said and ran her fingertips across his dark brows.

'And you have red veins everywhere my love.' It took a moment for it to register. Her mouth formed a perfect O before she struggled to free herself from him and knelt at his side. She lifted first one arm and then the other. Red veins could clearly be seen creeping toward each nipple. Slapping her hands to her belly she cried out with delight at the red veins doing the same toward her navel.

'We made a baby. Oh Aaron we made a baby.' Then burst into tears as he came to her side and wrapped his arms around her. 'A baby Aaron. Our baby.' She cried over and over.

Her parents were his first port of call after they had breakfasted and he had gone to get the midwife to ensure everything was in order. The first few days following conception tended to make the new mother somewhat sluggish. Aaron insisted therefore that she remain in bed. For once Aurora didn't argue.

The King and his Lady were seated at table having their own breakfast when he swooped in the window. His excitement was such that his wing tips were red. To the King's total astonishment he lifted him completely out of his chair and spun him around, then kissed him on the forehead. 'Your going to be a grandfather' he plonked him down in his chair and proceeded to spin the Lady Pearl around in giddy circles before he kissed her full on the lips. 'Good morning grandma.' Then returned her, with more dignity, to her seat. 'Aurora's fine, going to stay in bed for today at least. She'd love to see you I'm sure. Gotta go tell dad. Later.' Then he shot out of the window and was gone.

The King cleared his throat to restore his dignity. 'He appears to welcome the news my dear.' His eyes twinkled as he spoke and took his wife's warm hand.

Tears streamed down her face. 'A grandchild Salvax. I'm so happy. He will be a wonderful father.'

'Without a doubt. Come we will go visit.' They leaped from the balcony together.

Parlax was not at home but this did not stop his son from seeking him out. In the middle of a meeting he burst in and gave his father the same treatment as the King. Then was gone in a flash out of the window to find his sister.

There was a lot of backslapping and congratulations before the meeting got back to some order.

The house at the end of the orchard had a lot of visitors over the next twenty-four hours. Aaron was grateful for this as he was into the final preparations for the games.

Chapter Thirteen

As the delegates started to arrive Aaron at last got to see the opposition. His teammates had told him of course of the various nations, the breeds, but nothing of this telling came close to the visual impact of seeing with his own eyes.

He had heard of course of King Ruscul to the South. His people were the Sloo. Average height, thick set and powerful. They excelled in games of weight. Whether lifting or throwing. Then the Elfin people, Fayland's closest neighbours. Prince Nall was their representative. Short, stocky, sneaky in Aaron's opinion. The Elfin expertise lies in throwing. Aaron had seen them practising with a form of javelin. They were also good swimmers. The Lux, Nox, Honi and Dag were more in the line of Fayland. They were tall, slender and dark skinned. The strangest people came from a far off land named Ultar. Humanoid most certainly, but with a raised spin and short whip like tail. Their hands had very long fingers and two thumbs to each hand. They averaged about five feet tall. Aaron found them friendly and full of humour albeit that they were a sickly green colour. As yet he'd seen no wing spread from any of the invited delegates. Aaron made sure to look in on all the delegates and made mental notes of their expertise, as he was sure they did in turn.

At the state banquet on the evening before the games Aurora found herself sitting next to Prince Nall. She inwardly groaned at the prospect of spending even the shortest time in his company. He was arrogant to the point of being totally obnoxious. She looked longingly down the table at her husband who was seated between the beautiful Lady Renna from Honi and the equally lovely Princess Glush from Ultar.

The meal was entered into and much laughter was in evidence around the table. Aurora did her best to ignore the young Elfin prince in favour of Bud, the Ambassador from Sloo.

Although she wear the shift of a pregnant woman, Nall considered her fair game. He would not be put off by her father's rejection of his suit. In a few short weeks King Dard would be gone and the Elfin lands his. He considered Fayland a good choice to further his wealth and prestige. He would have preferred to have gained this by marriage, rather than war. But his armies were vast and could easily sweep any resistance aside. He, for one, could think of no reason why his suit had been rejected out of hand.

'You are looking well Lady Aurora.' He gained her attention as she sipped from a glass of water.

'I do feel well. I carry my husband's child. Nothing pleases us more.' Politely she turned her attention to him.

'I am surprised you took an off-worlder to your bed in preference to a blooded prince who offered for your hand.' Under the table he rested his hand on her thigh and squeezed gently. 'Surely the mongrel is of little importance to you.'

'Remove your hand from me before I cause a scene and have you thrown out and barred from the games.' She looked into his arrogant eyes and inwardly shuddered.

He shrugged and withdrew his hand. 'I wonder what you will think of him when he is defeated in all of his endeavours in the games. My team is superior.' His eyes raked her and came to rest on her breasts.

'It will be pleasing to me to see your team thrashed at every opportunity.' Her nerves were beginning to fray at the sheer malice in Prince Nall's eyes.

'When I win' his hand came onto her thigh again and brushed upward toward her centre. 'I shall ask for you as my prize. I think your father will agree.' His strong fingers squeezed hard around the tender flesh of her thigh. 'Then you will thrash about beneath me. I shall see to it.' He sneered, his nails digging into her flesh and drew blood. Aurora's hiss of pain made him smile. He knew she would not cause a scene.

Neither had seen Aaron leave his place at table. It was only when Prince Nall was lifted bodily from his seat and roughly tossed across the room by the irate husband that silence fell across the room. Aaron's wings were spread and flaming red as he swooped down on the Elfin Prince. Prince Nall's personal guards along with the palace guards came rushing towards the fray.

A raised hand from King Salvax had the guards halted in their tracks. He was curious to see how Aaron dealt with this situation. He had felt his daughter's disquiet from the other side of the room. Obviously there was more to this than at first he realised.

Aurora was physically restrained from rushing to her husband by the strong arms of her father. Hurriedly she explained what had happened. Her shift was ripped and blood smeared her thigh where the elf's fingernails dug deep into her fresh.

'Red rage' was the whispered comments around the room. Many backed away. Even Prince Nall's personal guards stepped back a pace when confronted with such fury. Lord Aaron's wings were starting to close around the Elfin prince whose screams of terror filled the hall.

At a nod from the King, Parlax hurried to his son's side. Aaron's eyes were blood red, far worse than his first experience with the red rage. He vibrated so hard his entire body shook.

'Can you hear me my son.' He spoke calmly. 'Be calm now. Prince Nall will be dealt with. Aurora needs you now.' Aaron made no response he simply hovered a foot from the ground, his wings started to inch closer to make contact with the terrified man at his feet. A soldier hurried to Parlax's side with a large white bag and handed it over.

'Aaron can you hear me. Can you look at me?' He was relieved to see his son's eyes blink. He was still very dangerous but Parlax was certain Aaron could hear him. 'This will be cold on your neck. It will take some of the heat away.' He had to reach up to his fullest extent in order to place the bag of ice on the back of his son's neck. Both hands were needed to hold it in place. It started to melt immediately.

'Put ice in the pool quickly' the King ordered and for this Parlax was grateful.

'Come down son. Let me help you.' Relieve flooded through him, and everyone else in the hall, as Aaron dropped toward the floor. A stray jet of flame scorched a hole in the marble tile close to the screaming man's feet as Aaron's wings vibrated strongly. Sparks flashed everywhere, as the young man seemed unable to control his violent trembling. 'That's it come down now. Try to relax' Another ice bag found its way onto his son's burning back by a palace guard, one of Aaron's team mates for the games.

'Get...him...out...of...my....sight.' Aaron's hands were balled into fists at his side. The guards dragged the terrified prince away immediately Aaron's feet had touched the floor. His wings spread wide and the volcanic red subsided to his normal brilliant blue. His eyes flashed both red and gold until they were back to his normal green. He was burning up, far worse than the first time. His head was spinning, his knees threatened to buckle, but with his last ounce of strength he raised his head and screamed his anguish to the world. It echoed around the hall and escaped via any exit available. Pearl clutched her daughter close to her side as she strained to go to her husband.

'He would be a formidable asset in battle.' Many whispered. 'He must have amazing control. I've never seen the like before.'

As the echoes faded and silence fell over the hall Aaron collapsed to his knees and then keeled over and lay inert. Parlax was at his side in an instant.

'We have to get him to the pool immediately.' King Salvax called his guards. 'Hurry now. Be careful of his wings.' There was a mad rush to help the King's son-in-law.

The guards were thankful for the gloves they wear on ceremonial occasions, as they should surely be blistered with too much contact with the burning man. Four lifted his body, with one either side to carry his wings. Dignity was forgotten as they hurried across the hall, down a short corridor to the pool. More guards dived in and reached up when the heavy man was lowered into the soothing water. Parlax took over and kept his son's head above water as the rest of his body was kept afloat by many willing hands. His wings shimmered against the chilly. Steam rose from around them as the ice melted almost at once.

'Can you hear me Aaron.' Parlax brushed cold water over his son's face.

'Ummm' Aaron's hands started to move under water.

'You need to close your wings son. We dare not let you go as too much damage could be done. Close my son.' He kissed his son's forehead. 'Float on your stomach. Close your wings.' He insisted. He looked up to find the King and guards standing by. 'Can you fetch Aurora. He will need to see her.' The King sent a guard immediately.

'Dad' Aaron blinked several times as he started to regain his senses.

'Do as I say son. Float on your stomach. Close your wings.' His voice was stern.

'Yes sir.' His wings closed, then he took a huge breath, Parlax and the guards let him go, and he sang beneath the surface like a stone.

Aurora rushed into the poolroom as Parlax heaved himself out of the water. Aaron broke the surface then and doggy paddled to orient himself with his surroundings. Without hesitation Aurora's shift hit the marble floor before she dived in to reach her husband. They were wrapped in each other's arms in seconds.

'I think it's safe for us to return to the banqueting hall now.' Parlax towelled himself dry.

'I will join you shortly.' The King signalled his guards and strode away.

When Parlax returned to the banqueting hall Lady Pearl had everyone seated and served wine and the cheese board. The hum of conversation stopped when he approached her side.

'All is well My Lady. His Majesty will join us shortly.'

'Aaron?' she asked. Everyone listened.

'I think it safe to say that the pool it nicely warm now.' He smiled sadly. 'I am totally amazed that he has such self-control. That he could hear me and respond when the rage was upon him is, to my mind, a miracle. Where his lovely wife is concerned he will tolerate no abuse what so ever, verbal or physical.' He took his seat to a chorus of 'here, here' in agreement.

The King returned twenty minutes later and addressed the table. 'My Lords and Ladies.' Silenced fell again. 'Once a year we join together in sporting activities to cement our alliances and to enjoy the games in friendly rivalry. To turn it into a blatant attempt to disrupt my household, to make vile treats and injure my daughter is an insult I will not tolerate.' His hands were fists at his side.

'Prince Nall and his retinue have been expelled from the palace and are being escorted from our lands. It is with some regret that I have also banned the Elfin team from the games. Their banner is at this moment being removed from the stadium. I would apologise to those at this table for this action.'

'I'd have his head Lord Salvax. He is a worm of a man and had brought shame to the House of Dard.' Many heads nodded in agreement as Ambassador Bud called from down the table.

'King Dard is an old friend and worthy of our respect. This is why I have sent my swiftest flier with word of what has happened here so that my old friend will hear the truth and not some twisted version of that truth from Prince Nall.' He smiled to the table. 'How is the betting going? I think this year Fayland may scrape a medal or two.' He resumed his seat and took his wife's hand in reassurance.

'Not a chance' was the chorus of replies and much laughter was in evidence once more.

Aaron and Aurora stayed in the pool for many long minutes. Steam had stopped rising from around Aaron and his heartbeat had calmed and his skin returned to its normal healthy hue.

'You should have linked with me when he first touched you.' Aaron managed to lift Aurora out of the water.

'Usually once rebuffed he leaves me alone. I have no idea why tonight he was so vicious.' She sat quietly whilst her husband wrapped a dry bandage around her slightly swollen thigh. Someone had thoughtfully left a first aid kit by her discarded shift.

'It doesn't look infected.' Aaron kissed the bandage before he sat back on his heel to look into her face. 'I don't have a bad temper you know.' He shook his head. 'I've never been one to fly off the handle at the least provocation. I don't understand why this 'red rage' comes over me so quickly. Did I hurt anybody?'

'No my love. Even Nall got away on his own feet, although he was dragged along by the palace guards.' Aurora said angrily. 'It appears that on both occasions I have been the catalyst. You have a very protective nature where I am concerned.' She ran her hands through his hair. 'We should go home and but you to bed. You have a bad headache don't deny it. I can see it in your eyes.' She rose and held out her hand. 'Come.'

He was too tired to argue and indeed his head was about to explode. So he followed meekly beside her as they left the palace. There was no way he could fly. Half way across the orchard however his knees began to buckle and he sank to the ground asleep. Aurora linked with her father who sent a couple of stalwart guards to assist her and carried her husband back to his bed. Like before he slept like a baby and woke refreshed ten hours later.

Chapter Fourteen

Aurora wore a shift of pale blue silk as she accompanied her husband to the games. Her father gave his speech of welcome. The banners flew and the competitors marched behind their flags. Cheers and applause rose all around from the thousands that filled the stadium. It was a successful start to the games. For the most part the activities resembled track and field events from his old world. Aaron was able to keep track of most of them as the Fayland team had representation in all of the events. It was however more fun than he had expected. Apparently cheating was the norm and accepted so long as you weren't caught doing it. They had referees, but obviously not enough to cover all the activities that were taking place at the same time around the stadium. The flying element would take place on the final day of the games.

'We've got to watch that big guy from the Sloo team.' Aaron pointed as his team congregated near the start line of the final foot race. The penultimate field event of the day. 'He's not fast but he has long arms and isn't afraid to use them to knock you on your ass.' It seemed to be what the Sloo were good at. They left stunned bodies all over the stadium.

'We're faster though.' A young man spoke from the centre of their huddle.

'True. So here's the plan.' They broke apart and went to their positions. It was a sort of relay race. The first member of the team set off on a flat out run for one hundred meters to the second team member. The second man then ran two hundred meters to the third team member. This man then ran three hundred meters to the fourth man, who ran the final leg of four hundred meters to the finish line. As Aaron was the anchorman he could call encouragement or deflect any sabotage. 'Stay focused. Good luck.'

A flag was raised then lowered and the race began. As expected there was a lot of pushing and shoving and a number of runners fell to the ground. Thankfully not the one from the Fayland team who had deliberately stayed to the rear of the pack to avoid any such happening. As the first marker was reached and the second runner started. The Fayland team were in third place behind the swinging Sloo and a dark skinned Honi. The rest were scattered all over the field. The noise level rose as the crowd of many thousands cheered on their favourite team. The royal party and visiting dignitaries had a place of importance by the finishing line. Aurora cheered on the Fayland team with great enthusiasm. The positions remained the same as the third team member started his run. He was only a slightly built young man but used his arms as Aaron had taught him to propel himself along and he nipped into second place as he reached Aaron. Thankfully the Sloo delegate had run out of steam and trailed in third. The dark skinned Honi streaked off down the track and Aaron gave chase. Aaron was by no means built to be an athlete but one thing he bought with him from his old life was the ability to run, and run fast. He had considerably more power in his legs than the slightly build Honi racing in front of him. As Aurora had stated weeks before, most people who flew more than they walked had thinner, less muscled legs. As they past the two hundred meter marker Aaron tucked himself in behind the leader and waited him out. The

Honi knew he was there and couldn't understand what he was waiting for. He picked up the pace, Aaron followed.

From the stands Aurora was on her feet cheering on her husband in a most undignified way.

'Come on, what are you waiting for. Flatten him, come on.' She thumped her hands on the stand barrier and lent out over it to cheer her husband on. The King took a protective hold on the hem of her shift to prevent her from toppling over the side. The roar from the crowd was deafening as the two racers turned into the final straight. With a burst of speed Aaron pulled out from behind the leader, pumped his legs and raced ahead to the finish line, pulling ahead a good ten meters at the end. Gasping in lungs full of air he rested his hands on his knees to regain his breath. Aurora was jumping up and down in the royal box and hugged her parents enthusiastically. 'He won, he won' she cried and burst into excited tears in her father's arms. 'So he did my daughter, so he did.' He patted her back and smiled broadly.

According to the scoreboard the team from Nox were ahead of Fayland, who were in second place. A position unheard of in there most recent history. The final game for the day was their version of the hammer throw. Six of the teams had a delegate entered. Aaron jogged over to the royal box for a few moments. 'You won, you won.' Aurora snatched his face in her hands and kissed him soundly. 'We're in second place!' she was so excited as she handed him a drink of water.

Aaron downed the water in a couple of swallows. 'I think I'm drawn in fifth place for this last event.' He still hadn't regained his even breathing yet. He had a towel around his neck as he was sweating heavily.

'You're throwing the hammer?' his wife said. 'I didn't know you were throwing the hammer.'

'I got shanghaied as I throw it further than any one else on the team in practise.' He kissed his wife. 'Luckily we only throw once, so I shouldn't be too long. Later.' And he jogged off to join his teammates.

'He is a man of many talents.' Lady Pearl observed.

'You're telling me.' Aurora smiled and sat calmly next to her father. 'How much did you beat?' she whispered in his ear.

'Just a small wager with some of my friends.' He winked at her then turned to watch the hammer throw. So far it had been a very good day. For all concerned.

The hammer, in this case, was exactly that. It weighed a solid ten pounds and measured four feet from the tip of the handle to the heavy end. As the contest began Aaron noticed that all of the competitors stepped up to the line, turned sideways on and swung the thing back and forth to gain some momentum before releasing it into the air. It was lucky that all the competitors were now safely behind the hammer throwers as the deadly weapon went flying in all directions. Most of the crowd were also ready to move swiftly out of the way as a hammer was known to fly amongst them.

For the most part the hammer landed in more or less the same place after each contestant had thrown. Aaron was up next and then finally the Sloo competitor that no one had beaten in the ten years he had been coming to the games. He was confident of a win.

When Aaron stepped up to throw a hush fell over the stadium. The only people who had seen him throw were his teammates. They had been sworn to secrecy.

'What's he doing?' Aurora stood up. 'He's facing the wrong way.' She lent forward to better see what was happening.

It was true Aaron had his back to the field and stood about four feet from the line. He's never been much good at the hammer at university but he knew the technique and applied it accordingly. He started by slowly swinging it back and forth until he had a good momentum going, not to high on the sweeps that it would throw him off balance when he started to spin. 'Here goes' he thought and bent his knees as he spun around on his heel so quickly the hammer was out of his hand before anyone realised it. There was absolute silence as it spun and lifted high in the air. Many rose from their seats to get a better look. It seemed to be airborne for ages. When it thudded to the ground it was meters ahead of any one else. The crowd went wild.

The Sloo contingent in the audience, loyal to their team, cheered loudly when the final contestant stepped up to the plate. It seemed to everyone concerned that he intended to try throwing the hammer as Aaron had done. Aaron immediately feared for the people in the stands directly behind them. He was thankful that most had moved to the sides in order to watch the final field contest of the day.

The hammer swung back and forth until the right momentum was reached. He bent his knees slightly and started to spin then released the hammer. He was astonished that he was still facing away from the field, the hammer flying towards the stands, luckily nearly empty of spectators. The hammer was in flight and had the few people remaining in their seats diving for cover. The force of the flight had the hammer hitting a flagpole and snapped it in half; luckily it fell outside of the stadium. The hammer disappeared from sight. The Sloo contestant was disqualified. Fayland won the hammer.

Bubbling with excitement Aurora snatched at her husband's hand the second he was close enough when he joined the royal party as they made their way to the pool area. 'I've never seen anything like that in my life. How on earth did you get the hammer to fly that far.'

Aaron by now had his arm around his wife's shoulders to stop her bouncing up and down as they walked along. He wasn't sure she should be this excited during the early stages of her pregnancy. He went on to explain the differences in the hammer event at the Olympics back on his old earth. 'The strategy is the same but adjustments needed to be made for the rigid handle. I'm not nearly powerful enough to throw the damn thing any real distance. Technique is the key.'

'You have good techniques my husband' she licked her lips. Her meaning completely different to his. He caught on instantly and gave her butt a playful swat as they took their seats. He was not taking part in the swimming. Each delegate could only take part in three events. They needed him for the flying tomorrow. The Fayland team came in a credible third thereby wiping out the gain from the hammer. Honi was still in first place, Fayland second. The team from Ultar were now third, having won the swimming event with comparative ease.

Just four teams were entered for the flying the following evening. The Dag, Nox, Honi and Fayland. The Lux team had withdrawn as one of their fliers had sustained a broken arm and was being attended to in the first aid marquee set up outside the stadium grounds. That particular area of the games had seen a steady stream of casualties following every event.

They drew lots for the order of flying. Fayland drew last which pleased Aaron immensely. He had a few tricks up his sleeve and his team had been practising very hard over the past two weeks. Each team was required to do set pieces.

Synchronised sets, tumbles, twists and turns and then an individual piece as a team for the finale.

Aaron watch closely as the teams went through their paces. The synchronised sets were flawless from all teams. The tumbles, twists and turns done with precision. The finale done with skill but lacked any real showmanship. Lots of cheers and applause filled the air. But nobody gasped, jumped up in their seat, pointed to the heavens. He planned they should do all that and more with his team.

'Now remember what we've practised. Win this and we win the games. Watch for my signals, remember your spacing and keep the timing in your head.' The other five members of the team nodded. They took up their positions.

The set pieces were a figure of eight and a star burst. Aaron found these the most difficult simply because he had to think about his flying and those around him. The twists, tumbles and turns were second nature to all of them. They did fly closer to the ground however so that the audience could better see each manoeuvre. Many instinctively ducked, gasped and applauded loudly.

'Okay guys here we go.' Everyone took up their positions for the finale. Those from the ground looked closely as one by one the team disappeared from the night sky. Aaron's brilliant blue shimmer was all that could be seen. Many got to their feet and pointed.

'Five, four, three, two, one' Aaron dropped like a stone, folded his wings slightly behind him to streamline his body. He was a blue blur in the sky as he headed for the far end of the swimming pool, around which the spectators gathered.

'Five, four, three, two one.' He called out again to his team when he was thirty feet from the ground and spread his wings. The dimmed wings behind him burst into light, the spectators gasped, when he skimmed the water surface before streaking back up into the sky and his team broke rank. Number two went left, three went right, four went left, number five right and number six followed after Aaron into the night sky. Everyone was on there feet cheering. The last performance of the day was the Dragon. This entailed holding onto the feet of the man in front of you and snaking through the sky, slithering from side to side before they approached the ground, straightened out and flew, for a short space of time, upside down. They landed beside the pool and were immediately mobbed by the crowd. Fayland had won the coveted chalice for the first time in five years.

Celebrations went on well into the night. Music played, people danced, laughed and made merry. The great hall in the palace was packed; the wide doors were open into the night and people spilled out onto the lawns to continue the revelry. Some however were fascinated by Aaron and his wife. To avoid the crush on the dance floor he took her in his arms and lifted them both into the air, wrapping his arms gently around her as they waltzed across the ceiling with their lips locked together.

'He should teach us how to do that.' Salvax looked up to the ceiling. 'It's very difficult. I can only manage a few meters myself. Pearl is by no means heavy. She hardly weighs more than our daughter.' He was talking to Parlax, who was himself observing the couple.

'From what your daughter has told me he did it within hours of learning how to fly. He comes by it quite naturally.' Parlax's voice rang with pride. 'His wings are exceptionally powerful.' As both men continued to stare the tips of Aaron's wings started to glow red when he nuzzled his wife's neck and she playfully slapped him on the arm and buried her face under his chin.

'Time for them to go home. He has other manoeuvres in mind I think.' Pearl said from behind her husband's back. Both men turned at the sound of her voice. She linked her arms through both of there's. 'They are a lovely couple. Send them home my husband.'

Aaron, distracted by the sudden hush that fell over the hall, looked down at his in-laws. The jerk of Salvax's head towards the orchard brought a smile to the young husband's face. He nodded politely then zoomed out of the double doors and was gone in a second. Aurora's happy laughter following in their wake.

Chapter Fifteen

Aaron had never been more pleased with his life as he was at this very moment. Four months after a successful games he was appointed as official teacher, would you believe it, of machinery repair and maintenance. He had set up in a large workshop adjacent to the foundry and enrolled a dozen young men and women onto an apprenticeship scheme. For a further two evenings a week he tutored the more senior personnel in the trade of repair and maintenance in the more modern ways of performing their routine tasks. Not that there work was inferior, not at all. But some of the machinery was very old and would need to be replaced, or in some cases redesigned altogether. They gathered around a large table for an hour with graph paper and pencils sketching out suggested designs for various machines, all of which were open to inter-pretation and amendment. Aaron wasn't ashamed to admit he learned a thing or two himself. For the most part it was fun. Seeing the young minds take on board more up-to-date ideas. To see the eager way they listened to his advice and crowded around to study his practical hands on examples. The evening classes were more interested in the designs of the tools he showed them that he had left back in his former life.

'This does what exactly?' a gnarled old man scratched his thin chest as he pointed at a particular design.

'It's what we call an electronic screwdriver. With a fuse in the handle so that if you touch a live wire whilst you're working, instead of getting a shock the fuse glows and warns you of trouble.' Aaron explained.

'My own apprentice could do with one of those he's forever blowing things up by mistake.' He chuckled and slapped his hand on the table.

'I can certainly try and rig one up for you. I've never tried before but I'll give it a go.' The conversation then turned to other tools and their uses.

In a comfortable chair to the rear of the classroom Aurora sat with her legs curled up beneath her. She was so proud of her husband. He had slipped into this life with apparent ease. Now that he had an official job he was amazing. Nothing was too much trouble, either for her or anyone who stopped him in the street for advice. He had built up a network of links and answered calls at all hours of the day and night. For herself she just loved him more and more each day. Being well over half way through her pregnancy the hot, hard and fast sex had been put on hold. Each morning, and every evening without fail, he made love to her with such passion and tenderness she wept openly and cried his name as he sent her soaring. Since she had conceived the sleep pouch was no longer needed. His body simply knew that she needed her rest and some gentle handling. She slept every night with his warm breath on her neck and his arms holding her gently.

'Where are you?' his strong fingers touched her cheek and she blinked. The classroom was empty.

'Just drifting.' She reached for his hand as he helped her to her feet. 'You have a very nice voice. Full of confidence and humour.' They walked to the door together and stepped through into the night air. Aaron closed the door behind him.

'Do you want me to carry you?' he swung an arm across her shoulders.

'No the walk will do me good.' He did however scoop her up and flew them to the outskirts of the city then put her down. They walked along looking into windows and talking softly to one another of nothing important just general chit-chat. A number of shops were still open so he parted with coins for a couple of bright red apples that they munched on as they walked along.

'We should have a cook out one evening.' Aaron casually mentioned, as they turned toward the road that lead around the orchard.

'I've heard about those, but I've never actually seen one. What does it entail?' She had at last given in and asked Aaron to carry her the rest of the way home. She had expected him to fly, but instead he continued walking.

'Anything you can throw on a grill really, chicken, sausage, burgers. We'll need bread rolls, fried onions, chips and salad. Hopefully beer.' He had been thinking about it for a while. 'Invite some people, sort of a party thing. What do you think?' They had reached the gate and he pushed it open easily. It swung closed with a click when he walked through with his precious burden.

'Whatever you say sweetheart. It sounds like fun.' She was placed on her feet just inside the doorway.

He never heard her scream, only felt the pain in his side then blackness before he hit the floor.

The serving woman who arrived at first light raised the alarm. She tripped over Aaron's inert body then slipped on the congealed blood at his side. Screaming in panic she fled the house and flew immediately to the King's private quarters. It was chaos for some time. The King's personal doctor was sent for before guards and the King himself went to personally see the extent of Aaron's injuries. The doctor arrived within seconds of the King and immediately set to work. There was considerable blood. Mostly from the knife that still protruded from his side and secondly from the crack on his head where he fit the floor.

'He still lives Majesty. I'll send for a cradle and take him to hospital.' The Doctor had padded the wound with thick cloth but had not removed the knife.

'Take him to the palace, its closer.' The King insisted as he hovered close by.

'No Your Majesty. He needs the hospital.' The Doctor simply continued working over the young man as the King paced back and forth. 'You should check on your daughter King Salvax, she should go with him.'

'Dear God!' he exclaimed as he turned and charged up the stairs to the master bedroom. It was still early and he hoped his daughter was sleeping, despite the noise from downstairs. In all of his anxiety he had completely forgotten about her.

'She's not here Your Majesty' the servant came hurrying toward him as he reached the landing. 'Their bed hasn't been slept in.'

'Search the place, search everywhere.' He turned and called for his guards. 'The Lady Aurora is missing. Find her.' He ordered. They were gone in seconds to do his biding.

'What can I do my King?' Parlax stood at the foot of the stairs. His son was on his way to the hospital.

'My friend you should go to the hospital, be with Aaron.' He hurried down the flight.

Parlax shook his head. 'He would not thank me for sitting by uselessly when his wife is missing.' Like his son his face was sheet white, his eyes full of grief and anguish.

'Your best tracker Parlax. Get your best tracker. From all accounts nothing has been disturbed. They were attacked the instant they stepped inside the door. They tried to kill Aaron and I believe they have taken Aurora.' He slumped down on the bottom step and placed his head in his hands. 'What do I tell her mother. How can I tell her this terrible news.'

Parlax linked with his tracker as he too took up residence on the stairs. 'Don't colour the truth. It is something you told me once, long ago. Say the words quickly, and then act. It is what you do best my friend.'

As the King raised his head Parlax closed his eyes and went very still. 'They are taking Aaron into the operating theatre to remove the knife.' He was linked to the doctor. 'They want me to go and give blood. Apparently we are the same type.'

'Then go. Instruct the quartermaster to assemble as many men with the same blood type as he can find and get them to the hospital. We won't lose him Parlax. My daughter would never forgive me. Go now. Hurry.' The King personally saw his friend to the door and watched as he lifted off and zoomed toward the hospital. Salvax was only too grateful that his wife had insisted her new son-in-law be tested and typed so that the information was on record for just such an incident as this. A very astute woman his Pearl.

The tracker landed a moment later and followed the King inside. Five minutes later he left with a piece of fine silk in his hand then lifted his face to the wind and breathed deeply. Aurora's scent was too strong around the house so he checked the ground for signs of a struggle. Found none so went further afield. He was best left to his own resources where he could concentrate on the task in hand. He was very good at what he did.

Parlax had given his blood when three guards came hurrying down the corridor to give theirs. Word had spread of the incident and many of Aaron's new friends came to make enquiries.

'Who would do such a thing? He hasn't hurt a sole? What of Lady Aurora?' These and many more questions spread through the crowd. The palace guards asked them all questions. 'Had they seen Lord Aaron last night? Where? What time? Who did he leave with?' They had a clear picture of his whereabouts to put in their reports.

'He bought apples from my shop just before closing last night.' The grocer offered. 'I closed shortly after nine o'clock. They seemed in a fine happy mood when they left.'

'Well at least we know they were both safe at nine last night.' The King watched his wife sit and speak quietly to Parlax, his daughter and family. Her eyes were still red and puffy from the tears she had shed. She had insisted on accompanying her husband to the hospital.

'According to the grocer they were in no particular hurry. Window-shopping as they ambled along. From what he tells me Lord Aaron spent some minutes kissing his Lady on the corner of the street before they walked on. I can only estimate that it would be another hour before they left the city. Fifteen minutes more to reach the house.' The sergeant of the guard gave his report in a whisper. 'Men have searched the orchard but could find no trace of where men may have lain in wait for them to pass by.'

'Osgood is tracking' the King began when the door to the operating suite opened and the doctor entered the waiting room. He wear a blue apron over his nakedness. Blood could clearly be seen smeared over the surface.

'My son?' Parlax could hardly speak.

'He lives.' He placed a strong hand on the older man's shoulder. There was an audible sigh in the room before Crystal burst into tears and collapsed into her husband's arms. Lady Pearl flung her arms around Parlax and they wept together.

'This is the knife' Doctor Wyn stepped towards the King who had had to sit down at the news.

'Sergeant go now and tell the people the good news. Assure them that an official statement will be made within the hour.' The sergeant hurried about his duty.

'It's not Fayland made.' The King studied the blade. 'The handle is horn, but could be from anywhere.' He turned the knife over. 'Elfin!' he hissed. 'See here the mark of Sethaul, smithy to the palace.'

'He makes many blades Your Majesty.' Wyn replied. The blacksmith was well renowned for his excellent weapons.

'Aye good doctor he does. But he never sells them to anyone outside of the Elfin kingdom.' He weighed the knife in his palm. It was a weapon designed to kill. The blade itself was at least six inches long. 'How did my new son survive a blade such as this?' he looked up at the doctor.

'It missed all of his vital organs. I can only assume the assassin was shorter in stature. Aaron wasn't directly sideways on, but turned slightly to the right. I think that he was probably carrying his wife and was setting her on her feet at his side. We've had to sew his innards back together and suck out some unpleasant bodily fluids but apart from some severe pain over the next few days he will make a full recovery. Any higher and it would have sliced right into his kidney, taken his lungs. We would have lost him by simply not knowing he was hurt. We can be thankful of one thing. They didn't pull the knife out. Although he lost considerable blood it would have been the end of him if they had removed it.' Dr. Wyn whispered.

'I think that information would be best kept to ourselves my old friend.' His Majesty agreed.

'Agreed' the good doctor turned to the waiting father. 'You can see him in a moment. We're just moving him into recovery. A nurse will come and get you.'

'Thank you doctor. Thank you so much.' Parlax shook his hand.

It was harder to see Aaron in a hospital bed with tubes and needles attached to various body parts. There was no colour in his face, chest and arms, whatsoever. He was almost translucent. But he was breathing deeply and evenly that gave everyone hope that he would indeed recover.

'We are going to keep him sedated for the next forty eight hours.' Wyn pointed to the fluid drips attached to Aaron's arm. 'This will keep him hydrated and fed until we allow him to wake up. Normally we only do this for twenty-four hours. But with Aurora missing the King feels the longer we can keep him unaware the better. He needs to heal in a stress free environment. When he wakes the trauma will be great, worse because he will be physically unable to do anything about it. So for his sake, we will do what we have to do to ensure his return to full health.' The doctor was matter of fact telling the family the course of action he was prepared to take.

'Do what needs be done doctor.' Parlax bent over his son and kissed his cool forehead. 'I've never known him be so cool, so still.'

'It was pass in a day or two. His body has been through quite an ordeal.' The doctor reassured.

'But he will be all right?' Crystal too kissed her brother.

'Be assured he will be well. He is in good hands.' The doctor escorted them from the room.

Osgood picked up a feint trail three hundred yards from the house and took off in pursuit. The Elfin peoples went bare foot, as did those of Fayland. But they favoured leather leggings rather than a loincloth. It wasn't so much the Lady Aurora's scent that he followed, although it lay softly on the breeze, but the strong smell of the leather and the more over-powering essence of elf. He was dogged in his pursuit. At one point Osgood came across hoof prints. They had obviously tethered horses nearby, as their wings weren't nearly strong enough to carry them any distance, let alone carry a strug-gling princess of Fayland. Now he was able to take to the sky to better survey the area. They were heading east to the nearest water. He would lose them for sure if they had a boat tethered. If they had just thirty minutes head start they could disappear into any number of inlets with overhangs of rock big enough to hide a vessel beneath, searching would take time but discovery inevitable. But they had hours. Hours where the kidnappers could disappear without trace over the open sea.

Instinct took him lower to the ground to pick up any slight sign of their passing. Then pain in his thigh, pain in his left wing, and he spiralled to the ground.

'I told you I saw someone fall.' A young lad dragged his father across the field to where the man lay.

'He's been shot.' An arrow protruded from his thigh. 'His wing is broken.' Another arrow had severed the bone between the backbone and the elbow.' Father and son hur-ried to his aid. 'Why it's Osgood.' The man exclaimed. 'Link to your brother at the palace my son, tell him what has hap-pened, and have a wagon sent out as soon as possible.' They made Osgood comfortable as they waited.

It was close to nightfall when the wagon rumbled across the field. A full regiment of guards flew in circles overhead to keep watch. Osgood, who was conscious now, was laid in the wagon; face down on thick blankets over layers of hay for comfort. His uninjured wing was folded down his back but the injured one would not respond fully to his commands, the pain was too severe. So it was laid very gently across the bed of the wagon.

'Send men east Sergeant' Osgood said urgently. 'They were heading east towards the sea.' He then sipped from a cup held to his lips and he was sedated within seconds. Half the regiment returned with the injured man. The Sergeant then led the remainder towards the east.

They found loose horses wondering along the shoreline and clear signs of where a boat had been beached and then returned to the water. The shimmer from their wings gave them sufficient light to see this clearly.

'Sir' a young corporal landed a few feet away and bent to pick something out of the sand. 'Mistress Aurora's engagement ring. I'm sure of it.'

'Your right. Good eyes corporal.' He looked out to sea. 'We'll do a sweep along the coastline and see if we can see anything, but in this light it will be doubtful. You men go north, the rest follow me south. Back in twenty minutes.'

They flew home with nothing positive to report.'

The ring was clutched in the King's fisted hand whilst he listened carefully to the report by his trusted sergeant. 'And Osgood?'

'Reports I have on him are good. No lasting damage. He will be unable to fly for several months and folding his wing will be impossible. I understand that my Lord Parlax will take him into his home when he can be released from hospital.' The sergeant stood relaxed next to his King.

The King nodded sagely. 'Parlax is a good man but if there is anything that he needs to ensure Osgood's full recovery take what money you need from the Treasury.'

The sergeant bowed. 'As you command My King.' He was soon gone.

'That worm Nall has her doesn't he' Lady Pearl's voice hissed from across the room. She was barely holding it together. Her nerves were stretched to breaking point. 'What can we do?'

'For the moment nothing' Salvax paced back and forth and was totally unprepared for his wife's hysterical ranting.

'Nothing! Call yourself King and stand there and tell me you can do *nothing*' her voice rose to the rafters. 'She's our daughter you must do *something*. Send your army and get her back, do you hear me, go and get her back. She's having our grandchild.' She picked up her footstool and hurled it across the room with such force it rebounded off a small table and smashed throw a window. Guards came rushing in immediately.

'Out! Get out!' she screamed. They did a brief bow, turned and fled.

As she looked around for something else to break or to hurl to vent her anger and fear her husband pulled her to face him and ruthlessly slapped her face. Then instantly snatched her into his powerful embrace and held her tightly as she slumped in defeat and wept and wept in his strong arms.

'My love, my love' he whispered into her ear as they both sank to the floor. 'Hush now' he stroked her hair. Never is all of the time he had known her, from childhood to wife had she ever fallen apart like this. She was his rock, someone *he* was able to turn to in times of crisis. It was *her* words that gave him courage and comfort. Now when she needed him the most he could not give her those words of comfort.

'What can we do husband. They've taken my baby.' She rocked back and forth in his arms. Both had tried, without success, to link with their daughter.

'Everything we know points to the Elfin people. If this is so then Nall will be responsible and held to account.' He lifted his wife's tear stained face. 'But my heart, we have no evidence at all. Only a few prints on the ground that could have been there for months, since the games, a knife and Aurora's ring. All are damning to be sure. The boat, if it is true she was taken aboard, could have taken her anywhere from that point.' His wife slumped again in his arms.

'I will send an emissary at first light and demand he be given an audience with King Nall.' Old King Dard had died shortly after the games earlier in the year. 'We will state our case and ask for his help in finding Aurora.' He didn't hold up much hope of a successful outcome. But he couldn't afford to antagonise the new King into doing something rash. He would need only the slightest provocation to start a war.

'Send Filo' Pearl's exhausted voice rose softly from his chest. 'He has a way of finding the truth amongst lies better than anyone I know.'

'That I will do, along with a regiment of my finest soldiers with strict instructions not to leave his side.'

'King Nall will see this as an insult.' Her voice sounded tired.

'As it was meant to be.' He stood and reached for her hand. 'Come my love you are exhausted.' They walked arm in arm from the room.

When assured his lovely wife was asleep Salfax slipped from the room to organise his men for the journey to Elfin and King Nall. He also set men to search the area where Osgood was injured. That sneaky Nall had obviously left men behind to deal with any tracker.

Chapter Sixteen

His brain was telling him it was time to open his eyes. Fatigue was telling him to sleep some more. The blackness that held him in quiet comfort was misting to greys and purples and swirling behind his closed eyes and made nausea rise in his throat. For hours it seemed he couldn't get past the fog in his head. He could hear voices, distant voices then a cool cloth on his forehead his throat and chest. And there was pain everywhere. His head pounded, his body screamed in pain with every slight movement. The inside of his mouth was like a dry sandpit. He surmised he couldn't be dead, for surely death didn't hurt so much.

'I think he's coming round.' A soft voice filled the room. Crystal rose to her feet from the chair beside the bed and brushed a hand down the side of her brother's face. A nurse watched from nearby.

'Are you in there Aaron? Time to wake up now. Open your eyes.' She moistened a cloth and gently wiped his eyelids and face. His eyelids fluttered a little and he tried to speak, but his tongue was dry and stuck to the roof of his mouth.

'Give him a sip of water, not too much now.' The nurse supervised as the sister lifted a cup to her brother's lips and dribbled a few drops into his parched mouth. When it seemed safe she let him have more until half the cup was consumed. His eyes opened slowly.

'There you are' the nurse looked closely into his blinking eyes. 'I'll get the doctor' she told Crystal as she left the room. Crystal linked with her father immediately.

'Can you see me Aaron?' she squeezed his hand. 'Don't try to move.'

'Can't focus' he mumbled 'Headache.' His eyelids drooped again.

The doctor came then and asked Crystal to wait outside whilst he examined his patient. Parlax arrived soon thereafter and waited with his daughter until the doctor came out and spoke to them.

'I've put drops in his eyes his vision should clear very soon.' He sat with them a moment. 'We've removed some of the drips and tubes now so he should be more comfortable. His wound is healing nicely. His headache is probably due to enforced sleep. I think that four days is enough now. Any more could be harmful to his recovery.'

'Does he know of Aurora?' his father asked.

'I thought it best you speak with him.' The doctor rose to his feet. 'I've arranged for him to have something to eat and several more glasses of water. Give him a few minutes before you go in.' He strode off.

'Do we tell him father?' Crystal clutched at her father's hand.

'He must be told my daughter. It would be best for me to see him alone. Go home to your husband and family.' He kissed her cheek. 'Thank you for being with him.'

'Tell him I will see him tomorrow.' She squeezed his hand again then left.

Parlax let his son eat a bowl of nourishing soup and a thickly buttered roll. Aaron ate with the deliberation of a man trying to stay awake. His eyelids were prone to close and he was forced to make a concerted effort to keep them open.

The food helped, as did the tall glasses of water. He hadn't expected to find Aurora sitting at his bedside, as the strain on her back would have been uncomfortable. But as he cleared his plate he had a tightness around his heart that he couldn't explain. His father had not mentioned her the entire time they had chatted around his meal.

'What's wrong?' Aaron pushed his tray to one side. 'Where is Aurora?' He shifted his position slightly to ease the soreness in his side.

'No one knows my son' Parlax came and sat on the bed at his son's side. 'Tell me what you remember of the night you were attacked?'

'What do you mean no one knows?' Aaron snatched at his father's arm, hissing at the pain that coursed through his body.

'Tell me what happened?' Parlax looked his son in the eyes. 'Now!' The hand that fastened around his arm relaxed and slid to the sheet, then balled into a fist.

Aaron went through the events of that night. His eyes never left his father's. There was a knot in his stomach he felt sure would make him lose his meal at any moment. She couldn't possibly be gone. He had to find her.

Parlax reached into a small bag he had brought along with him and showed his son the knife that had been so carefully removed from his side. 'It is Elfin made of that there is no doubt. Whether it was wheeled by an Elf is another matter.' Parlax watched his son closely.

'Did the King send a search party?' Aaron asked urgently. 'They couldn't have gone far.'

'My tracker was sent. You remember Osgood?' Aaron nodded. 'He followed a trail, picked up Aurora's scent, a strong smell of leather and then horses.' Parlax told his son of the events of four nights ago.

'Four nights!' This time the young man couldn't stop his voice from filling the room. 'You've kept me unconscious for four nights whilst my wife is in God knows whose hands.' His wings started to unfurl without conscious effort. Pain tore through his side.

'Stop now.' His father commanded. 'Aaron close now. Do it!' Once again his father was astonished that his simple command would be obeyed instantly. Aaron shook violently for some minutes until he brought himself under control. His face was screwed up with pain; beads of perspiration covered his brow. His eyes were tinged with red.

'It was for this exact reason we kept you sedated my son. Believe me when I say we are doing everything in our power to locate her. The emissary that our King sent to Elfin should return tomorrow with news. If Aurora is being held there we will know tomorrow. Nothing gets past Filo.' He placed a reassuring hand on his son's shoulder.

'Have you linked with her?' Aaron asked in defeat. He was as weak as a kitten and knew it.

'Many have tried.' He shook his head. 'Rest now I will return tomorrow with news.' He left immediately.

Aaron slumped back against his pillows. Four nights. Four long nights. 'Where are you my love?' He sat back up again, wincing with pain as he crossed his legs and rested his open palms on his knees and let himself drift into meditation. It was as familiar to him as simply breathing. He concentrated on relieving his pain, expelling it from his body with each cleansing breath. A nurse came into the room to remove the tray but he did not hear her. She made notes on his chart before she left.

Within an hour he had taken the edge off his pain. Then he turned his mind to finding his wife.

'Aurora' he simply thought about her, sending his love though the airwaves hoping for a connection.

Aurora came to full consciousness to the rolling motion aboard ship. She was disorientated and nauseous. She was not a good sailor. It was almost totally dark in her room, or more likely her prison cell. Feint light came through a grill in the far wall. Beneath her was a thin pallet, which sat directly on the cold wooden planks of the floor. She was covered in a thick blanket of furs. Her first reaction was that of panic as she quickly let her hands clutch at her stomach and was relieved it was still swollen with her child. A deep sigh escaped her dry mouth.

She remembered being forced to drink some bitter fluid, then being past from hand to hand. Being carried in strong arms, being lifted onto a horse behind a leather covered back and tied securely in place. Her attempts to scream for help were muffled by a leather gag and together with a blindfold had her totally disorientated and filled with terror. They stopped only once and she was given more of the brackish water before the gag was replaced. Fatigue drained her body of strength shortly afterward and she was easily lifted and strapped in place so that the kidnappers could carry her away. Her mind was a swirling vortex of colours and left her unable to think.

She was vaguely aware of being lifted from the horse and pushed to the ground. Damp sand under her feet and the smell of the sea indicated her proximity to the ocean. They must be travelling east; Fayland had cliffs to the west. Panic seized her when rough hands pulled her to her feet. She screamed beneath the gag, kicked with her feet, struggled violently until she was overpowered by sheer weight of numbers. Bound hand and foot she was dumped unceremoniously into a boat that rocked alarmingly. They were taking her from Fayland, away from her family, away from her homeland. She prayed that they would not find her engagement ring that she had slipped from her finger and tossed into the sand. It broke her heart to do it, to lose something so precious. She had worn it often. Aaron would find it, she was sure.

'Aaron' she gasped and with that thought the panic and agony of loss swamped her. She had seen the movement from the corner of her eye. Had watched in horror the blade plunge into her husband's side, his groan and fall to the floor. So much blood, so much blood. She knew she had screamed but after that nothing, she had feinted.

She drew her knees up as best she could to cradle her unborn child and to wrap her arms around them and let the tears fall. How long she sat and rocked and cried she had no idea. Her mind was in turmoil. She drifted between awareness and deep depression. Her wonderful Aaron was dead. Her heart simply died albeit kept on beating.

She came to awareness when a small light appeared at the base of the wall. As she watched a plate of food was slipped into her cell along with a glass of liquid. Her child's survival eventually made her crawl across the floor to find the food. It was barely palatable but she forced it down and drank the sweet liquid. She crawled back to the pallet and under the furs and let herself dissolve into misery.

Many days past with little change. Every other day a bucket was left and one removed. Food arrived four times a day and this Aurora ate regardless of her lack of appetite. She had not been able to bathe, her body gave off an unpleasant smell, her hair was listless and lank and fell in greasy tangles down her back. Her shift could hardly be called the lovely blue silk she had worn that night. It was deplorably dirty but it was all she had. During the entire time of her captivity she had seen no one, except a hand that delivered her food and took away the bucket of waste. She prayed for death one minutes and prayed for life the next as her child moved within her. Every waking minute she relived the all to brief time she had with her husband. The early part of their marriage when he was full of lust and passion and would often simply flip her onto her back and bury himself inside her willing body and give her hot hard sex. They panted and then laughed and did it all over again. The times when his tender side took over and they made love, slowly, tenderly, passionately until she had begged for release, unashamedly begged. When they played like children, and then took to the skies to fly in dizzy circles. Swimming was a pastime they both enjoyed. But always every activity ended with his magnificent body covering hers. The way he had taken to teaching. The way he gave knowledge and soaked it up in return. He had many new friends and was well liked. So why, oh why, did someone take his life, simply to kidnap her. She had no enemies that she knew off. The only one that came to mind was King Nall. But the hand that took the bucket and pushed in the plate was not Elfin. White skin, three fingers, and one thumb. Slender limbs.

It must be night she thought as the activity over her head had stopped as it did at nightfall. Exhausted she crawled beneath the furs and turned onto her side and stared into the darkness. She had tried to link with her father, but every time she tried her head would ache. A side affect of the drug she thought, so in the end she didn't even try. She gave up. Without her husband it didn't matter where they took her, she was dead inside and would stay that way. Eventually she drifted toward sleep and heard him. It was such a shock that she sat up in panic. 'Aaron' she said aloud. In total confusion she looked around her thinking to see him appear at her side out of the darkness.

The jolt to Aaron's system when he linked with her would have sent alarms beeping if he had been attached to a heart monitor.

'Sweetheart' he thought 'I've found you. Where are you? Are you safe?'

'You're alive, oh Aaron you're alive.' She cried, simple heart felt sobs racked her slender body. Tears in rivers ran from her eyes. The headache was throbbing but she determined not to lose this precious link with her husband.

Feeling her anguish Aaron felt completely helpless. Control now however was more important. He couldn't let the red rage take him over. Breathing deeply he relaxed his tense body and was able to send his thoughts calmly to his wife. 'Ssssh sweetheart, please don't cry.' All he could do was sit quietly and send his love and reassurance to her. Eventually she calmed. Her voice hitched a couple of time as she wiped away her tears with a grubby hand, leaving a smear across each cheek.

'Are you all right?' she asked eventually.

'I'm in hospital sweetheart. They kept me sedated for four days because they wanted me to lie still. The wound was severe but my life is not threatened.'

'I saw the knife go into you. The blood was everywhere. I thought I'd lost you.' Her breath shuddered into her lungs.

'Not going to get rid of me that easily.' He felt her smile. 'Do you know where you are?'

'On a ship, going east. That's all I know. They haven't spoken to me or let me out of this cell. It is dark all of the time. I only have one barred window set high in the wall. I can't spread my wings to fly up and see, the cell is too small.' Her head was thumping with pain.

Aaron could feel her pain and exhaustion. Her mind was going fuzzy. 'Aurora are you getting enough to eat. Our child?' On a ship, for four days. Where the hell were they taking her?

It cleared her mind when he spoke of their child. 'I still have our child within me. I have food on a regular basis. It is bland and the same with every meal but I make myself eat it so that I can be strong for myself and our baby. I'm so tired all the time; they don't give me water to wash. I sleep on a thin pallet on the floor with a fur blanket. I want to come home.' She began to cry all over again.

'I'm going to find you sweetheart. Whatever it takes I will find you. Are they Elfin?' Tears welled in his eyes when he felt her hopelessness.

'No. They have three fingers and a thumb, white skin.' Her mind was clouding over again.

'Don't give in to this. Be strong. Wait for me.' He could feel the red rage beginning to take hold again and ruthlessly shut it down. Now was not the time.

'I'm sorry my husband.' Her reply was soft but with an endearment that sent his heart into a rapid tattoo. 'I'm so afraid.'

'I know sweetheart, but try to sleep now. I'm going to speak with your father. He's been trying to link with you since the first moment he discovered you gone.'

'I never heard him.' Anguish filled her thoughts for her parents.

'It doesn't matter. Sleep now. When they next bring food try and see outside the door. Everything you can see I need to know about.' His mind caressed her. 'I love you. Be safe.'

'I love you. I will.' She lay down and slept immediately. For once her heart and mind at rest. It took Aaron some minutes to control his uneven breathing and rapid heartbeat.

In the main council chamber members of the military, along with the King and his ministers gathered. Across the huge table a map was spread.

'There is no evidence that leads us to believe the Lady Aurora is still in Fayland. Every inch of coastline around our entire country has been searched. All evidence points to a vessel of some description being beached and launched from the east. Every inlet, cave and overhang, regardless of size, has been thoroughly searched. Nothing was found.' General Vont gave his report. 'I would say that we had so many volunteers from the people our task was completed with some haste.'

'They are good people. My daughter was much respected and loved, as is her husband.' The King studied the map. 'It doesn't help us find her however.'

'She's on a ship.' Aaron had flown into the room via an open window and landed next to the King. His skin was pale and he had a thick bandage around his waist.

'What the devil are you doing out of hospital?' The King turned on the younger man. 'You can hardly stand!' His voice was stern, not so much in annoyance that his son-in-law was out of bed, but simply to control his own anxiety. Aaron's pallor was a sickly grey.

'I can fly.' He said through gritted teeth. He had a hand on the back of the King's chair for support. Sweat beaded his forehead.

The King personally filled a glass with water. 'Close and sit.' He commanded. Parlax came to Aaron's side in support.

'Sit my son.' He rested a hand on a warm shoulder as Aaron's wings closed. 'Tell us what you know.' Aaron nodded and sat with care in the nearest chair. He drank the water and accepted a refill.

'I linked with her.' He ran his hands through his hair. 'She is still aboard ship.'

'Still?' The King turned his attention back to the map. 'If that is the case she isn't headed for Elfin. Under full sail two days is all it takes to reach their shores.'

'Not Elfin' Aaron continued. 'White skin, three fingers and a thumb.' He downed the rest of his water. He felt a little better. In pain obviously, but manageable.

'I don't know a species with three fingers.' Vont ventured.

'If they were headed east.' Aaron rose, assured his father he was fine. 'Here' he jabbed a finger on the mountains to the east. 'This is where we'll find my wife. Here.' He sighed 'somewhere.'

'It's too far to fly.' Many muttered.

'We will need ships that can carry an army. We can send our scouting parties that we can base aboard ship. The last thing we need is for our men to fall exhausted into the sea.'

'I'm going now.' Aaron walked carefully across the room. His father caught his arm.

'No son you are not strong enough. Go back to the hospital, rest, and heal. We will be ready to go in a few days. We will find her.'

'Do you honestly think I will stay one moment longer than necessary. I can fly, so I will go now.' He snatched his arm from his father's hand. 'It would be a foolish man to try and stop me.' He turned to retrace his steps to the window, clutching his side.

'You will do as I command' the King roared 'or find yourself incarcerated.' It was obvious his son-in-law was in a great deal of pain. He doubted very much if he would even make it to the coast in his condition. He signalled his guards who immediately surrounded Lord Aaron. 'Do you think that your wife means more to you than my daughter to me?' he accused.

'No my King' he used the formal salutation. 'But she is my wife. She carries our child.' His wings spread instantly, vividly blue tinged with red. 'They stole her from me. Why? Does anyone know?' He rose with amazing agility into the air and hovered above them. 'They keep her in a filthy hole' his voice vibrated with rage. 'They made her cry!' his voice filled the room, his wings turned volcanic red. 'I shall find her and slaughter the bastards who took her.' His eyes turned red and in a flash he zipped out of the window. Everyone spilled out onto the balcony as Aaron shot straight up into the air. A streaking red comet. He hovered a moment. Then filled his lungs and screamed into the night sky.

'My son.' Parlax stumbled to his knees. 'My son.' The sound vibrated across the heavens for long moments. Then it stopped. The red blur in the sky sparked reds and gold before it shot off toward the east. 'We have to stop him. He'll be killed.'

'No my friend' the King helped his friend to his feet. 'We follow.' He turned to his generals. 'Ready the boats; we sail on the next tide. Summon your troops, full armour and rations.'

'Yes my King' they answered in unison before taking to the sky.

'We have two hours until the tide.' He turned to Parlax. 'You wish to travel with us?' Although he knew the answer he asked it regardless.

'Yes my King.' He bowed deeply.

'Very well' he addressed the council members. 'In my absence I charge you all with the welfare of my Lady Pearl and the people of Fayland.' Then he strode away to inform his wife of the new happenings and that he would be leaving shortly to head his troops in the search for their daughter.

Fayland's army was relatively small. Their navy even smaller. But with the help of the loyal people of the kingdom, who volunteered in droves, the ships were loaded with water and food enough to feed the entire army twice over for at least two weeks. In all four ships were crewed and readied. Each ship would take a total of one hundred soldiers plus crew. Without exception they sailed with the tide and headed northeast, towards the mountains. Over two hundred soldiers remained at the Palace to guard Lady Pearl and the people of Fayland.

Chapter Seventeen

Aaron made it to the eastern shore and had to rest. Sweat poured down his face, pain left his body weak, and anger drained him of good sense. The strain of his long journey had cooled his temper and returned his magnificent wings to their usual blue.

He glided around for a suitable place to land, where fresh water was available and set down by a small cottage next to a slow running stream. He drank his fill, closed his wings and stretched out to sleep under a tree on the cool grass.

He woke abruptly to a strong hand shaking his shoulder. He winced as he sat up and rubbed his hands over his face and through his hair. Days of stubble covered his jaw.

'Are you hurt sir?' a strong voice asked. When Aaron turned his head he saw a man crouched down at his side watching him closely.

'Just tired.' Aaron rose to his feet with the man. They were roughly the same age. But whereas one was dark the other was fair. It was then the man noticed the chain around Aaron's neck. 'Would you be Lord Aaron?'

'That's me' Aaron held out a hand, which was taken immediately in a strong grip. 'And you sir?'

'I'm Streff My Lord, this is my farm.' He swept his arms wide. 'Please come to the house, eat breakfast with us.'

'I would appreciate a good meal. Thank you.' He followed the farmer toward his home.

He was received warmly into the cosy home of Streff and his wife Trina. Although well along in her pregnancy she bustle about and placed fresh bread, cheese omelettes and bowls of fruit and cream before them. A pitcher of fresh milk sat in a basin filled with ice in the centre of the table. Sparkling glasses sat at each setting. All had a hearty appetite.

'We heard you were near to death my Lord and that the Lady Aurora was taken from us.' Trina asked as she poured the milk.

'As you see I may not be back to full health, and yes my wife is missing. I was able to link with her only yesterday. They have taken her east. She is still aboard ship.'

'Still?' Streff looked concerned. 'My Lord there is nothing to the east but a vast ocean and then the mountains that I am told are too steep to climb. They stretch for miles, for as far as the eye can see.'

'You've been there?' Aaron's interest peeked immediately.

'Before my opening two years ago I was a fisherman. We trawled as far east as we felt it safe to go. The catch was always good. There's a strong undercurrent close to the mountains, very treacherous.' He concluded. 'You think that's where they've taken her?'

Aaron nodded. 'Landfall to the north, to Elfin, can be reached within two days. The only other course is west to more mountains or to circle back south to King Ruscal's lands. Evidence was discovered that indicated they took her east.'

'King Nall's ruthless all right, but he's not stupid enough to take a woman from the royal household. To bring King Salvax's wrath down on his head. The people would come to arms My Lord to aid you and return your wife to your side.'

The simple statement humbled Aaron. 'Do you have a boat that I could borrow' he said at last. 'I have to go and see for myself.' He winced when he got to his feet. Trina looked across as her husband with wide eyes. He smiled and nodded.

'My Lord I am trained in healing. I have herbs and salve that can ease your discomfort.' She offered.

'I would be grateful for your help.' He sat patiently as his bandage was removed. He had bled a little and the thick protective padding was stuck to his skin. With gentle care Trina bathed the pad with warm water until it was safe to ease it from the sore wound. 'This will sting My Lord.' She placed a hot cloth soaked in herbs against the raw wound. Aaron sucked in his breath and let it out slowly as the stinging eased.

He turned a reddened face to her and smiled. 'You're telling me.' She giggled in reply, making her husband smile.

'There is a little infection, but I think a drawing poultice will clear that up.' She hurried to the fire and began to mix water and herbs together into a paste.

'When is your child due?' Aaron asked quietly as the men watched her work.

'By end of next week.' He said with some pride. 'The midwife will come and stay a few days when the labour starts.' He noticed Aaron's sad smile. 'When is your lady due?' he asked tentatively.

'About nine weeks' he shook his head. 'I want her home long before that happy event takes place.'

'I have a boat sir. Not very large, single mast and sail. Trim in the water and has good speed. Do you sail?'

'In my former life I did some sailing. I can manage well enough. Thank you.' He turned his attention back to Trina as she place a warm mixture on his skin and a thick padding before she bandaged him snugly. She handed him a small pot with a cork stopper some strips of bandage and several more pads. 'The mixture should be heated, but it is not strictly necessary. Change the dressing again tomorrow. After that if the wound is clean and healed, cut out the stitches, wash the wound in sea water and leave it to the air.'

'Thank you' he kissed her cheek and she blushed crimson before hurrying about her daily duties. 'You are a lucky man Streff. She is very lovely.' The men walked outside.

'Don't I know it.' His grin was wide. 'Can you fly? The mooring is just up the coast.' He spread his wings. Not as wide as Aaron's but a brilliant shade of yellow, streaked with silver.

Aaron nodded and spread his own. Streff's eyes were huge in his face. He had heard, of course, but hadn't expected to truth of it to be standing right in front of him.

'This way' and he took off and headed north east along the coast. In less than three minutes they landed on a mooring dock, to which five boats were bobbing calmly on the swell. A number of houses sat nearby alongside an icehouse and workbenches. Men and woman stood beside the benches gutting and cleaning the fish and packing them in crates of ice ready for shipping.

Streff excused himself when he left Aaron to inspect his boat. He hurried to the men and woman at work and spoke with them. Within seconds they dispersed to various locations. Two of the men went inside the icehouse and returned rolling a large barrel. This they proceeded to load onto Streff's small boat and strapped it against the mast. On investigation Aaron discovered it was filled with ice that would slowly melt and give him a good supply of drinking water. The women arrived shortly afterwards bringing with them all manner of supplies. Bread, cheese, honey, biscuits, fruit, vegetables, dried fish and meat, tea and coffee. Aaron was overwhelmed with their generosity. Streff spend a few minutes showing Aaron a small galley in the stern where he could heat water and cook a meal. In the bow was stored a set of oars and a spare sail along with a rolled up pallet and some blankets. Steering was via a rudder to the rear of the galley. Aaron made a link with Streff just in case he got into trouble or if he received any news of his wife. With a firm handshake Aaron put to sea.

He set a course east once out in open water and for the remainder of the day the small craft set a spanking pace across the waves. In the quiet times Aaron meditated and tried to link with Aurora. Something was wrong. He could sense her, feel her mood of lethargy, could see the swirls of colour that had her mind confused.

'They've drugged her' he said out loud. Dear God what might they be doing to her at this very minute. 'Be safe my love.' He thought and said aloud. 'Be safe I'm coming.' With those words hardly out of his mouth he secured the rudder to keep the boat on a steady course and lighted a lamp that he hung from the mast. It was pitch black, with clouds covering the moon; he would never to able to find the boat again without a beacon to guide him. Then he took to the sky rising quickly into the night air, higher and higher until the low clouds misted his vision. Then he simply spread his wings and glided. Eventually his vision cleared as he scanned the ocean below him. There was nothing. No lights to indicate another vessel was anywhere in the immediate area. When he was practically skimming the surface of the water he once again rose high into the sky and glided again. He covered many more miles simply gliding than he would have done using all his strength flying at a lower level. After a fruitless search he returned to the boat. The small welcoming light guiding him safely home.

'My Lord Aaron' Streff linked with him shortly after he landed.

'Yes my friend' Aaron sat in the warmth of the galley and heated water for a hot drink. It was much colder out at sea than on dry land.

'Four ships of the royal navy are headed in your direction. There are many soldiers aboard each ship. Your father and the King are amongst them. They have been unable to link with you.'

'I haven't been listening.' Was all Aaron said. This was not exactly true. He had just ignored them. He would make amends when he found his wife. Not before.

'Your father asked me to tell you to be careful. They are only hours behind you.' Streff didn't tell him that the King was still furious and demanded the young man return to Fayland immediately. He thought it best to keep this information to himself. He surmised Aaron already had a good idea of the King's state of mind. 'Are you well My Lord?' he added for himself.

'I cannot link with her. I think they may have drugged her. Her mind is confused.' He ran his hands through his hair. 'And I am tired now. Thank you for the information. I shall keep a weather eye out for the navy.' Then he simply switched off.

He ate to keep his strength up and sleep to rest his aching body. By morning his boat had covered the many miles he had flown in the night.

Dawn of the third day brought a little rain and choppy seas, but at least the wind was blowing. He set full sail and forged ahead. The rain stopped and so did the wind toward mid-afternoon to add to the young man's frustration. Using a long spyglass that he had discovered in the forward storage area he scanned the horizon. There was a heavy mist away in the distance. This he felt sure would indicate land of some description. To the south he saw tiny dark specks on the horizon. The King was fast approaching. Or at least he would be if the wind picked up again. But then again if they had seen him, and he doubted very much if the King didn't have lookouts posted aboard every ship, the King would send his best fliers to get him.

When he was just thinking to take off and to hell with the waiting Aurora linked with him.

'Aaron' it was a soft gentle call. Not unlike when she woke from a long sleep. Still a little sluggish and not quite fully awake.

'I am here my love.' He answered immediately. 'Where are you?' He sat abruptly and tried to concentrate. To clear his mind of everything but her voice.

'Under the land.' She tried very hard to clear her mind. She had been awakened in the night and blindfolded before being dragged from the cell and taken above decks. They forced a cup to her mouth but she spat most of it out and struggled weakly as she was lifted in strong arms and lowered into a smaller boat and rowed ashore. She heard oars in the water. Enough of the liquid had slid down her throat to disorientate her and blur her vision. 'Not in prison.' She fought sleep as tears fell. 'Echoes.' Then she was gone.

'Don't cry sweetheart. It kills me, please don't cry.' He sprang to his feet and fisted his hands in his hair as rage overtook him. His wings flashed open and were red instantly.

'Do you see that?' the corporal of the guard asked the man next to him. 'The only person I know who has the red rage is Lord Aaron. Summon the King.' He kept the glass to his eye.

Within minutes the King and Parlax were at his side. He handed the glass to his King who was just about to raise it to his eye when the sound hit them.

'He's flying' Parlax said as the sound of anguish whirled all around them and as he watched the red streak shoot into the twilight sky. 'Come to us my son. Let us help you.' He thought.

'Oh no.' he gasped as the streak stopped abruptly and simply tumbled and fell towards the cold cold sea. He spread his wings and took off immediately, closely followed by four guards and the King. Parlax knew they wouldn't be in time. They were simply too far away. With his wings out of control he would hit the water hard, do untold damage to them and possibly lose consciousness in the icy sea and drown.

As all eyes were on the plummeting Aaron they were amazed to see him straighten out, dim and close his wings and hit the water straight as an arrow.

'The bloody young fool. Friend or not Parlax I'm going to put him in chains.' The King did an immediate about turn and flew back to his ship. The guards had to scramble to keep up with him. Parlax stayed behind to watch over his son as he ploughed through the surf toward the naval vessels.

His temper had cooled and his body was free of stress as he hauled himself aboard the King's ship. Willing hands leaned over the side to give him assistance as he scrambled up the rope ladder. Other hands, not so friendly, caught hold of him and snapped heavy irons on his ankles before he had a chance to move.

'What's the meaning of this.' Aaron barked. 'Get these off me.'

'The meaning you young fool is this!' the King stepped into Aaron's face. 'You do not defy me. You do not take it upon yourself to start a war by your foolishness.'

'I haven't….'

'Silence!' Salvax had never been so angry. 'Do not speak another word. I am your King and you will obey my commands to the letter or suffer the consequences.' He hissed into Aaron's angry face. 'Just nod your head so that I know you understand.' Oh there was such defiance in those brilliant green eyes. Such anger. The battle that was being raged behind them was all to clear to the man in his face. Salvax half expected the red rage to start building. Aaron was angry enough; his breathing was harsh and short. Yet strangely he seemed able to control it at this particular point. Something had obviously happened on the smaller boat that had set the anger in motion, but it would appear it had nothing to do with this particular kind of anger. Odd.

Aaron eventually nodded after a full five minutes of silence. His breathing slowed and the tension left his shoulders, his fists opened at his side.

'I would have your word Lord Aaron.' The King stepped back a pace 'that you will do nothing without first consulting with me and then I will decide what action should be taken. Do you agree?'

'Yes my King.' Aaron held his head high. As far as he was concerned he had acted appropriately. Aurora may be the King's daughter but she was first and foremost his wife.

A jerk of the King's head had the irons removed. 'Follow me.' He indicated Aaron, Parlax and General Vont. He led the men below to his cabin. Aaron found a towel thrust into his hands and he dried himself briskly. Parlax handed him a dry loincloth that he changed into quickly.

'What do you know?' The King personally poured each man a glass of wine. 'Sit.' They gathered around a table.

'She's not coherent. I think they maybe using some drug to keep her calm while they transport her. All I see is a swirling cloud of confusion.' He looked into his glass of rich red wine for some minutes. No one interrupted his thoughts. 'She linked, very briefly. She was trying.' This time he took a sip then pushed the glass away. 'She said 'under the land' and 'not in prison' and 'echoes'. I sensed that she was afraid, for herself and our child. They made her cry.' His voice was hardly audible, but his body was vibrating and his eyes started to redden before he squeezed them closed. His fists thumped the table as he fought his body for control. Thankfully his wings did not open.

'You were angry before, with me on deck yet the red rage did not come.' The King spoke softly and rested a large hand on Aaron's tight fist. It seemed to calm him and the fist relaxed. Salvax pulled his hand away.

'I don't have a temper, never have. I can get angry, sure I can, but to be so filled with rage has never happened until I came here.' He rested his elbows on the table and combed his fingers through his damp hair. 'Sometimes' a smile crossed his face 'when we make love she cries. When she wraps herself around me and takes me in she destroys me, and she cries. Tears stream down her face and she whispered my name over and over and we're both lost in the moment.' He looked up at the King. 'Those tears I can take, those tears are beautiful to see, to experience.' He had to get to his feet now and pace. 'But when her tears are caused through hurt or fear something comes over me and my control slips away. Right now' he faced the table and the three man 'right now my lovely Aurora is afraid and crying and I can't find her, I can't help her. My wife's frightened tears are what brings on the red rage. Nothing else. I'm going on deck. Excuse me.' He bowed to the table in general and hurried from the cabin.

'Gentlemen' the King sat back in his chair. 'I think we have our next Oracle' he lifted his glass and saluted the closed door out of which his son-in-law had departed.

'It had crossed my mind' Parlax sighed heavily. 'I've been studying the ledgers and writings.'

'That will have to wait for now.' Salvax rose and retrieved a rolled map and spread it over the table. 'Aurora said 'under the land' caves come to mind. What do we know of the base of these mountains.'

On deck Aaron braced his hands on the port side of the railing and looked out to sea. The wind now filled the sails again and the trim vessel was picking up speed and continuing east toward the bank of mist on the far horizon.

'What news my Lord Aaron?' a young man came to stand at the railings following the gaze of his team leader.

'She's out there Jon.' Aaron turned a sombre face to the young man next to him. Jon now wore a loincloth and was happily married to a gorgeous little red hair. 'I just can't get a fix on her exact position.'

'You must be the only one who has been able to link with Lady Aurora. None, as far as I am aware, have been able to do so.' Jon placed a comforting hand on Aaron's shoulder. 'At least we know where to start our search. The team are ready to follow you my Lord. You have but to ask.'

It was tempting, very tempting, but had to be resisted. 'I gave my word. I will wait for the King's directive. Rest assured that if I am given the task, the team will come with me.' Jon nodded.

'There is a good place for meditation on the top of the steerage house' he pointed astern, bowed, and then left.

An hour later when the King emerged with Parlax and General Vont Aaron's smaller craft had been tied to the stern and trailed along in the bigger ship's wake. The crew worked efficiently even with the many soldiers that crowded the deck. The only place that appeared to be free of personnel was the steerage house and this was primarily because Lord Aaron sat crossed legged on the roof on a pile of spare sails, hands open on his knees and his magnificent wings spread wide. The blues were vibrant and shimmered in the twilight now encroaching all around. Although he sat upright, his body held no tension or stress, he was relaxed with his eyes closed, his mind elsewhere.

'He meditates every day so I am told.' The King dismissed his general as he and Parlax walked the deck.

'From childhood he told me. It is something that comes naturally to him. It frees him from pain, clears his head and allows him to sleep should it be necessary.' His father informed his King. 'Since my Opening I do not meditate nearly enough. Maybe once or twice a week.' He freely admitted.

'Very few of us do once we mature' the King agreed. 'It may be why he has such control over his red rage.' Parlax agreed with the King's statement.

They were not the only ones to notice the change in Lord Aaron. Forty minutes had past since the King had come on deck. He was studying the charts with his navigator when Parlax touched his arm. 'My King' was all he said as Salvax turned in his direction and saw where his friend was looking.

'He's linked with her I think.' Parlax said softly. All work had stopped aboard ship. It was utterly silent except for the water running down the side of the hull and the wind in the sails.

Aaron's wings were vibrating gently, his back had stiffened and his head fell back on his shoulders.

'Can you hear me my love' her gentle thoughts filled him.

'Always sweetheart' his senses filled with her. 'Are you safe?'

'Yes. We have made camp for the night. We are still underground in a labyrinth of tunnels' her mind was clear and relaxed.

'Are you hurt' he could feel her drifting. Had they drugged her again?

'No just tired. They do not know I can link with you. They think they are safe now. They do not drug me anymore.'

'But where are you Aurora? I am close. Your father and his army are with me. We headed east and are approaching the mists and the mountains.' He tried not to push her too hard but he needed the information, as much as she could give him.

'I don't know. The blindfold was only removed when we were in the tunnels.' She yawned and curled protectively around the child that grew within her.

'Think Aurora!' he demanded. 'Anything you remember regardless of how insignificant.'

'Walked all day, so tired Aaron. But the boat I was put in scrapped against the rocks when the oars were in the water. I love you. Come and find me. So tired. I don't know these people, they are strangers to me.' She sighed.

'Sleep now. I will find you. I love you.' Then she was gone.

He wasn't a man who shed tears easily. But when his body started to tremble and his breath hitched, he was unable to stop them. 'I will find you. I will. I promise.' He sobbed. In his anguish he hadn't realised he had spoken aloud. As his body filled with longing just to simply hold her in his arms, the rage began to build. His wings vibrated strongly and tinged with red. When at last the tears subsided and he opened his eyes. The brilliant green were vivid red. Those closest to him backed away fully expecting his wings to change colour completely and the red rage to take him over.

He got slowly to his feet, braced them apart for balance, turned his face to the heavens and roared 'Why do I feel so fucking helpless.' The sound filled the night sky and boomed like thunder all around them. Screaming his anguish into the heavens was a safety valve he found very effective and aided his control.

'Can we do something?' the King whispered to his friend.

'Do not worry my King' Parlax stood straight at his side. 'He has it under control.' A sad smile crossed his face.

And so he did. Although his wings still vibrated and were tinged with red his mind, this time, was in control. Aaron did not let his rage consume him. He banked it, stored it away, for another time. When he found those responsible for his wife's abduction, then, he promised himself, he would let it loose. Then God help them all because he simply wouldn't be able to control it. He closed his wings and when he opened his eyes they were his usual green. With new information he returned below decks with the King.

Two hours later Aaron stretched out on a pallet on deck and tried to sleep. A plan had been formed and agreed. Links were made with the other ships so all would be in readiness for the dawn.

'It gets cold at night' a member of the crew placed a blanket over him.

'Thanks' he said and closed his eyes.

Chapter Eighteen

He hadn't expected to sleep so was stunned when he was prodded awake by a naked foot.

'Come have breakfast my Lord Aaron' a tall soldier indicated a table spread with the morning fare.

When he stretched his cramped muscles and stood at the railing he was surprised to find himself facing a granite wall of mountain reaching high into the clouds and as far as the eye could see to right and left.

The morning dawned to bright sunlight and a warming breeze. By seven o'clock four boats from each ship were lowered into the sea each with a seven man crew. One in the bow with a plumb line to record the depth, two to row, and four soldiers. They spread out in a long line and when the signal was given started to row steadily towards the rocks.

'Shallow depth, two meters' the man in the bow of Aaron's boat called out. Over the side nothing could be seen but black water.

'Shallow water, five feet. Lift oars.' The two men rowing did it instantly. It would seem all the other small boats had encountered the same obstacles below the water line as all oars were pulled clear of the water.

'Scrapping, shallow water, four feet.'

'Okay I'm going in.' Aaron immediately slide over the side into waist deep water and onto jagged rocks and smooth pebbles. He inched around until he had a firm footing and was standing at the bow. He was thrown a rope that he took in a firm grip as the other end was fastened to the boat. As Aaron guided, the rowers used the oars to punt the boat away from any rocks as Aaron indicated. This appeared to work quite successfully. The King had forbidden any man or woman to enter the water without a safety line. Those in the water had to be within easy reach of their boat at all times. Aaron was grateful for this because as he inched closer to the rock surface he saw a large black hole in the side of the mountain. He turned to indicate his find to the others and missed his footing. His knees scrapped the bottom and jarred his cold legs as he went beneath the surface. The current took him and lifted him to the surface and threw him, none to gently, at the rock face. He was kept from being swept away by the strong undercurrent by a firm grip on the safety line.

Cursing colourfully he indicated he wasn't hurt, all that much, and pointed to the cave entrance. The boat immediately turned in that direction and battled the current to go inside. Three other boats, from Aaron's ship followed. Two other caves were discovered and the remaining boats divided into two teams and headed under ground. When Aaron linked with the other teams he was told that one swimmer had been knocked unconscious when he too hit the rock face and another had broken a finger. Aaron had sustained a nasty gash to his left arm and this was soon bandaged when his team joined him. He had discarded the bandage from around his waist only that morning. The stitches had been removed and the wound pronounced clean and healthy. His knees were scrapped and bruised, but all in all he wasn't too bad.

When he had hauled himself from the water he cautiously spread his wings to fill the cave with light. There was sufficient room for his full spread after a cursory inspection. He saw another boat pulled clear of the water and pushed up against the wall. Beside this a basket sat filled with torches and a flint stone. The medic had just completed his treatment of Lord Aaron when the rest of the men hauled the boat ashore.

'This looks promising' Jon came and stood at his side. He gave Aaron the once over to assure himself that the medic had done his job.

'That it does my friend. The other boats should have landed by now. Link with them and see what they have found.' He moved further down the tunnel to allow the other boats to land and his men to scramble ashore.

'All report a landing sight and a single boat with a basket of fresh torches to one side.' Jon reported.

Aaron nodded. 'Tell them to make there way inland but to have a care for there safety. Hopefully our paths will cross further along the tunnel.' He struck a flint to stone to get a spark and lighted a torch then closed his wings. Jon relayed his orders.

'Are the boats secure?' he called to the rear.

'Yes my Lord' came the reply.

'Right. The men from the last boat will wait ten minutes before they follow the main group, which I will lead. If we encounter trouble along the way I expect the rear guard to rescue our sorry asses.' He was sure it wasn't the usual way to address soldiers on a mission but it seemed appropriate for this specific campaign.

'Oh I think we can manage to do just that my Lord' there were affirmative nods and grins from the seven men that would make up the rear guard. Torches were lit and past around.

'Okay then, lets move out.' The young husband led the way. As he walked along Aaron linked with General Vont to say stage one was operational. Soldiers from each ship would now take to the air and scout the height of the mountains and further a field.

General Vont was at that moment making additions to the map to indicate the three caves they had discovered. His airborne troops had just reported the discovery of a narrow crack in the mountainside about three quarters the way up. It was wide enough for them to fly through and reconnoitre.

'There's a tree filled valley on the other side' he indicated the area to his King. 'Sheer mountains on three sides, the west, north and south. It tapers to a narrow gap to the east and more trees and vegetation can be seen further inland.' He reported. 'My troops are in hiding awaiting instructions but report no sign of life but also that the canopy is thick and without further investigation cannot be certain.'

'This is excellent news General Vont' Salvax studied the amended map closely. 'Can an estimate be given as to how far down the valley sits in the crater. That would give us an indication as to where the exits might emerge into daylight.'

'That cannot be ascertained unless I put men on the ground my King.' He was chafing a little at being left behind.

'Then do so. Send an entire regiment. Cover as much ground as possible. They are not to engage the natives, observe only. Who is your best man?' The King ran a strong hand through his hair.

'Captain Dirk' he said without hesitation. 'An engineer by skill. He has a good eye. The men respect him.' Vont had every confidence in the younger man.

'See it done General.'

'Yes my King.' He hurried from the cabin.

Salvax then sat quietly and linked with his wife to give her an update knowing she would inform the council in due course.

'Get up woman' a kick landed on her thigh and bought her painfully awake. She scrambled to her feet and backed up against the wall in fretful distress, her hands clasped over her swollen belly. The man laughed as she cringed away from his strange face.

All of them were at least six feet tall. Four males and two females. All were bald. Their eyes were large and dark with hair that grew thick and long over both upper and lower lids. Aurora thought they might be light sensitive. They only ever used one torch. Their noses were long and wide with a mouth that had thin lips and sharp pointed teeth. Although covered with some sort of cloth their frame was reed thin with arms far longer than any Aurora had seen before. All had three long fingers and a thumb. Their long legs looked too thin to carry their weight but they never seemed to tire. All of her jailers, the females included, had huge appetites not only for food, but for sex. The women were used repeatedly between all of the males whenever the opportunity arose. It would never be allowed in Fayland. The gene pool would be totally corrupted. Maybe that was why, to Aurora's eyes, they looked identical.

'Eat we leave shortly' a skin of water was dropped at her feet and a plate of food pushed carelessly across the stone floor. Aurora hurried to obey. As yet she hadn't said a word. She drank deeply and ate her fill before she stepped away down the tunnel to relieve herself. Even her toilet was watched over by a guard.

They pushed on hard today. The weight of her child sapped her strength and in the semi darkness she stumbled often. They only stopped when one of the males pulled a female to the ground for a quick bout of sex. They were hardly consummate lovers. A water skin was thrown at her feet when she sank to the floor. She drank automatically;

water was essential to her wellbeing and that of her child. She could go without food for a day or two but not water. The planned short break lasted an hour as the males decided that they each, again, needed a turn on the females so Aurora spent a quiet hour with her eyes closed and tried to block out the grunts and moans. She was immensely relieved she hadn't been forced to perform that particular repugnant service.

As the final man grunted and withdrew she was hauled to her feet and dragged along the tunnel. The men were always more talkative after their sexual interludes but as they spoke their native tongue she was unable to understand. They were obviously educated as they spoke perfect Fayland when addressing her. The females didn't seemed to care one way or the other.

The bright sunlight hurt her eyes when they pushed through a thick tangle of vines into the open air. Relief flooded through her as she closed her eyes and turned her dirty face towards the sunlight. Her captors didn't like it at all. And dragged her struggling body down a crumbling path and into the cool shade of the nearby forest. They continued for many miles until darkness crept over the land and Aurora's thought turned to escape. In the open she could fly. Not far in her current state, but far enough to avoid capture. If she could fly, she felt sure that Aaron would eventually find her.

As if reading her thoughts one of the females came up behind her and snapped a thick metal collar around her neck, attached to this was a long metal chain. Although she wanted to struggle and fight them, she stood placidly whilst the end was looped around a strong sapling and a lock put in place. Whether or not they knew she had wings was debatable but as she was taken from Fayland she thought it likely. They were taking no chances, leaving her no avenue of escape. She was given food and water, and then tossed a blanket to take her rest as best she could. She dragged the chain as far as it would go and lay down behind a fallen tree. At least she didn't have to look at them.

As she curled up to sleep she linked with her husband.

'We have left the tunnel. A thick curtain of vines covers the exit. The path we were travelling leads out onto a narrow path and down into the forest. I could hear running water to the north but I never saw it as we headed away. East I think from the way the sun set in the sky.'

'Good girl' he inwardly sighed. 'We are in the tunnels now. Three teams are travelling from different locations and hopefully we will meet up soon. There are already sixteen sol-diers in hiding in the forest. A full regiment under Captain Dirk is on its way.' He relayed the information. 'Any chance you can get away?' he asked hopefully.

'None. They have fixed a metal collar around my neck with a long chain and a lock. I was trying to think of a way to spread my wings but whether or not they know I can fly I have no idea. The collar went on within minutes of our leaving the tunnel.' She had to smile and he felt it. 'I was extremely, how do you say it, pissed off.'

Aaron laughed aloud for the first time in a long time. His men looked at him strangely as they hurried along the tunnel. They hadn't stopped to rest but ate and drank on the move. 'How many nights were you in the tunnel?'

'Only one I think, one night of sleep anyway.' She checked the sky. 'It is full dark now.'

'With any luck we will be out of the tunnel by daybreak. Do you know why you were taken? Have they said anything?'

'Nothing of importance. They speak in their own tongue most of the time. A language I don't know, have never heard before. They all speak perfect Fayland however when they give me orders.' She twitched a bit and Aaron felt this also.

'Are you all right?' His thoughts were filled with anxiety.

'Our baby is kicking. He seemed impatient to wait the remaining eight weeks.' She smiled to herself.

'Well you make sure he does. I want to see our child born and welcome him or her into the world.' He smiled as he hurried along the tunnel.

'You would not mind if we had a daughter?' She had always assumed their child would be a boy.

'Mind, of course I wouldn't mind. She would be beautiful, just like her mother. Now go to sleep. I will see you soon. Good night my love.' Her spirits were high, for this he was extremely thankful.

'Good night. I love you.' Then she was gone.

Aaron called a halt. 'We'll take thirty minutes to rest.' Men were already lowering to the hard rock.

'Why were you laughing my Lord' someone dared to asked.

'My wife, the lovely Lady Aurora, is, and I quote, extremely pissed off.' A ripple of laughed filled the tunnel. 'Her captors are taking no chances and had put a collar around her neck attached to this is a long metal chain. Her plans to spread her wings have come to naught and she is quite cross.' There was an annoyed murmuring down the tunnel when they heard this news. 'The bastards' was the most popular curse.

They pushed on. As yet they has found no evidence that a party had travelled this way. No evidence of a campfire, places were a body had lain down to rest. Nothing. They met up with the other two teams when the three tunnels converged about five hundred yards from the exit. They burst out into the pre-dawn sky. No vines covered the entrance. To

Aaron's estimation they were too far south. Directly in their path was a deep slope that lead into the valley and the forest. Aaron sent his men down into the trees to snatch a couple of hours rest.

'You made good time my Lord' Captain Dirk linked with Aaron.

'Where are you?' he looked both right and left.

'Above you' Dirk was hanging over an outcropping of rocks with a spyglass in his hand. 'I'll come down.' He got to his feet and glided down.

'We pushed hard. Need a couple of hours sleep.' They shook hands. 'What news?'

'No sign of the natives. The original scouts have been sent to set up a watch to the east' he indicated the narrow pass between the mountainsides. 'Half my men have taken up places of concealment to the north and south. Any sign of the Lady Aurora will be linked immediately. Airborne reconnaissance is out of the question; the canopy is too thick. What we did find was a city in the next valley. Lots of trees, lots of shade. Not much surface building. From what we have been able to see these people prefer to live below ground.'

'Aurora thought they may be light sensitive. Large black eyes with thick lashes.' Aaron concluded as they made their way down the slope into the trees.

'And very promiscuous from all accounts. They appear to be at it like rabbits.' Dirk spoke quietly.

'Aurora said as much.' Both men smiled.

'Get some sleep. I'll wake you in a couple of hours.' He nodded then turned and walked back up the slope. Aaron was asleep as soon as his head touched the hard cool ground.

Whilst Aaron and his men slept it was reported to Captain Dirk that the vine-covered entrance from which Aurora had left the mountainside had been discovered.

Trackers were sent immediately to that location to begin a thorough search.

'Lord Aaron' a hand touched his shoulder. 'Time for breakfast.' One of his men was crouched at his side.

'Yes thank you. I'm awake' he accepted the hand that pulled him to his feet. 'I miss my bed' he rotated his neck and shoulders to relieve the cramp.

'As do we all my Lord' the soldier chuckled. 'Captain Dirk has news' he gestured to the top of the slope were the Captain was giving orders and pointing off to the north with a chunk of bread. As Aaron approached a full score of men took to the air and headed in that direction.

'We found the exit of vines' Dirk said as Aaron approached and knelt in the dirt and used a stick to draw. 'It's about six miles south east of here. The path is crumbling which leads me to believe it's not a regular route. There is a swift running, although shallow, river running to the east from the north.' He drew as he spoke.

'We're in the wrong place' Aaron said unnecessarily and lifted his head to look further south.

'I've got trackers in place. I'm going to cut across the valley to a point just north of the eastern exit into the next valley. It would appear to be the most likely avenue to intercept them.' He marked his crude map with the pointed stick. 'My men report no activity through the passage since they took up station.' Both men rose to their feet. 'I've sent men to the north and south sides of the passage to find the river's course and any other passage ways through the mountain side. Any they find they will station two men on look out. The remainder will station themselves in hiding across the mountainside and await my instructions. If Lady Aurora is spotted we will know immediately. They won't leave this valley' Captain Dirk said with confidence as he watched Lord

Aaron digest this information. 'I'm going to fly the rest of the men to this point' he jabbed his stick into the ground near the eastern entrance to the mountain. 'From there we'll spread out and converge west. I should be hearing from the trackers soon and better know the best course to set.' He turned to Aaron. 'I would like you to remain with me.'

Aaron's head whipped around, his eyes were now blazing. 'If you expect me to…'

Dirk cut him off. 'But I don't think I could cope well with your red rage at this juncture. My sergeant is expecting you to join his troops on the eastern mountainside. I would ask you to listen when he advises, to consider his strategy and adhere to reason.' Dirk placed a hard hand on Aaron's wide shoulder. 'He is a good man, well experienced. I will take it much amiss if any of my men are hurt because you cannot hold your temper.' He spoke as one husband to another.

'That's a very affective way of cutting a man off at the knees without bloodshed.' Aaron nodded his understanding.

'If it were my wife I would move heaven and earth to get her back.' He stepped back as Aaron unfurled and opened his wings. 'This is what I do, and do well, trust me.'

Again Aaron nodded. 'When I'm in situ I'll try and link with Aurora she should be awake now.'

Captain Dirk nodded as Aaron lifted effortlessly into the air and zoomed off. It was true what everyone was saying. Lord Aaron was a natural; flying was as easy as breathing for him. Calling his men to order the sky was soon filled with his troops as they headed northeast. They would soon land and cover the entire eastern side of the valley and head inland.

The flash of a blade against sunlight drew Aaron down to an overhang of rock on which several men were hiding. He soon joined them. Sergeant Dia was a man of middle years with a tall muscular body. He explained he had two men to the north and two to the south of their position covering passages that were found leading into the mountains.

'Haven't seen a soul my Lord. Heard strange grunting and snuffling that we think might be pigs but they could be anywhere under the canopy of trees. We had a look at ground level and the undergrowth is denser there. Anything or anybody moving through it we will be able to hear.'

'Good. I'm going to try and link with my wife to see if they are on the move yet.' It was still fairly early, maybe eight o'clock.

He moved a short distance away and sat in his favourite position. Those nearby thought it odd that he still meditated. Most gave it up after their Opening ceremony. Having no need of the practice once the pain was gone. Many thought the red rage had something to do with it. Keeping Lord Aaron calm would be of utmost importance.

'Wake up sleepy head' Aaron tried to link. 'Time to wake up my love.'

'I am awake. Have been for some time.' She let her senses fill with him. 'Where are you?' She was sitting on the ancient tree trunk observing the campsite.

'Close I think. I'm with Sergeant Dia on the mountain face to the east. Trackers and Captain Dirk and his forces are coming from all directions. If our luck holds you will be in my arms at the end of the day.' He let his mind wonder to where his hands would wonder and felt the ache of her longing for his caress. His blood warmed.

'Don't be cruel Aaron' her face flushed with heat. 'I miss you so' she didn't cry however, she was calm, knowing rescue was at hand. 'They don't appear to be in any hurry. They gave me food and water at six this morning. Now they simply sit around a small fire and talk and….have sex.' She glanced toward the fire and sure enough they were at it again. It made Aaron smile at the image she sent him. 'I think they're waiting for something, or someone. I overheard the females talking in English before they saw me watching them. They think they should get a larger share of the fee for ……services rendered.' It was the politest words she could think of.

'Sit tight then. See if you can hear this.' Aaron lifted his head, put two fingers into his mouth and whistled shrilly into the air.

'Yes!' her excited thoughts filled his mind. 'So clear you can't be too far away.' She got to her feet and casually walked the length of the log and back to better see the camp. 'They hear it to. They're looking around nervously.' She sat on the log again looking sullen at the guards as she pulled her knees up to her chest and wrapped her arms around them.

'They should be fucking terrified' his mind snarled. 'Just a moment' and he was gone.

Trusting him to link back Aurora took in as much of her surroundings as possible. There was little in the way of variance from any side. Their campsite was on the only patch of open ground that she had seen since entering the forest. Trees seem to grow in uniform rows with hardly an arms spread between them. Flying, now she thought seriously about it, would be impossible. Climbing one of the lofty giants would be the only way to gain open space enough to spread her wings. 'Not a good idea' she thought. There was one thing. A tree was cleaved almost in half from what appeared to be a lightning strike. They had made camp near by.

'Sweetheart are you there?' Aaron asked.

'Yes Aaron. What's happening?'

'A covered wagon and a group of men have come through the passage and are heading west into the forest. They should pass our position shortly. I and a dozen men will follow.'

'They come for me?' she asked apprehensively.

'Seems like Aurora. Do not be afraid. When you see the wagon, know that I will be close by and be able to see you. Be calm, don't give us away.' He said earnestly.

'I'm not stupid Aaron. I can keep my feelings guarded.' She said with some annoyance. 'Just get on with it so we can go home. Oh and tell Captain Dirk, if he is close, to look for a Y shaped tree, been struck by lightning I think. The camp is at its base.'

'Yes ma'am' he smiled in his thoughts and so did she. Then he was gone.

With something more positive to do the men waited the arrival of the wagon and guards. Aaron linked with Captain Dirk and gave him Aurora's location. Once the wagon passed this spot the kidnappers and the wagon would be surrounded.

Captain Dirk reported he was already in situ and could see the campsite and the Lady Aurora. Everything was relaxed and gave the Captain ample opportunity to surround the area with his men. He agreed with Aaron that he would hold his position until the wagon and additional forces arrived and for Aaron to secure the rear.

'Lady Aurora can you hear me?' Dirk risked a link as he crouched just feet behind the tree to which the King's daughter was chained.

Instantly alert, her heart suddenly pounding, the young woman straightened her back against the tree. 'Perfectly Captain Dirk. You made good time.' Her eyes scanned the camp for any sign they may have noticed her sudden intake of breath or her stiffening spine. Thankfully they had not.

'We have the camp surrounded on three sides. Your husband is following the wagon and will secure the rear. As soon as the wagon appears, stand and duck behind the tree you are leaning against. It will provide sufficient cover should arrows start to fly.'

'I pray it doesn't come to that' she said with feeling. A stray arrow could find any number of the palace soldiers, possibly even Aaron. Now she started to seriously worry.

'As do I. Be prepared my Lady.' Then he was gone.

Be prepared she thought. How prepared could anyone be in this sort of situation. To calm herself she rose to her feet and paced from side to side as if to stretch her legs and gently making soft circles over her extended belly as her child stirred within her. One of the females looked across at her but seeing nothing untoward returned her gaze to the small fire. Not even the habitual sex was distracting the guards this morning. The relative safety of the tree was soon denied her as the chain was unlocked and she was hauled toward the fire and pushed roughly to the floor. Her knee caught on a rough stone and started to bleed from a deep cut. Her silence was broken as she cursed them long and loudly.

'So she speaks' a female jeered.

'Yes I speak when I have something to say.' Disdain was clearly in her eyes when she swept the female from toes to bald head. 'When my father comes he….'

'Your father' the words spewed from the wide thin mouth 'doesn't even know where you are or who took you. You are lost to him and that new husband of yours.' Her gaze rested on Aurora's swollen belly. 'Just maybe your new master will allow you to keep that brat, but then again I think not.'

'I have no master! Will never be slave to some man who thinks that all he has to do is kidnap me from my home. Does he think I will literally fall at his feet and worship the ground he walks upon when he snaps his fingers? He'd be better to run and hide from me for my wrath will be formidable.' Her voice remained soft and gentle, but her eyes were blazing making the female guard think that maybe her new master would have his hands full with this one. But it was of no importance to her. All she wanted was the money to buy her freedom.

'There will be no rescue for you' the female crouched down beside Aurora and looked directly into her eyes. 'No one has ever been inside our mountains and valleys' long fingers snatched at Aurora's greasy hair and yanked it painfully. 'You will spend the remainder of your life on your back with your legs spread or on your hands and knees taking the weight of your new master. Your husband will be a distant memory and will probably drive you insane with longing.' She laughed. 'Think on that my lady' she said and pushed Aurora to the ground.

When she stood over the prostrate woman she was stunned by the bright smile that crossed her face. 'We will see' her smile widened 'The men of Fayland are most persistent.'

The female guard grunted then moved away. Aurora was pleased to note that her eyes were constantly on the move, searching the undergrowth and trees for any sign of pursuit. Maybe they weren't as confident as it appeared.

It was only moments later that the wagon was heard approaching. It was forced to stop twenty feet from the campsite, as the trees were too dense for easy passage. The team was immediately un-harnessed and moved to the rear of the wagon. The cross beam un-pined and attached to the rear. It was obviously something that had to be done on a regular basis. The eight-man guard strolled toward the camp and greeted their fellows like old friends. Much chatter was in evidence. Food was the next priority. After kicking Aurora out of the way, they ignoring her completely as they gathered around the fire. From various bags they pulled large chunks of meat, cheeses and bread, skins of wine and several other foods Aurora had never seen before. As the foodstuffs were shared, the remaining driver and guard joined the feast. The driver, who carried a little more weight than the other men, was more inclined to have sex rather than eat. He simply caught hold of a female, pushed her down on her hands and knees, lifted her tunic, pushed his own aside, and thrust into her energetically. As he worked to please himself he was laughing and joking with the other guards. One of whom handed him a huge drumstick of meat, which he chewed on as he thrusted.

Aurora was pleased when she realised it was the female who taunted her earlier. When they made eye contact Aurora just smiled and shrugged at her, the female looked away.

He had finished his meat, drank two mugs of wine before he grunted his completion and withdrew. The female was given a mug of wine and a large chunk of meat to chew on when another took the driver's place. The other female, by this time, was similarly occupied.

'Now is the time Aaron whilst they are distracted' Aurora thought. No sooner had the words filled her mind, than the deed was done. Fayland soldiers rose from cover and swamped the campsite. A violent battle followed. Knives flashed in the dappled sunlight, fists connected to flesh, blood splattered the ground. The trained soldiers of Fayland however easily overwhelming the guards. There were no fatalities, but the medic was called on to treat a number of minor wounds on both sides.

With rescue at hand Aurora sat quietly whilst her collar was removed and the captives bound and left under guard. Search as she might she could not find her husband amongst the victorious. Worry for his safety filled her mind.

'Captain Dirk. My husband where is he?' she called across the short distance separating them.

'He will be along. He is just doing a mopping up exercise a short way off. Sergeant Dia and some men are with him. Have no fear my Lady.' He gave instructions to his men before he turned back to her. He for one would not like to find *his* wife in such a deplorable state. A short distance from the camp a small cubical of sorts had been erected. Inside was a warming fire, basin, cloths and soap and thick towels. Standing in neat rows were buckets of nicely hot water. Hanging on a low branch was a clean shift. Captain Dirk lead her away and smiled broadly at her delighted squeal of surprise as she rushed inside and the rough woven door pushed back in place. A female guard stood ready to assist Lady Aurora should it be necessary. Captain Dirk went about his duties. The first being to link with his General to report the success of his mission and to give a status report.

It had been reported to Sergeant Dia that a second, smaller, contingent of men had entered the valley via the tunnel closest to the pass. Six native guards, fully armed and more alert than the ones with the wagon, guarded a cloaked, richly garbed figure that rode a horse. Behind the horse four other cloaked men walked. Smaller and stockier in stature.

'That's not one of the indigenous people' one of the guards spoke softly as the column pushed through the undergrowth. 'Too short in stature.' He concluded as he gestured with his head to the rider. Nobody disagreed with him.

Aaron, Sergeant Dia and six men watched the small caravan approach. The guards protecting this dignitary were more alert however and scanned the surrounding undergrowth constantly. As they watched a buzzing insect swarmed around the nose of the horse and it tossed it's head and caused the rider to adjust his seat and take a firm grip on the reins. His hands were then clearly seen. The four others behind the horse could not be seen at this point.

'Elfin' Aaron snarled. 'Fucking Elfin' how he remained crouched in hiding he will never know. His body began to shake, his eyes turned red. He snatched at the knife he had strapped to his waist. He had need of a weapon if he could not spread his wings.

'No Lord Aaron' Sergeant Dia took a firm hold on his arm. 'Patience man. A few more minutes, then by God you can have the bastard. We'll clear the way.' At his signal he and his men launched themselves from cover and engaged the enemy. The horse reared with fright and was then harshly pulled around and raced off the way it had just come. Aaron was hot on his heels and came face to face with the four Elfin mercenaries that had been hired as escort. Two died within minutes of one another. Aaron's blade buried itself deep in the throats of the two as the remainder fled into the undergrowth.

He may not have been able to spread his wings, but the speed he was able to force from his legs would have done an Olympic sprinter proud as he raced after his quarry. For all of his height and weight, he was light on his feet. The blood lust was high, his eyes were volcanic red. His blood was at boiling point.

Chapter Nineteen

Freshly scrubbed and sweeter smelling, hair clean and shining and a soft clean shift in place the Lady Aurora returned to camp. Every man and woman from Fayland rose to their feet at her approach and loud applause filled the arena. She smiled and laughed with delight then bade them sit and return to their meal or their duty. It was on this happy scene that Sergeant Dia approached with the additional guards trussed up. One of his men was hurt but seemed cheerful enough when Aurora asked how serious was his wound.

''Tis nothing my Lady. Lord Aaron would say I zigged when I should have zagged. Couple of stitches and I'll be good as new.' She walked with him to the doctor to assure herself that his statement was true and was pleased it was.

'What of my husband Sergeant Dia?' she was anxious now to actually see him. His absence was very unnerving. Sergeant Dia had joined them when he reported the outcome of his mission.

'Elfin!' shock covered Aurora's face. 'But who would do….King Nall' she swayed a little and was instantly lowered to a tree stump and a small cup of water placed in her hands. 'He's surely lost his mind to think he could get away with this?' Aurora asked no one in particular. There was no answer.

'Lord Aaron obviously thought so. But in all honesty we did not see his face.' He looked across at his Captain and jerked his head toward his Princess.

'Continue Sergeant we will hear all of it.'

'The red rage had started' he spoke gently to Aurora. 'When the cowardly…..' he inhaled deeply. 'When the fighting started he turned tail and ran. Lord Aaron gave chase. Whoever it is, he will not escape.' He wanted to touch her, to hold her in his strong arms until her husband returned, but it was not his place.

'He'll kill him' her voice was whisper soft. 'He wouldn't be able to stop himself this time.' She but her face in her hands and wept quietly.

'My Lady' Captain Dirk crouched at her side. 'He would face public execution if he is captured. He knows this. Should the worst happen and he is killed, it would be because Lord Aaron defended himself.' He reached out and pulled her hands gently from her tear stained face. 'Every man and woman here. Every man and woman in Fayland would fight for you and their King. Not because of duty or fear. Because of love. Fayland has a good and strong King. His daughter is much loved. Although new to this life Lord Aaron has many loyal friends, a family that love him. But you, my Lady, you are his life. He would gladly lay down his life for you.'

'I couldn't bare to lose him.' She sniffled.

'I say would gladly lay down his life, not foolishly give it away. Take heart Aurora, that little worm doesn't stand a chance.' It did as he had hoped and made her smile.

She had dried her eyes and was sitting by the fight nibbling on a piece of bread when a scream filled the air. She shot to her feet, plate and food spilling into the fire.

'Stay calm my Lady.' Captain Dirk was instantly at her side.

'The sky' a trembling finger pointed to the dabbled light filtering through the canopy. 'The sky is red.' She feinted.

Aaron's anger was sufficient to carry him into open space and he was able to spread his wings and quite literally snatch the escaping kidnapper from his labouring mount and take to the sky.

'Unhand me you ruffian' the struggling elf commanded. 'Do you know who I am?' His bravado was holding up reasonable well albeit he was soaring into the sky in the hands of a madman. The gold he had in his saddlebags would surely buy his freedom.

'Aye I know who you are you weasel.' Aaron hissed in his ear.

Hearing the voice King Nall turned his head and look into the flaming red eyes of death. 'You!' he screamed. 'How did you get here? She's mine now you cannot have her." His eyes were rolling around in his head. 'I've paid good money for her. Fayland will be mine.' With strength born of desperation and madness he twisted around and pulled a short blade from his belt and swung it at his adversary drawing blood from a shallow cut across Aaron's chest. It was all it took to totally enrage the young man. He may have been able to control his growing anger up until that point but not now. Now he let the savagery of the red rage take hold. His wings vibrated and turned red. King Nall screamed and saw death in those vivid red eyes.

'You cannot buy true love you worm." His eyes flashed red and gold as Aaron roared into the snarling face of the Elfin King. "Money will only get her hatred. King Salvax has the love and respect of his people. What do you have?" Aaron was able to deflect another slash of the Elfin blade as King Nall struggled violently to be free. "Aurora would grind you into the ground. You are no match for her. You are no match for me. She is mine' was all Aaron said as he closed his wings around the Elfin King and literally let the rage take control. The blast of heat from his wings kept him airborne as his roar of uncontrolled fury drowned out the dying screams of the man being burnt alive within the folds of his wings. When there was nothing left but a chard husk he let the lifeless corpse fall to the ground. He cared not where.

Blind with rage and totally out of control he flashed across the sky. Red and gold flames shot from his huge wings as his screams of victory filled the sky.

There was total silence in the camp as all eyes turned toward the heavens. The normal blue of the sky was filled with swirls of red and gold and flashes of silver, similar to lightening.

'I'm glad Lady Aurora can't see this.' Sergeant Dia spoke quietly to Captain Dirk as both watched the flaming display across the sky. They watched for a full ten minutes.

'I never thought to see it." He freely admitted when at last the sky began to clear.

'There' Sergeant Dia pointed to the south. "Lord Aaron appears to have regained control.' A blue comet flashed across the sky.

With his rage released he calmed. Remarkably there was no trace of burning on his body or wings, just a bloodied slash across his chest. He was light headed and over hot, but the debilitating weakness that usually came over him at such times did not take hold of him now. So he rose higher into the sky where it was colder and glided around until he felt civilised once again. His first calming thought was of Aurora and turned east to go find her.

Aurora woke from her feint to twilight. A crude shelter had been erected around her with a piece of cloth serving as a door. She was warm and cosy in the strong arms that held her. She knew it was Aaron. Nobody had that wonderful smell that surrounded him. Nobody would dare nibble on the back of her neck and make her giggle. Nobody but her husband. She turned slowly to face him. They met nose to nose in the middle of the thin pallet.

'Husband' she could just make out his handsome face.

'Wife' she was deep in shadow, but her smell was unmistakable.

Then she was pulled urgently to his chest and kissed with such thoroughness tears started anew. 'Take me. Take me now.' She started to pull up her shift over her extended belly.

'No sweetheart, no.' He groaned in frustration. 'Much as I would love to lose myself in you it is far too dangerous so near your time.'

'It is safe Aaron' she shifted to her side and nestled her bottom in his lap.' Please. I need you.'

He rose up on an elbow to look down at her. 'Are you sure this is all right?' Having had no experience in such matters he had no knowledge to draw from.

'Perfectly.' She turned onto her back again and reached for the buckle of his loincloth, undid it and pushed it down his thighs until it got stuck against the pallet. Not satisfied she tugged at it until she could release his manhood and was delighted when it sprang to life in her hand. It was long and heavy and in perfect working order.

On her side again he easily slipped inside her. There was an audible sigh from both parties as they settled in for a nice steady ride toward completion.

Aaron woke alone. He thought he had only slept a short time, as it was still twilight. Thinking to find Aurora he wriggled into his loincloth and left the shelter. The smell of food has his stomach rumbling. In was dawn. He had slept a full eight hours.

It took months of hard diplomacy to satisfy King Salvax that all those responsible for his daughter's kidnap had been brought to justice. The supreme council of Peak, the valley people, summarily executed the natives from the mountain valleys. The two elfin mercenaries, discovered to be army deserters, were returned to Elfin and sent to the mines. A sentence many thought worse than death. The governing council of Elfin were dismissed as it was discovered that many knew of King Nall's intent to kidnap the Lady Aurora and stood by and did nothing. A Queen was now on the throne. A distant relative of the good King Dard had been located and crowned Queen to the cheers and relief of the Elfin people. She determined that peace would reign between Elfin and Fayland and set about weeding out, from all walks of life, every corrupt individual she could find. She ordered restitution for all and any damage done by the previous King to the people of Fayland.

King Salvax and Lady Pearl were invited to her wedding and were received in regal splendour and greeted with the generous hospitality, so lacking under King Nall, but always present under the old King Dard. A trade agreement had been signed and peace was assured by a simple handshake, monarch to monarch.

The Peaks people agreed to collapsed all and every tunnel leading from the valleys through the mountains into the sea. Their lands beyond the mountains were vast and fertile and something they would guard jealously from outside interference. Peace was guaranteed, as they had no intention of building an international relationship with any other country.

Chapter Twenty

'Before I met you' Aaron sat beside his wife in their wide comfortable bed. 'I thought that I would spend my life fixing cars and fire engines, being uncle to Philip and Julia. Never being able to take a wife, father a child. Living off the love of my friends and their children.' He reached over and brushed his hand over his son's head as he suckled at Aurora's breast.

'Now you have both' she smiled across at him. 'A wife who loves you beyond anything she could possibly have imagined and a son who will grow to love you with equal measure.' Their son Jax had been born only six hours ago. Seven months to the day from when her red veins began to show.

'I can't wait to take him for his first flight' the new father bent down and placed a soft kiss on his son's head. 'I didn't think I could love this deeply, this completely.'

'Welcome to the club' Aurora yawned as Aaron took their son and placed him in a crib close to her side of the bed. He was a good healthy seven and a half pounds in weight, with a mat of dark hair and long sturdy limbs. 'Going to be tall like his father.' She snuggled down in the bed when Aaron tucked the covers around her. Her body temperature had dropped after the birth, all perfectly natural so he was informed, but it would mean that she needed extra clothing or to stay in bed for at least two weeks, until her body recovered. Aaron liked the idea of the bed rest. Aurora hadn't complained.

'I have to go and see the Oracle' Aaron crouched beside the bed to better she her face. There were some fatigue lines across the beautiful surface, but again he was told this was perfectly natural and would disappear with enough rest.

'Is something wrong?' she tried to sit up but he pushed her gently down.

'Nothing. Your father and mine seemed to think I should talk to him. From all accounts he is the only other person ever to have the red rage with such destructive powers.' He would never regret the death of King Nall and the two mercenaries, but it did worry him a little. The fact that he could, and did, kill without a seconds thought.

'Was his body ever found?' she hide a yawn behind a small hand.

He shook his head. 'Apparently the wild pigs in the valley will eat anything.' He smiled at his wife's screwed up face. 'Go to sleep little mother' he kissed her smiling mouth. 'Your mother will be here shortly.' She was asleep before he got to his feet and left the room.

The oracle's home was situated on a small plot of land north of the palace grounds. There was a well-tended garden spread over three sides, a well and outbuilding to the rear. On a hill behind the outbuildings a stone structure could be seen. What it was was unclear but it looked to be very old.

Aaron landed on the path leading to the front door. He felt a little uneasy. Why, he had no idea. He was simply asked to speak with the man. So here he was.

'I don't bite Lord Aaron.' A tall middle aged man stepped from behind a bramble bush were he had been collecting berries. He had watched the man land gracefully. Admired his magnificent wings.

'Forgive me sir; I do not know your name. I was directed here to speak with the oracle. Would that be you?' Aaron crossed the garden toward the man as he closed his wings.

'I have that distinction. I am called Leo' he held out a hand that was taken immediately. 'Come walk with me' he headed toward the rear of his house, leaving his basket on the back step. They walked toward the stone structure.

'I have to confess I expected a man of more mature years. My preconception of oracle is of an ancient old man, bent over and walking with a cane. You definitely don't fit the bill.'

Leo laughed. 'I'm glad to hear it. Tell me about yourself?' It wasn't a command but Aaron felt obliged to retell his story. Leo listened closely as they reached the summit of the rise and sat on a stone bench. The view was worth the short walk. Rolling fields, distant forests, a river to the west and brilliant sunshine.

Aaron sat next to the older man.

'I come to meditate here. To listen here. I heard you singing. It was so melancholy, so sad and yet so alluring. The Valspec heart song is one of the most beautiful of sounds.' He turned to Aaron. 'Can you not hear your son?'

'What?' Aaron automatically turned his head toward his home.

'Your son is singing. Babies do for the first month after birth it was how I found you. Once heard, it is never forgotten. Even in sleep he sings.' Leo watched the young man get to his feet and pace.

'I don't hear him. If this is a natural thing for new fathers, why do I not hear him? Is something wrong?' There was a deep frown on his face when he faced the oracle.

'Forgive me. I forget that for the first thirty years of your life you were not given the opportunity to hone your senses.' He rose and walked closer to the structure. 'Sit here with me. Meditate with me. I will see if I can link to your son so that you might hear for yourself.' They sat facing one another. Aaron took up his usual position, pleased that Leo did the same.

'Let your mind empty, relax. When I touch your hand think of your son. Asleep now, safe by his mother's side. Relax' Leo was amazed at how responsive Aaron was. He was absolutely fascinated when within a few minutes, seemly without effort, Aaron rose to his feet as his wings opened and spread wide. He then resumed his position on the ground. The base of his wings just brushed the ground behind him.

'Amazing' Leo thought as he felt Aaron go deeper into his meditation. He settled himself for a moment then reached across and touched Aaron's hand. The change was barely noticeable. His chin lifted a little, his back straightened, his breathing deepened. The two men linked. And for the first time Aaron heard his son's heart song. Leo watched as Aaron's breath hitched, tears formed and ran down his face and a smile appeared. It was one of the most rewarding of sights to see a young father so filled with love.

'Do you hear him Aaron?'

'Yes' he said with reverence.

'Link with him. His song will only last a month now. When he is older and it is time for his opening you will hear it again and be prepared.' Leo closed his eyes. 'Break the link now, let him sleep. Clear your mind.' Aaron's breath evened out his body relaxed.

'Do you hear me Lord Aaron.' He did not link but spoke the words.

Aaron nodded.

'I want to try something. Relax now, no harm will come to you.'

'I'm safe here, I know that.'

'Close your mind to Fayland. Open your mind to the world you left behind. Think of Mike Townsend, your life long friend, your brother. Think of him now. What he would be doing, where he would be. Don't force anything, just think about him. Relax.'

'It's Saturday right.' It was a statement, not a question.

'It is'

'Cook out in the back yard. Sophie will be mixing drinks, the kids will be playing on the swings we made.' He smiled he could see it clearly. 'Oops grills on fire. Too much lighter fuel buddy. Sausages are burnt.'

'A little charcoal never hurt anybody.' Mike dropped the tongues he was using to tend the meat and spun around. He saw his children on the swings and his wife coming from the back door with a tray of drinks. 'Too much sun, losing it here.' He picked up the tongues, wiped them clean and added burgers to the grill.

'What's happening?' Aaron asked Leo. 'I can hear him, I could see what he saw.'

'You've made a link with him. I have a number of friends I speak with on your earth. They keep me informed of what's going on down there. It is permitted. Not too often as you will get severe headaches. Link with him now and explain. I will see you back at my house.' He rose and left.

Taking a huge breath Aaron linked again with Mike. 'Stay calm buddy. It is me. I've made a link. Like making a phone call.' A headache was making itself known.

'Aaron?' Mike couldn't stop his head from swivelling from side to side.

'Who else could get inside that thick skull of yours?' Both men smiled. 'Listen I'm told I can link with you once in a while, too often and my head will blow up or something.

I just wanted to know how you are. Is everything okay down there? Don't speak aloud, just think it.'

'Miss you buddy, no denying it.' He turned the meat on the grill. 'Everyone was devastated when you were reported missing but they found your car eventually and everything you left behind. The blood was a good touch by the way the cops found your backpack covered in it. Aurora's pack was torn and dirty but no blood, no bodies. Car was well into the water and it was high tide when it was found. Official verdict accidental death.'

'Sorry to have put you through that Mike, but it was for the best. The insurance pay up and everything?'

'We had to wait a month before they released the policy but no hassle after that. We've got over fifty thousand dollars invested for the kids college fund. We decided to leave the utility shares for the time being, prices are going up.'

'Could make you a millionaire maybe.' Aaron rubbed his temples to alleviate the pain.

'Dream on buddy.' Mike smiled to himself. 'Tell me how you are.'

'Aurora and I are married. I have a son Mike, can you believe it. He was born just seven hours ago. His name is Jax. Mother and baby are just terrific.'

'Way to go buddy.' He mentally did a high five.

'Mike can you just hear me or can you see anything?'

'Just you in my head bro. No visions.' He was sorry for that. He would have loved to see him.

'Before I go will you turn around so that I can see the kids and Sophie. You can tell her of the link if you want to. But not the kids okay.'

'You will link again though. Keep in touch.'

'You bet. Two, three times a year if I can. Turn around Mike, let me see them.'

Mike turned and called to his family. 'Grubs up kids. Come and get it.' They scrambled from the swings and dashed to their father's side and filled buns and rolls with charcoal sausage and burgers. Sophie came forward with a tall glass in her hand filled with ice and some amber liquid. 'One of these days we'll get a cook out that isn't burnt to a crisp.' She gave him a smacking kiss however and filled a bun with a thick well-cooked burger before going back to the kids.

'They look great Mike, really great.' His head was beginning to spin. 'Gotta go buddy. Until next time.' Then he was gone.

Back in Leo's house he was given a cup of some brown liquid that tasted ominously like he thought dirt might taste like but his headache vanished almost before it could get a good hold.

'So young Aaron. Looks like you'll be the next oracle.' Leo sat back in his chair and watched the shock form on Aaron's face. 'Red rage, formidable control, linking to your earth. No better prophesy in my opinion.' His smile was all knowing.

'You gotta be kidding me' Aaron slumped back in his chair with his mouth open.